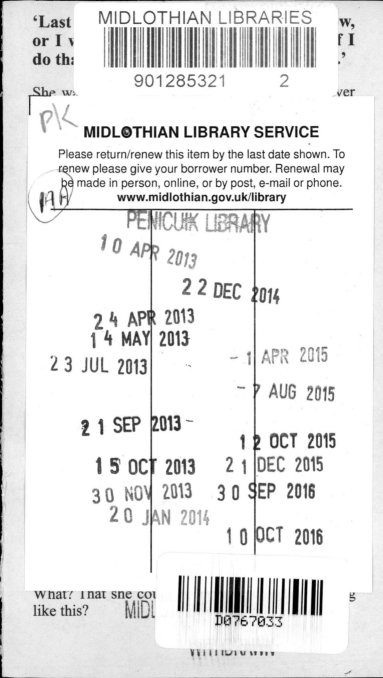

'Last ... w,
or I v ... f I
do tha ... '

She w ... ver

What? That she cou ... g
like this?

NEVER TRUST
A RAKE

Annie Burrows

MILLS & BOON

First published in Great Britain 2013
by Mills & Boon, an imprint of Harlequin (UK) Limited.
Harlequin (UK) Limited, Eton House, 18-24 Paradise Road,
Richmond, Surrey TW9 1SR

© Annie Burrows 2013

ISBN: 978 0 263 89805 7

Harlequin (UK) policy is to use papers that are natural, renewable
and recyclable products and made from wood grown in sustainable
forests. The logging and manufacturing process conform to the
legal environmental regulations of the country of origin.

Printed and bound in Spain
by Blackprint CPI, Barcelona

Annie Burrows has been making up stories for her own amusement since she first went to school. As soon as she got the hang of using a pencil she began to write them down. Her love of books meant she had to do a degree in English literature. And her love of writing meant she could never take on a job where she didn't have time to jot down notes when inspiration for a new plot struck her. She still wants the heroines of her stories to wear beautiful floaty dresses and triumph over all that life can throw at them. But when she got married she discovered that finding a hero is an essential ingredient to arriving at 'happy ever after'.

**Do you know that some of these novels are also
available as eBooks? Visit www.millsandboon.co.uk**

With thanks for all the help and support
the Novelistas of North Wales provide.
You are a great bunch of ladies.

Chapter One

Ye Gods, he'd known it would not be easy, but he hadn't expected them all to be quite so predictable.

Lord Deben strode out on to the terrace, deserted since the night air was damp with drizzle, made it to the parapet and leaned heavily on the copingstone, where he drew in several deep breaths of air blessedly unadulterated by perfume, sweat and candle grease.

First to run true to form had been tonight's hostess, Lady Twining. Her eyes had practically popped out of her head when she'd recognised exactly upon whose arm the Dowager Lady Dalrymple was leaning. He had only ever once before had anything to do with a come-out ball, and that had been his own sister's—a glittering affair which he'd hosted himself some four years ago. He could see Lady Twining wondering why on earth he had suddenly decided to accompany such a stickler for good form to such an insipid event, held in the home of a family who would never aspire to be part of his usual, racy set.

While they had slowly mounted the stairs, he'd watched her rapidly working out how to deal with the dilemma his attendance posed. She could hardly refuse to admit him, since she'd sent his godmother an invitation and he was evidently acting as her escort. But, oh, how she wanted to. She clearly felt that letting him in amongst the virtuous damsels currently thronging her corridors would be like opening the henhouse door to a prowling fox.

But she didn't have the courage to say what she was thinking. And by the time he'd arrived at the head of the receiving line, it was all *what an honour to welcome you into our home, my lord,* and *we did not think to have such an august presence as yours...*

No. She had not actually said that last phrase, but that was what she'd meant by all that gushing and fluttering. The presence of a belted earl was such a social coup for her that it far outweighed the potential danger he posed to the moral tone of the assembly.

And as for those assembled guests—his lip

curled in utter contempt. They had divided neatly into two camps: those who reacted solely to his reputation by clucking and fluttering like outraged hens in defence of their precious chicks and those, he grimaced, with an eye to the main chance.

He'd felt their beady eyes following his progress into the house. Heard the whispered swell of speculation. Why was he here? And with Lady Dalrymple, of all people? Was it a sign that this Season he was at last going to do his duty to his family and take a wife?

On the outside chance that the most notorious womaniser of his generation, the most dangerous flirt, was actually going to look about him for a woman to take her place at his side in society, as his legally wed countess, the most ambitious amongst them had promptly begun elbowing each other aside in their determination to thrust their simpering charges under his nose.

The fact that they'd guessed correctly didn't make their approaches any less repellent. Which was why he would have to attend more events such as this and endure the vapid discourse that passed for conversation and the gauche mannerisms…and sometimes even the spotty complexions. How else could a man be absolutely sure that his first child, at least, was of his own get unless he married a girl who'd only just emerged from the schoolroom? And the duty he owed his proud lineage made that an absolute imperative.

But did they really think he'd propose to the first chit he met, at the first event he attended since he'd made up his mind it was time, and past time, he knuckled down to the fate his position made inescapable?

He leaned back and tilted his face to the rain. It managed to cool his skin, even if it could do nothing to soothe the roiling bitterness churning in his guts. Nothing could do that.

Unless... He stilled, as the most fantastic thought occurred to him. He didn't think he could face many more such events as this. And what was there to choose between all those pallid, eager, young females, after all? Why the hell shouldn't he just propose to the very first chit to cross his path when he went back inside? That would at least get the whole unpleasant business over and done with as quickly and painlessly as possible.

What would it take—a year out of his life? Propose to one of those girls who'd been paraded before him like brood mares at Tattersalls. Get the banns read, go through the travesty of a ceremony, bed her, then keep on bedding her until he could be certain she was increasing. Hope that the child was a boy. Then, with the succession sorted, he could return to his carefree existence and she could…

He sucked in a short, sharp breath, bowing his head again as he considered what his *wife* would get up to, left to her own devices.

Anything. Anything and everything. Nobody knew better than he just how far bored young matrons would go in the pursuit of sexual adventure.

With an exclamation of impatience he pulled his watch from his waistcoat pocket and turned to catch the light from the ballroom windows so that he could check the time. His brow raised in disbelief. Had he only been in this house for thirty minutes? It could be hours before Lady Dalrymple was ready to leave. She would want to watch the dancing, gossip with those of her cronies who were present and take supper.

So be it. His mouth twisted with distaste. He had to fill in the time somehow, so it might as well be following his impulse to deal with the marriage situation as swiftly and cleanly as possible. He *would* return to the ballroom and ask the first girl to cross his path to dance with him. If she accepted, and if he didn't find her too repulsive, he would locate her father and start talking settlements.

There. The whole abominable, damnable thing settled. He would not even have to alert the *ton* to his intent by setting foot in that hell-hole known as Almack's.

And yet, when he replaced his watch in his pocket, his feet remained welded to the spot. And his gaze stayed fixed straight ahead, though his eyes were not seeing the dampening gardens below the terrace, but the abyss into which he was about to throw himself.

It would *not* matter if he could not grow to like the anonymous chit who waited for him inside that house very much, as long as he could contemplate bedding her for the requisite amount of time to get an heir. If he didn't grow fond of her, she wouldn't have the power to hurt him. Humiliate him. He could watch her carrying on her love affairs with the same kind of amused indifference displayed by all the husbands he'd cuckolded over the years. Whose bored, dissatisfied wives had been actively seeking younger, more energetic men to provide them with the spice their dutifully contracted marriages so singularly lacked.

Within the bounds of such a lukewarm arrangement, he might even be able to tolerate her offspring. Perhaps even treat them with kindness, rather than calling them bastards to their face. And they'd think of each other as brothers and sisters, and care for and support each other, instead of...

A swell of music issuing from the ballroom pulled him abruptly from the maelstrom of negativity that always churned through him whenever a stray thought escaped its confines and crept back towards his childhood.

He turned slowly, annoyed to have his brief interlude of solitude interrupted, though he hadn't expected to see a *female* silhouette in the doorway that led back to the house.

'Why, Lord Deben!'

The girl gasped and raised her hand to her throat in a dramatic gesture, intended, he supposed cynically, to betoken surprise.

'I did not think anyone else would be out here,' she said, glancing along the length of the otherwise deserted terrace and back.

'Why, indeed, would anyone venture forth in such inclement weather?'

Undeterred by the dryness of his tone, she advanced a step or two and giggled.

'I should not be out here with you, all alone, should I? Mama says you are dangerous.'

Now that she was closer he could see she was quite a pretty little thing. Good features, clear skin, expensively and fashionably clad. And well used to male attention, to judge from the way she was preening under his leisurely, not to say insolent, perusal of her assets.

'Your mama is correct. I am dangerous.'

'I am not afraid of you,' she said, sashaying right up to him. She came so close that the perfume she wore wafted to his nostrils from her hot little body. She was breathing hard. She was excited. A little nervous, too, but mostly excited.

'You have never been known to harm a virtuous damsel,' she said breathily. 'Your reputation has all been gained with young matrons, or widows.'

'Your mama should have warned you that it is not the thing to discuss a man's *amours* with him.'

She smiled. Knowingly.

'But, Lord Deben,' she murmured, sliding one hand up the lapel of his jacket, 'I am sure you want your future wife to understand these things. To be understanding...'

He gripped her hand and detached it from his clothing, filled with a gut-deep revulsion.

'On the contrary, madam, that is the *last* thing I want from the woman I shall marry.'

It was no good. He was more like his father than he'd thought. Even if he took the greatest care never to fall in love with his own wife, he wouldn't be able to bear the thought of her being *understanding*. Of expecting him to carry on as though he was still a bachelor, so that she could enjoy her own sexual adventures.

In short, of becoming a cuckold.

'You had better return to the ballroom. As you yourself said, it is quite improper of you to be out here, alone, with a man like me.'

She pouted. 'It is absurd of you to preach propriety, when everyone knows you have never had any time for it.'

Then, in a move so swift it took him completely by surprise, she flung both arms about his neck.

'God dammit, what are you about?' He reached up and tried to disentangle himself from her hold. He managed to prise one hand off, but then she dropped her fan, leaving her other hand free to find purchase. When he stepped smartly back in a more determined effort to evade her grasping hands, she clung tighter, so that he found himself dragging her with him.

'Let go of me, you impudent baggage,' he growled. 'I do not know what you think you will achieve by flinging yourself at me like this, but...'

There was a shriek. Light flooded the terrace as the doors from the house burst open. The girl who had been clinging so tenaciously slumped against him, pressing her cheek to his chest.

'Lord Deben!' A well-built matron stalked towards him, her jowls quivering with indignation. 'Let go of my daughter this instant!'

He still had his hands on her wrists, from

when he'd been trying to prise her off. As he attempted to push her upright, she gave a little moan and arched theatrically backwards, as though in a faint. Instinctively, he caught her as she began to fall. And though part of him would have dearly liked to let her slump into a crumpled heap on the damp flagstones, another part of him knew that were he to give in to such a base instinct, it would only make the situation look worse for him.

At any moment, another person might take it into their heads to come outside, and what would they see? The wicked Lord Deben standing over the prone body of a shocked, half-ravished innocent? Or the wicked Lord Deben standing with the swooning victim of his attempted seduction clasped in his arms? With the indignant mother demanding the release of his supposed victim?

Whichever tableau they would see, the outcome would be the same. These two females would expect him to make reparation by marrying this scheming little baggage.

He had never been so angry in his whole life. Caught in the kind of trap a greenhorn should have seen coming. And on his first foray into the world of so-called innocents! How could he have so woefully underestimated the predatory nature of womankind? He'd dismissed those virtually indistinguishable white-clad girls in the

ballroom as vapid, brainless ciphers. But this girl
had a quick mind. And an immense amount of
ambition. He was the wealthiest, youngest, most
highly ranking man she was ever likely to get
within what he guessed was her limited social
reach. And she had taken ruthless advantage of
his momentary lapse of concentration to compromise him. She didn't care a whit for his character. Or have a qualm about marrying a man she
believed was incapable of fidelity. In fact, she'd
told him she would *condone* it.

What was worse, the chit was not to know he
was, in actual fact, looking for a wife. For all she
knew, he was still an obdurate rake.

And yet she had persisted in setting out to
ruthlessly snare him.

Cunning, ambitious, ruthless and amoral. If
his mother were still alive, she would have seen
this girl as a kindred spirit.

'It is quite obvious what has been going on out
here,' said the girl's mother, drawing herself up
to her full height. Then, just as he'd expected,
she said, 'You must make amends.'

'Offer marriage, you mean?' That did it. He
no longer cared if the old besom did think him
ungallant. He thrust her clinging daughter from
him with such determination she tottered a few
steps and had to clutch at her mother to prevent
herself tripping over.

Had he really been toying with the idea of proposing to the first apparently eligible female to cross his path? Was he mad? If he married a creature like this one, history would repeat itself, with the added twist that he would never be entirely certain who had fathered *any* of the children for whom he would be obliged to provide.

He leaned back against the balustrade and folded his arms. He was just about to inform them that no power on earth would induce him to offer this girl his name when another voice cried out, 'Oh, please, it is not what it looks like!'

The three of them at his end of the terrace whirled towards the shadows at the far end, from whence the voice had emanated.

He could just make out a slender female form wriggling out from between two massive earthenware planters, behind which she had clearly been concealing herself.

'For one thing,' the still-shadowed girl said, reaching down to free her gown from some unseen obstruction, 'I was out here the whole time. Miss Waverley was never alone with Lord Deben.'

Having freed her skirts, she straightened up and walked towards them. She hovered on the fringe of the pool of light in which they stood, as though reluctant to fully emerge from the shadows. But he'd glimpsed moss smearing the regulation white of her gown as a corner of it had fluttered into the light. And there was what looked like dried leaves caught in the tangled curls which tumbled round a pair of thin shoulders.

'That's all very well,' the outraged mother of the scheming Miss Waverley, as he now knew her to be named, put in, 'but how did he come to have her in his arms?'

Miss Waverley was still clinging to her mother with the air of a tragedy queen, but on her pretty face he could see the first stirrings of alarm.

'Oh, well, she…' The dishevelled girl hesitated. She darted a look towards the worried Miss Waverley, then drew herself upright and looked the older woman straight in the eye. 'She dropped her fan. And then she sort of…stumbled up against Lord Deben, who naturally prevented her from falling.'

Well, she'd certainly presented the whole sequence of events in such a way as to put an entirely different complexion on the matter. Without telling an outright lie.

In fact, it had been very neatly done.

He pushed himself away from the balustrade and took the two paces necessary to reach the fan, which he bent down and retrieved.

'No gentleman,' he said, having decided to take his cue from the girl who, for some reason, reminded him of autumn personified, 'not even one with a reputation as tarnished as my own, could have permitted such a fair creature to fall,' he said, returning the fan to the set-faced Miss Waverley with a flourish. He had no idea why the Spirit of Autumn had decided to put a stop to Miss Waverley's scheme, but he was not about to look a gift horse in the mouth.

Miss Waverley's mother was looking pensively at the uneven edges of the damp flagstones on which they stood.

Miss Waverley's eyes were darting from him to the girl who had emerged from the shadows. He could almost see her mind working. It was no longer a case of her word against his. There were two people prepared to swear nothing untoward had occurred here this night.

'Sir Humphrey should get these flags attended to, don't you think?' He smiled frostily at the girl who had attempted to compromise him. 'Before somebody comes to grief. But at least I have the satisfaction of knowing that you have not come to any lasting hurt from this night's little encounter.'

She flung up her chin and glowered at him.

Her mother, however, was more gracious in defeat.

'Oh, well, I see now how it was, of course. And I do thank you for coming to my daughter's aid, my lord. Though why she was out here with Miss Gibson, I cannot begin to imagine. She is not our sort of person. Not our sort of person at all.'

The matron shot the bedraggled nymph a look of contempt.

Did he imagine it, or did she shrink from the scrutiny, as though she was half-thinking of ducking behind the ornamental urns again?

'Nor can I imagine how my dear Isabella has come to be on such intimate terms with her. Really, child,' she said, addressing her daughter, whose mouth was pouting sulkily, 'I cannot think what on earth possessed you to accompany a person like that out here, where you might have soiled your gown. Or caught a chill. How on earth,' she said, rounding on the hapless Miss Gibson, '*did* you manage to persuade my daughter to come out here? And what were you doing, hiding at the end of the terrace down there, leaving my daughter alone with a gentleman? Have you no notion how improper your action was? How selfish?'

Though he couldn't help wondering himself how Miss Gibson would answer that barrage of questions, he had his own list, which were far more pertinent, given that he knew what had actually occurred.

The one which was uppermost, however, was

to wonder why she had not taken the chance to expose Miss Waverley for the scheming jade she was, if she was so keen to put a spoke in her wheel. Her description of the sordid little scene had been so neatly wrapped up that Miss Waverley would walk away from this encounter with her reputation untarnished. Yet concern for Miss Waverley's reputation could not have been what prompted her. She'd come out of hiding before he told them he would never offer her his name, no matter what tales they told. His reputation was already black as pitch, so he had nothing to lose. But the Waverley chit would most definitely have got her just deserts if this pair of designing females had attempted to cross swords, socially, with a man of his standing.

All Miss Gibson had needed to do, so far as she was concerned, was to stay concealed behind her plant pots and wait for them all to go away. Had she acted from friendship, then? Had she wanted to save a friend from a disastrous marriage?

No...he didn't think that was it either. Miss Waverley had, at no point, looked as though she felt anything...friendly about the girl who'd thwarted her ambition. She certainly had not expected her to be out here. She had scanned the terrace for witnesses before staging her attempt to compromise him. And been furious when the

Gibson girl had emerged and scotched her plans to bag herself an earl.

Enemies, then? No…from what the mother had said they barely mixed in the same social circles. Which meant they were not likely to have had opportunity to become either enemies, or friends.

Whichever way he looked at it, he kept on returning to the same unsettling conclusion. Her actions had nothing to do with Miss Waverley at all.

She had been attempting to rescue *him*.

He leaned back against the parapet once more, one hand on either side of him, and watched her in fascination. She was not making any attempt to defend herself while Miss Waverley's mother rang a peal over her. She scarcely seemed to notice either the tirade, or the poisonous glances Miss Waverley kept darting at her.

She was just standing there, shoulders slumped, as though she simply did not care what anyone thought of her, or said of her. As though she wasn't even fully attending to the vitriol being poured upon her innocent head.

Right up until the moment when Miss Waverley's mother said, 'But, then, what can one expect from somebody hailing from such a family as yours?'

At that, the change which came over her was

remarkable. She lifted her head and stepped forwards, so that she was for the first time fully illuminated by the light streaming from the ballroom windows. All the colours of autumn glowed in her wild tresses. Rich conker browns, threaded with gold and russet of leaves on the turn. And her demeanour was so fierce, it was like witnessing a storm whipping up out of nowhere, blasting away all shreds of one of those drear November mornings which so depressed him.

'One can expect *honourable* behaviour,' she said. 'I was concealing myself only because I did not wish anyone, especially not a gentleman, to see that I had been crying.'

Now that he could believe. Miss Gibson did not weep prettily. Her nose, which was a shade too large for her rather thin face, was red and running. Her cheeks were mottled and streaked with what looked like not only tears, but horrifically like the effusions from that abomination of a nose.

It made it all the more remarkable for her to have exposed herself to view, in order to intervene in the affairs of two people who were neither her friends, nor, in his case, even a remote acquaintance.

'I might have known,' the matron snapped. 'I hope you are thoroughly ashamed of yourself,

young lady. You see what comes of giving way
to such a vulgar display of emotion? Not only do
you look an absolute disgrace, but your selfish,
wilful behaviour has exposed my own, blameless daughter to a situation that might very easily have been misinterpreted!'

Miss Gibson clenched her fists. She looked at
the *blameless* Miss Waverley and took a breath.
She was just about to blurt out the truth that
would send shock waves rippling through the
tranquillity of Miss Twining's come-out ball,
when he saw a look of chagrin cross her face.

Ah. She had just worked out that she could
not now tell the complete truth without exposing
herself. That was what happened when a woman
began to spin a web of lies. She only had to
put one foot wrong, to run the risk of becoming
hopelessly enmeshed herself.

At least she had the intelligence to see it. She
closed her mouth, lifted her chin and regarded
the mother in stony-faced silence.

He felt his lips twitch as the gale blew itself
out. Really, this was better than a play.

It was perhaps unfortunate that Miss Gibson
glanced at him at the exact moment he began to
see the humour in the situation. She caught his
amused expression and returned it with a scowl
that could have curdled milk.

'Well,' said the matron, who had missed the

exchange of glances, because she'd been busy placing a comforting arm about her thwarted daughter's shoulders. 'I can see that you were motivated by the kindness of your heart, my dear, but really, it would have been better to have sought out Miss Gibson's chaperon and let her deal with it.'

His brief foray into amusement at the absurdity of it all was over. The matron's attitude was almost as offensive as that of her daughter. Here was a young female, so distressed that she'd run outside to give way to her emotions, and all she was getting was a lecture. It was not right. Somebody ought to be offering her some comfort. After all, females did not weep with such abandon, not in private, without having very good reason. They must know that, surely?

He looked at the mother. At Miss Waverley herself. And frowned.

He did not have much in the way of empathy for the sensibilities of females, but he was clearly the only person out here who felt even the tiniest scrap of it towards the bedraggled Miss Gibson. Not that he would dream of attempting to deal with her personally. He'd never had any success soothing weeping females. On the few occasions he'd attempted to offer consolation to one of his sisters when indulging in a fit of tears, his brand of rational argument had thrown them into something bordering on hysterics.

She needed a sympathetic female. The chaperon that the Waverley woman had mentioned— that was the woman who would know how to deal with her.

He pushed himself off the balustrade. 'Allow me to rectify that error,' he said, 'by performing that office this very minute. If one of you would be so good as to furnish me with her name?'

'Oh,' said the matron with a sneer, 'she is a Mrs Ledbetter. I dare say you would not know *her*, my lord. Indeed, I cannot think how a woman of her station in life came to secure an invitation to an event such as this.'

He smiled. 'Indeed. One attends private balls in the expectation of only encountering a better class of person. Mrs Waverley, is it?'

'Lady Chigwell,' she simpered.

'Lady Chigwell,' he replied, with a bow of acknowledgement. As he straightened up, he caught Miss Gibson's eye and gave her a wink. But if he had thought she might have relished the thinly veiled snub he had just administered, he was disappointed, meeting only disapproval in her gaze.

Perhaps she had not understood the gesture he had made on her behalf.

'Miss Gibson,' he said, closing the distance

between them so that he could take her hand, 'may I tell Mrs Ledbetter you will wait for her out here?' In an undertone, he added, 'What does she look like?'

Miss Gibson blinked up at him with eyes that, at close quarters, he could see were still swimming in unshed tears. He squeezed her hand gently, trying to offer her both his gratitude and, somewhat to his surprise, some reassurance. There was not another female in the world, to whom he was not related, who could testify that Lord Deben had shown the slightest hint of concern for her welfare.

But no man, not even one as immune to fellow feeling as people often accused him of being, could fail to be moved by her plight. She had come out here to indulge in a private fit of tears, only to find herself obliged to have her breakdown exposed, and, to crown it all, to have not only her own character, but that of her chaperon quite unjustly ripped to shreds.

'She is wearing a purple turban,' she hissed in an undertone, 'with one white and one purple ostrich feather in it. You really cannot miss it.' And then, snatching her hand from his, she said, 'I think it would be for the best if I wait out here.'

'Yes, indeed,' put in Miss Waverley in a sugary-sweet voice. 'You would not want to walk across that ballroom, not as you are. You really need to give your face a good wash before you let anyone see you.'

Miss Gibson hastily swiped at her cheeks with the backs of her hands. The effect, since her gloves were as badly soiled as her gown, was unfortunate.

'Allow me,' he said, producing a square of monogrammed white silk from his tailcoat pocket with a flourish and offering it to her.

'Thank you, sir,' she said gruffly and proceeded to take it from him with such reluctance that he suspected she would have refused it altogether were she not so desperate.

Why was that? he wondered. If she had taken a dislike to him, as seemed to be the case from the way she glared at him, after blowing her nose with a very unladylike thoroughness, then why had she come to his aid in the first place?

Or perhaps, as she had stated, it was just that she did not like to have any gentleman see her in such an unbecoming state of distress.

That must be it.

He turned, satisfied that he had accounted for the unwarranted hostility he could detect in her attitude, and made his way along the terrace, back to the ballroom.

Now all he had to do was find a woman of advancing years, in an ostrich-feathered purple turban, pass on the information that Miss Gibson was outside awaiting her assistance and he could lay the whole matter to rest.

Although he could not quite shake off an unfamiliar feeling of wishing he could do something to alleviate Miss Gibson's distress. He'd realised, in the instant the threat of becoming leg-shackled to a creature of Miss Waverley's calibre loomed before him, that he would rather die than face a marriage such as the one endured by his own father. And he was becoming more and more convinced that Miss Gibson had intervened to save him from just such a fate.

That must be it. She could not bear to see anyone forced into a marriage that was not of their own choosing.

Perhaps that was why she was out here crying. From what Lady Chigwell had said, she was not from a very good family. Perhaps she was being coerced to marry 'well' in order to advance their social standing. Perhaps that was what she was doing here tonight. Being put on display, to be sold off like a slave at auction. He had not seen her at her best just now, but her very youth, her very vulnerability, would hold enough appeal to interest several men he knew who were casting about them for wives this Season. It was the way of the world. Older men with money and status could more or less have their pick of the young virgins who came up to town each year to find a husband. The families of said virgins practically sold them off to the highest bidder, no matter what their feelings.

Denied choice in the matter, they eventually rebelled and took lovers of their own choosing.

Having freedom of choice was the one benefit that, as a man, he had which many women were not permitted. And he'd almost thrown it away.

It had been Miss Waverley who had shocked him out of the apathy that had almost led him to make a disastrous error. He held such cynical views of marriage that he'd been on the verge of allowing fate to take the choice out of his hands. Like a gambler, who tossed a coin to determine his next move. He'd thought it would simplify things to remove the element of choice from the equation. No such thing. Marriage, once entered into, was an inescapable bond. Reluctance to enter that state did not excuse a cavalier attitude towards the choice of bride. Though he still could not imagine finding any real pleasure for himself, in marriage, he owed it to his children to thoroughly investigate the character of the woman who would bear them. He would never knowingly foist a parent like his own mother upon poor innocent children. Nor a woman like Miss Waverley.

She might have jolted him out of his fatalistic attitude this evening, but it was only because she epitomised all he most despised in females.

He felt no gratitude towards her whatsoever. And yet, in spite of her intervention being quite unnecessary, the fact that Miss Gibson seemed to have acted out of concern for him did make him feel as though he wished he could repay her in some way.

For nobody, male or female, had ever attempted to rescue him from anything.

Good God. He stood stock still, smiling with unholy mirth at the thought that suddenly struck him. He'd just been rescued by a damsel in distress.

Not that anyone could, by any stretch of the imagination, think of him as a knight in any kind of armour. He fought his battles in the House of Lords, with cutting words rather than at tourneys, with lance and mace.

He turned, he was not entirely sure why, to take one last look at her—and caught Miss Waverley shooting her a look of pure venom.

He'd already ascertained that she was amoral and ruthless. And though Miss Gibson clearly possessed a great deal of courage, she appeared to be socially inferior to the scheming Isabella. Which rendered her vulnerable to the kind of attack he had no doubt the girl would launch at the first available opportunity.

He had wondered how he might repay Miss Gibson for helping him preserve his liberty. Now he knew. Over the next few weeks, at the very least, he would keep a discreet watch over her.

Or heaven alone knew what twisted form of revenge the thwarted Miss Waverley would exact.

Chapter Two

Another day in London.

Henrietta looked out of the drawing-room window at the row of houses across the street from the one her Aunt Ledbetter inhabited, repressing a sigh.

Too many buildings squashed together, too many people thronging the narrow streets, too much noise and bustle, and an overpowering concentration of smells. She had only been here just over a month and already she longed for the peace and quiet of Much Wakering: the wide skies, the sound of birdsong and the scent of blossom.

From her bedroom window she could see just one tree, if she hung out over the windowsill and craned her neck. One miserable, stunted sapling that looked as out of place in its environment as she felt.

'What did you think of the performance, Miss Gibson?'

Henrietta started and pulled her attention back to her aunt's guests. Or at least, the one guest who was trying to include her in a conversation to which she had not been giving her full attention. She had hoped that going to sit on a chair on the fringes of the room would have been enough to deter people from obliging her to talk. But Mrs Crimmer was not an easy person to deter from any course upon which she set her mind.

'The performance? Oh, I, um...' They had gone to the theatre the night before. In truth, if she were in a better frame of mind, she would have enjoyed the spectacle. But ever since Miss Twining's ball there had been a cold lump of misery lodged just beneath her breastbone, which not even the most skilled of clowns could alleviate, and a fog of depression hanging round her through which everything she saw seemed grey and unappealing.

As unappealing as she knew herself to be.

The only thing that managed to make her haul herself out of bed in the mornings was the knowledge that if she lay there all day feeling sorry for herself, her aunt would worry. Mrs Ledbetter had done so much more than just accept

the responsibility when her father had written to
his cousin to ask if she might supervise a Season in London. Mrs Ledbetter had flung herself into the task with an enthusiasm which had
taken Henrietta by surprise. At first, she'd been
inclined to feel a bit offended by the way 'Aunt'
Ledbetter had shaken her head and clucked her
tongue as she'd watched the maid unpack her
clothes. But then she'd never had a female rela-
tive supervise her wardrobe, at least not since
her mother's death so many years ago. And any
offence soon melted away under the discovery
that Mrs Ledbetter did not just enjoy shopping
for clothes, but derived enormous pleasure from
discovering which colours or styles became her
the most. When she wasn't taking her shopping
for garments and all sorts of accessories Henrietta had no idea were absolutely essential, she
had hired people to round her off in other ways.
A *friseur* had come to the house to cut and style
her hair. A dancing master visited regularly to
teach her the steps of all the dances she had always wished she might be able to do, but had
never had the opportunity to learn.

And her kindness continued, day after day.
She organised trips to the theatre or the latest exhibitions, and took her to musical evenings and
dinner parties where she introduced her to all
her friends and acquaintances. Nothing was too

much trouble. And, considering her own daughter Mildred was at an age to be considering matrimonial prospects herself, she might easily have treated Henrietta as a rival, or a threat, or even just an imposition.

Neither mother nor daughter had done any such thing. They had welcomed her into their circle with open arms.

For their sakes, Henrietta drew on all her reserves of will-power and mustered up a wan smile.

'We have nothing like it in Much Wakering, Mrs Crimmer,' she said quite truthfully. 'So many talented acts, one after another. It was quite, um…'

'Overwhelming, was it, my dear?'

Mrs Crimmer, the wife of one of Mr Ledbetter's business contacts, nodded her head in a sympathetic manner. People who lived in London all year round, she had swiftly discovered, tended to look upon *provincials* with a mixture of pity and contempt.

If Mrs Crimmer had spoken so patronisingly to her three days ago, she would have made a withering retort. Or at least, she corrected herself, she would have bitten one back, for the sake of Mildred's prospects. For Mr and Mrs Ledbetter were hoping that Mildred would look favourably upon young Mr Crimmer's suit.

She glanced across the room to where the red-faced young man was paying court, rather bashfully, to Mildred, while Mildred was looking decidedly unimpressed.

Her aunt and uncle, for so she had come to think of them, might have hopes in that direction, but Mildred was looking for more from life than a prosaic match to cement a business alliance. She was looking for romance.

But then Mildred was pretty enough to have romantic aspirations. She had lovely golden hair, wide green eyes and a delicate little nose that made her look like an angelic kitten.

Perhaps that was why they had all accepted Henrietta into the household so readily, she sighed. With her gawky figure and plain face, she posed no threat to her distant cousin. When the pair of them walked into a room, all masculine attention went to Mildred.

Which had not bothered Henrietta in the slightest. She did not want masculine attention. Or at least, she had only ever hankered after the attention of *one* man.

But even he was beyond her reach now. Three nights ago, he'd finally forced her to accept the fact that she'd been a complete fool to follow him to London. And now she could no longer even pretend to herself that, deep down, she *did* mean something to him.

She could never have meant anything to him, for him to treat her as he had. She reached out and took a biscuit from the plate set on the table between her and Mrs Crimmer.

She was stuck in town until the end of June, at the very earliest, for she could not bring herself to slink home. Especially not in the light of what he'd said.

You belong in the country, not in a rackety place like London, had been the opinion he'd expressed upon the only occasion he'd called upon her. *I shouldn't wonder at it if you aren't soon aching to get back to Much Wakering.*

It was galling to admit that, in a way, he was correct. She *did* miss the trees and the tranquillity, and the fact that everyone knew everyone else.

But that didn't make her a country bumpkin.

It had been a shock to hear Richard—her Richard, as she'd still been thinking of him then—speak to her in such patronising tones. She had only been in town one week, after all, and of course she'd still been a bit wide-eyed and excited.

But that did not mean she would *never* be able to cope with the sophistication of London society. Why, Richard himself had only acquired his town bronze after several trips. At first, the difference had only been apparent in his appear-

ance. He'd begun to look very smart in clothes
bought from a London tailor. And then the way
he'd had his hair cut, well, it had drawn gasps of
admiration all round. That shock of unruly curls
had been tamed into a style that took much of the
boyish roundness from his freckled face. He'd
no longer looked like the easy-going son of the
local squire, but, well, just as she'd always en-
visioned Paris, the man so handsome goddesses
had squabbled over him. But, gradually, she'd
sensed an inner change, too. She'd begun to feel
uneasily as if he was drawing further and further
away from her. And this last Christmas there had
been a veneer of sophistication about him, expressed in languid mannerisms which were so
unlike those of the blunt, honest boy who had
run tame in her house for years that he had made
her feel positively naïve and tongue-tied.

She ought, she reflected gloomily as she
snapped her biscuit in half, to have taken heed
of his withdrawal then and spared herself the
humiliation she'd endured at Miss Twining's
ball. Or recognised his reference to her return
to Much Wakering as a hint that he didn't want
her in town. Instead, she had persuaded herself
that his words were an awkward expression of
concern for how she would cope. Oh, why was
she so stupid? Why hadn't she seen? If he had really been concerned about how she would cope,

he would have escorted her everywhere. Haunted the Ledbetters' house and taken steps to shield her from all the undesirable elements he warned her stalked London society.

Well, now she knew better.

She popped one half of the biscuit into her mouth, consoling herself with the fact that at least she had not confided her romantic aspirations with regard to Richard to anyone. Which meant she was the only one who knew what a stupid, pathetic fool she'd been.

Unfortunately, it also made it quite impossible to go home. If she were to start talking about leaving, everyone would want to know why she wanted to cut her stay short. And she had no plausible excuse to give. She couldn't possibly offend her dear Aunt Ledbetter by letting her think she was in any way responsible for her present unhappiness. And she was absolutely never going to let anybody know what a fool she'd made of herself over Richard. Her heart might be bruised, but at least her pride was still intact.

And that was the rub. If she insisted on going home without confessing the full truth, they would all assume she wanted to go back to the countryside because town life was, indeed, too much for her.

Given the choice between looking like a silly

girl who'd pursued a man who didn't love her to London, or a feeble-minded ninny who couldn't cope with being more than five miles away from her parish church, or putting a brave face on it and staying in town when all the lustre had gone from the experience, Henrietta had decided on the latter course. She would stay in town.

Besides, she owed her aunt and cousin even more since her ignominious departure from Miss Twining's ball. They had been so gracious about it. They had fussed over her in the coach when they'd seen her tears, and expressed the kind of sympathy for the fictitious headache she'd claimed which she had never in her life experienced before. She would never have invented a headache to explain her distress if she'd known how concerned they would be. She had just assumed they would pat her hand and send her to her room for a quiet lie down, like her brothers or her father would have done.

Instead, they'd come to her room with her, with vials of lavender water to dab on her temples, and had stayed with her while she drank a soothing tisane, sharing anecdotes about their own monthly fluctuations in health until she'd been almost crushed with guilt.

Particularly as they'd both been so thrilled to get an invitation to the house of a genuine baronet—Aunt Ledbetter so that she could gossip over the details of the interior of a baronial town house with her circle of friends and Mildred because she hoped to attract the attention of one of the sons of the lower ranks of the nobility who were bound to fill the house. She had robbed them both of at least half their pleasure, just because she'd been unable to control her temper when she'd seen that cat Miss Waverley attempting to snare yet another poor unsuspecting man in her clutches.

Even when she'd tried to apologise, their response had heaped coals of fire on her head.

'We would not have spent even that one hour in such elevated company had you not become friends with Miss Twining,' Aunt Ledbetter had said. *'In fact, I thought it most gracious of her to include us in your invitation at all.'*

'Yes,' she had replied weakly. *'Miss Twining is a lovely person.'* Which short statement had been the only truthful remark she could make about the entire affair. For she really had liked Julia Twining for the way she had not looked down her nose at Henrietta's London connections, nor made any disparaging remarks about their background.

Unlike some people.

'I cannot help wondering where on earth your father dredged up this set of relatives,' Richard had said, eyeing her aunt askance on the one

visit he'd paid to this very drawing room. *'Never heard of 'em before you took it into your head you wanted a Season. And now I've met 'em, I'm not a bit surprised. Oh, not that there's anything wrong with them, in their way. Cits often are very respectable. It's just that they're not the sort of people I want to mix with, while I'm in town. And if your father ever took his nose out of a book long enough to notice what's what, he'd have known better than to send you to stay with people who can't introduce you to anyone that matters, or take you any of the places a girl of your station ought to be seen.'*

Had she really been so idiotic as to interpret that statement as an expression of concern for her? He was not in the least bit concerned for her. He was just worried that she might pop up somewhere and embarrass him with her humble relations, or perhaps her countrified ways, in front of his newer, smarter, London friends.

But, she consoled herself, stuffing the other half of the biscuit into her mouth, at least she'd had the spirit to object to the disparaging way he'd spoken about her father.

'Papa cannot help being a bit unaware of what London society is like,' she had said, firmly. *'You know he hardly ever comes up to town any more, and when he does it is only because he has heard that some rare book has finally come on*

the market.' After all, she could not deny that Richard's accusation was, in part, justified. She had not been a week in town before realising that because his cousin had married a man of business, she did not have, as Richard had so scornfully pointed out, the entrée into anywhere even remotely fashionable. *'And anyway,'* she'd continued, loathe to admit to her disappointment, *'if he did know, he would probably think it highly frivolous. He never judges a man by his rank or wealth, as you should know by now. How many times have you heard him say that a man's real worth stems from his character and his intellect?'*

She reached for another biscuit, feeling rather pleased with herself for taking that stance, even when she had still been Richard's dupe. But then nothing would make her tolerate any criticism of her father, from whatever quarter it came.

Besides, he already felt badly enough about the discovery that she had somehow attained the age of two and twenty without him having done anything about finding her a husband.

The slightly bewildered look had crossed his face—the one he always adopted when forced to confront anything to do with the domestic side of life—when she had first tentatively broached the subject of having a London Season. *'Are you quite sure you are old enough to want to think of getting married?'* He had then taken off his spectacles, and laid them on his desk with a resolute air. *'But of course, my dear, if you want a Season, then you must have one. Leave it with me.'*

'You...you won't forget?' It would have been just like him. And he knew it, too, for instead of reprimanding her for speaking in such a forthright manner, he had smiled and assured her that, no, when it came to something as important as his only daughter's future, he most certainly would not forget.

And he hadn't forgotten. He just hadn't got it quite right. But since she had not the heart to disillusion him about the wonderful time he hoped she was having, she had kept her letters home both cheerful and suitably vague.

Mrs Crimmer was still chattering away, but Henrietta had not heard a word for several minutes while she had been alternately woolgathering and munching her way methodically through the entire plate of biscuits. Her mind had not been able to do much more than go over and over the night of Miss Twining's ball for days. It had all been so very much more painful, she had decided, because she'd pinned such hopes on it. And on Miss Twining herself. She really had hoped they might be friends. It hadn't seemed to matter to *her* that she was staying with unfashionable relatives in the least. Miss Twining had even said she might call her Julia, she sighed, reaching for the last biscuit.

But the incident at the ball had destroyed any possibility that friendship could blossom between them, even if they'd had anything in common, which there hadn't been time to find out, for she had left the ball before Miss Waverley, so that it would be Miss Waverley's version of events that everyone would hear. And she knew such a schemer would not waste the heaven-sent opportunity to blacken her enemy's reputation.

Not that she cared. She had no wish to step outside her aunt's social circle *ever* again.

What was the point?

'I say, what a bang-up rig,' remarked Mr Bentley, who was lounging against the frame of the other window, amusing himself by watching the passing traffic. He was a friend of Mr Crimmer junior. She rather thought his role today was not only to provide moral support during the gruelling ordeal of attempting to make Mildred smile on him, but also to bear him company to the nearest hostelry, once they had stayed the requisite half-hour, to help revive Mr Crimmer's battered spirits.

'Pulled up right outside, as though he means to pay a visit here. By Jove, he does, too. He's coming up the steps.'

On receipt of that information her aunt, to everyone's astonishment, leapt from the sofa upon which she had been sitting and reached the window in one bound.

'Oh, my goodness,' she exclaimed, having thrust Mr Bentley aside and peered out. 'He said he would call, but I never dreamed for one moment that he *meant* it. Even though he asked so particularly for our direction.'

Henrietta froze, the last biscuit halfway to her mouth. From her vantage point she, too, had seen the stylish curricle pull up in front of the house and had already recognised its driver.

'Henrietta, my dear,' said Aunt Ledbetter, whirling round to face her, 'perhaps I should have mentioned it before, but…' She paused at the sound of the front door knocker rapping. 'Lord Deben said he might call, to see how you were, after…' She checked, as though only just recalling that her drawing room was full of visitors. 'After you were taken ill at Miss Twining's ball.'

Voices in the hall alerted them to the fact that Lord Deben had entered the house.

Aunt Ledbetter sprinted back to her sofa and sat down hastily, arranging her skirts and adopting a languid pose, as though she had earls dropping in upon her every day of the week.

All conversation ceased. Every eye turned towards the door.

'Lord Deben,' announced Warnes, their butler.

Lord Deben strode into the room and paused, looking about him down his thin, aristocratic nose.

Henrietta's hackles rose. He'd walked into Miss Twining's house wearing just the same expression, as though he couldn't quite believe he'd graced the place with his presence. Back then, she hadn't known who or what he was, but the impression he had made on the others, his knowledge of it and his contemptuous reaction, had given her an instant dislike of the man.

His gaze swept her aunt's drawing room with an air that somehow conveyed the impression he did not see anyone until his eyes came to rest on her.

'Miss Gibson,' he said, crossing the room to where she sat, 'I trust I find you in better health today?'

It was all Henrietta could do to bite back an enquiry as to whether he had ever had any manners, or whether he just did not see the need to employ them today. What kind of man ignored his hostess, let alone the other occupants of the room?

But then Richard had behaved just like this when he'd come here, too. Richard had thought himself too good for this company. Richard had not deigned to speak to any of them either, dismissively referring to them as a bunch of clerks and shopkeepers. Though even he had, in deference to good manners, at least given Aunt Ledbetter a perfunctory bow before giving his undivided attention to Henrietta.

So she was not in the least bit flattered by the way Lord Deben bowed over her hand. When it looked as though he meant to kiss it, she raised it to her own mouth instead, shoving the last of the biscuits defiantly between her teeth.

She heard Mildred gasp.

Lord Deben's expression did not alter one whit.

'You still look a trifle peaked,' he informed her, shutting out the other occupants of the room by the simple pretext of standing with his back to them all. 'I shall take you out for a drive in the park. That should put the bloom back in your cheeks.'

'You will take me out for a drive,' she repeated. What unmitigated gall! Did he think she was so stupid she couldn't see how he was snubbing her poor dear aunt? Besides, what if she didn't want to go out? What then? She was just about to inform him that nothing on earth would induce her to leave this room, in the company of a man who clearly thought he was too good for it, when Mr Bentley burst out,

'My word, what I wouldn't give for a chance

to tool that set-up round the park. Or even sit up beside you, my lord.' He shot Henrietta a look loaded with envy. 'You lucky, lucky girl!'

Lord Deben's heavy lids lowered a fraction. He turned towards Mr Bentley, his lip curling. 'I do not generally invite young gentlemen to escort me in the park during the fashionable hour,' he remarked in a crushing tone that instantly reduced his admirer to red-faced silence.

He hadn't invited her, either. Issued an order, more like.

'And it is very generous of you to invite Henrietta,' said her aunt, shooting her a look loaded with meaning. 'Such an unlooked-for honour. It will not take her but a moment to run upstairs and put on a bonnet and coat.' She made shooing motions towards Henrietta behind Lord Deben's back. 'Will it, my dear?'

No, it wouldn't. And it would be better, much better for her aunt if she got him out of the house to tell him what she thought of his manners, than create a scene in her aunt's drawing room.

'Make haste,' he said to Henrietta brusquely, finally succeeding in grasping her hand and using the hold he gained upon it to lift her to her feet. 'I do not want to keep my horses standing.'

His horses! Well, that put her in her place. He rated their welfare far higher than such a paltry consideration as her sensibilities!

Who did he think he was? To come in here and comprehensively insult everyone like that?

Henrietta swept out of the room on a surge of indignation that completely banished the lethargy that had made even walking require a huge effort of will-power since Miss Twining's ball.

Not keep his horses waiting, indeed! She marched up the stairs and flung open the door to her room.

And to crush poor Mr Bentley, she fumed as she strode across to the armoire and yanked it open, who'd only been expressing the kind of boyish enthusiasm for the splendour of his horses that any of her brothers might have done.

And to ignore her aunt and her cousins like that! Just because they were connected to trade! Because he thought they were common.

Well, she'd show him common.

She stuffed her arms into the sleeves of her mulberry redingote, then marched along the corridor to her aunt's room, where she ruthlessly plundered her selection of furs until she found the fox. She slung it round her shoulders, pausing before the mirror only long enough to assure herself that it did indeed clash with her coat as horribly as she'd hoped, before making for Mildred's room and the high-crowned bonnet, topped with a pair of bright red ostrich feathers, which had only arrived the morning before.

* * *

When she reappeared in the drawing room, not five minutes after she'd left it, Mildred's jaw dropped. Her aunt made a faint choking noise.

Lord Deben, who was standing at the window, next to Mr Bentley, cocked his head to one side as his lazy brown eyes scanned her outfit.

'More colour already,' he drawled with a perfectly straight face, 'just at the mere prospect of taking the air.'

'Oh, yes,' she agreed with a smile as she stalked towards him. 'I am so looking forward to being seen driving round the park with you, at the *fashionable* hour.'

This would serve him right! He looked just the type of man who would hate being seen driving about with someone who looked positively vulgar. He might have lowered himself by inviting a girl to drive with him who was well outside the circles in which he normally moved, but he had taken the greatest care over his own outfit. She knew enough about male fashion to guess that his clothing hailed from the most expensive, exclusive tailors. And he had shaved, very recently. His cheeks had that sheen that only lasted an hour or so after the event, and besides, when he had bent over her hand to attempt to kiss it, she had smelled oil of bergamot.

'How little did I think,' she simpered, 'when I

came up to town that I should have the honour of being taken driving by such an *important* man. In such a…a *bang-up* rig, too.'

His face, she noted with savage pleasure, was growing more wooden by the second.

'I shall be sure to give you a full account of my treat, Mr Bentley—' she beamed at the youth whose eyes were swivelling from the immaculately clad earl, to the ostrich feathers adorning her borrowed hat with something like horror '—next time you call upon us.'

Lord Deben gestured for her to precede him into the hall and, with her ostrich plumes bobbing in time to her martial stride, they set off.

Chapter Three

So what if he had finally found some semblance of manners and opened the door for her? It meant nothing. Except, perhaps, that he couldn't wait to escape the presence of people he considered so far beneath him.

So what if he was a good driver? Just because he could weave in and out of the heavy traffic with an ease of manner that made it look effortless, when she knew it required great skill, did not make him any less unlikeable.

She was almost glad when, having swept through the park gates, he repeatedly cut people dead who were trying to attract his attention. It made it so much easier to cling to her bad humour, which the thrillingly rapid drive through the teeming streets had almost dispelled.

'You are not an easy person to run to ground,' he said suddenly, just when she was beginning to wonder whether the entire outing was going to take place in silence. 'I looked for you at the Cardingtons' and the Lensboroughs' on Tuesday, the Swaffhams', Pendleboroughs', and Bonhams' last night. And I regret to say that I do not have much time to spare on you today, even though it is imperative that we have some private conversation regarding what happened at that débutante's ball whose name escapes me for the moment. Hence the abduction.' He turned and bestowed a lazy smile upon her.

She felt a funny jolt in her stomach. There was something in that look that almost compelled her to smile back. Which was absurd, since she was very cross with him.

Reminding herself that he could not even recall the name of the girl she'd hoped might have become a friend was just what she needed to bolster her resentment.

'On Tuesday night,' she therefore retorted, 'I was at a dance held by the Mountjoys. They are vintners. I don't suppose you know them. And last night we went to the theatre in a party with most of the people who were sitting around the drawing room just now.'

'Mountjoy...' he mused. 'I think I do know

of them. I have a feeling they supply my cellars at Deben House.'

'I shouldn't be a bit surprised. They boast of having the patronage of several of the more well-heeled members of the *ton*, though not the entrée into their homes.'

'Ah,' he said.

'And before you ask how I came to be at such an exalted affair as *Miss Twining's* come-out ball, it was entirely due to the offices of my brother Hubert, who serves in the same regiment as her brother Charlie. Charlie wrote to her, asking if she wouldn't mind calling on me, because I wasn't likely to know anyone in town just at first.'

Not that *he'd* thought of it as an exalted affair. To judge from the look on his face, he'd regarded attendance as a tedious duty, probably undertaken out of some kind of obligation to the elderly lady he'd been escorting.

While for her it had been an evening that should have brought nothing but delight.

Well, neither of them had got quite what they'd expected.

At the time he'd walked in looking all cynical and bored, she'd still been full of hope she might run into Richard there. Miss Twining was bound to have sent him an invitation, since he, too, was friendly with her brother Charlie. And she was

fairly sure that he would have called in for half
an hour, at least, to 'do the pretty', even if he did
not stay to dance. She had so hoped that, seeing
her all dressed up in her London finery, with her
hair so stylishly cut, her brother Hubert's best
friend would at long last see that she had grown
up. See her as a woman, to be taken seriously,
and not just one of his childhood playmates that
he could casually brush aside.

'Had I known how you are circumstanced,'
said Lord Deben, interrupting her gloomy reflec-
tions of that fateful night, 'I would have called
upon you sooner.'

'But you did know how I am circumstanced.
Lady Chigwell took great pains to let you know
that she considered I was intruding amongst my
betters.'

'I assumed that was spite talking and dis-
counted it. Particularly when I looked you up
and discovered that you have a much more impressive pedigree than Lady Chigwell, whose
husband's title, such as it is, is a mere two generations old.'

'You looked me up…?'

'Of course. I had no intention of asking around
and raising people's curiosity about why I wished
to know more about you. When I found that you
are Miss Gibson of Shoebury Manor in Much
Wakering and that your father is Sir Henry Gib-

son, scientist and scholar, member of the Royal Society, I naturally assumed you would be attending the kind of events most débutantes of your age enjoy when they come up to town for their Season.' His mouth twisted with distaste. 'Had I known that you would not, no power on earth would have compelled me to attend any of them.'

He'd spent two consecutive evenings haunting places he did not want to go to, merely because he had thought she might be there? And now she was obliging him to drive round the park, at the fashionable hour, while she was dressed in such spectacularly vulgar style?

For the first time in days, she felt almost cheerful.

'What a lot of time you have wasted on my account,' she said, with a satisfied gleam in her eye.

'Well, it is not because I have been struck by a *coup de foudre*,' he said sharply. 'Do not take it into your head that I have an interest in you for any sentimental or…romantic reason,' he said with a curl to his lip as he glanced at her out of the corner of his eye.

'I wouldn't!' The coxcomb! Did he really believe that every female in London sighed after him, just because Miss Waverley had flung herself at him?

'Let me tell you that I wouldn't *want* to attract that kind of attention from a man as unpleasant and rude as you,' she retorted hotly. 'In fact, I didn't want to come out for a drive with you today at all. And I wouldn't have, either, if it wouldn't have meant embarrassing my aunt.'

His full lips tightened in displeasure. Nobody spoke to him like that. Nobody.

'It is as well I gave you little choice, then, is it not?'

'I do not see that at all. I do not see that there is any reason for you to have looked for me, or investigated my background, or dragged me out of the house today...'

'When you were clearly enjoying the company so much,' he sneered.

She blinked. Had her misery been that obvious?

'It was nothing to do with the company. *They* are all perfectly lovely people, who have very generously opened their home to me...'

He frowned. He had dismissed the suspicion that she had taken him in aversion on that accursed terrace, assuming she was just angry at the whole world, because of some injustice being perpetrated upon her. But he could not hold on to that assumption any longer. From his preliminary investigation into her background, and that of her father, and the people with whom she was living, he could find no reason why anyone should attempt to coerce her into marriage. He had not yet managed to find out why she was living with a set of cits in Bloomsbury, when she had perfectly respectable relations who could have presented her at court, but she clearly felt no ill will towards them for not being able to launch her into society. She had just referred to *them* as perfectly lovely people, putting such stress on the pronoun that he could not mistake her implication that she excluded him from the set of people she liked.

In short, his first impression had been correct. She really did not like him at all. His scowl landed at random upon the driver of a very showy high-perch phaeton going in the opposite direction, causing the young man such consternation he very nearly ran his team off the road.

'Then I can only deduce that whatever is still making you look as though you are on the verge of going into a decline had its origins at Miss Twining's ball.'

His scowl intensified. He was inured to enduring this level of antagonism from his siblings, but he had no experience of prolonging an interaction with a person to whom he was not bound by ties of family who held him in dislike. It was problematical. He was not going to rescind his decision to provide a bulwark against whatever malice Miss Waverley chose to unleash upon her, but he had taken it for granted she would have received his offer of assistance with becoming gratitude. After all, he was about to bestow a singular honour upon her. Never, in his entire life, had he gone to so much trouble on another person's behalf.

The usual pattern was for people to seek him out. If they didn't bore him too dreadfully, he generally permitted them limited access to his circle, while he waited to discover what their motives were for attempting to get near him.

He turned his glare sideways, where she sat with that beak of a nose in the air, completely shutting him out.

The corners of his mouth turned down, as he bit back a string of oaths. What the devil had got into him? He did not want her to fawn over him, did he? He despised toadeaters.

It must just be that he was not used to having to expend any effort in getting people to like him. He didn't quite know how to go about it—

Hold hard—like him? Why the devil should he be concerned whether this aggravating chit liked him or not? He had never cared one whit for another's opinion. And he would not, most definitely not, care about hers either.

Which resolve lasted until the moment she turned her face up to his, and said, with a tremor in her voice, and stress creasing her brow, 'I don't, do I? Please tell me I don't look as though I'm going into a decline.'

'Well, Miss Gibson—'

'Because I am not going to.' She straightened up, as though she was exerting her entire will to pull herself together. 'Absolutely not. Only a spineless ninny would—' She shut her mouth with a snap, as though feeling she had said too much.

Leaving him wishing he could pull up the carriage and put his arms round her. Just to comfort her. She was struggling so valiantly to conceal some form of heartbreak that his own concerns no longer seemed to matter so very much.

Of course, he would do no such thing. For one thing, he was the very last person qualified to offer comfort to a heartbroken woman. He was more usually the one accused of doing the breaking. And the only comfort he'd ever given a female had been of the hot and sweaty variety. With his reputation, and given what he knew of her, if he did attempt to put his arms round her Miss Gibson would no doubt misinterpret his motives and slap his face.

'This is getting tiresome,' he said. 'I wish you would stop pretending you have no idea why I sought you out.'

'I do *not* know why you should have done such a thing. I never expected to see you again, after I left that horrid ball. Especially not when I found out that you are an earl.'

'Two earls, if you count the Irish title. Not that many people do.'

'I don't care how many earls you are, or what country you have the authority to lord it over, I just wish you had left me alone!'

'Tut tut, Miss Gibson. Can you really believe that I would not wish to take the very first opportunity that offered to thank you for coming so gallantly to my rescue?'

'To *thank* me?' He had gone to all this trouble to express his thanks?

He watched her subside on to the seat, her anger visibly draining away.

'Oh, well...'

'Miss Gibson, I do thank you. From the bottom of what passes for my heart. It is not an exaggeration to say you saved me from a fate worse than death.'

'Having to get married, you mean?'

'Oh, no, never that. Had you not intervened, I would merely have repudiated Miss Waverley, stood back and watched her commit social suicide by attempting to manipulate me,' he corrected her. 'Absolutely nothing would have induced me to tamely fall in with her schemes. I would rather take a pistol and shoot myself in the leg.'

'Oh.' To say she was shocked was putting it mildly. She had grown up believing that gentlemen adhered to a certain code of morals. But he had just admitted he would have allowed Miss Waverley to ruin herself, without lifting so much as a finger to prevent it.

'Oh? Is that all you have to say?' He had just, for some reason, confided something to her that he would never have dreamed of telling another living soul. Though for the life of him he could not think why. And all she could say was *Oh*.

'No. I...I think I can see now why you wished to speak to me privately. That...kind of thing is not the...kind of thing one can talk about in a crowded drawing room.'

'Precisely.' He didn't think he'd ever had to work so hard to wring such a small concession from anyone. 'Hence the ruthless abduction.' Well, he wasn't going to admit that a large part of why he'd detached her from her family was because he still harboured a suspicion there could be some sinister reason for her having been sent to them. It would make it sound as though he read Gothic novels, in which helpless young women were imprisoned and tyrannised by ruthless step-parents, and needed a daring, heroic man, usually a peer of the realm, to uncover the foul plot and set them free.

'I had hoped to find you at the kind of event

where I could have drawn you aside discreetly and thanked you before now.'

'Oh.' She wished she could think of something more intelligent to say, but really, what was there to say? She had never met anyone so utterly ruthless. So selfish.

Except perhaps Miss Waverley herself.

'I regret the necessity of being rather short with your estimable relation and her guests, but I am supposed to be working on a speech this afternoon.'

'A speech?'

'Yes. For the House. There is quite an important debate currently in progress, on which I have most decided views. My secretary knows them, of course, but if I once allowed him to put words into my mouth, he might gain the impression that I was willing to let him influence my opinions, too. Which would not do.'

He frowned. Why was he explaining himself to her? He never bothered explaining himself to anyone. Why start now, just because she was giving him that measuring look?

On receipt of that frown, Henrietta shrank in shame. Her aunt had positively gushed about what an important man Lord Deben was, and how people had stared to see him being so gracious to them when Henrietta was 'taken ill', and the more she'd gone on, the more Henrietta had resented him. She'd thought he was just high and mighty, looking down his nose at them because he had wealth and a title. But now she realised that he really was an important, and probably very influential, man. And he was telling her that he took his responsibilities quite seriously.

She could not wonder at it that he looked a little irritated to be driving such a graceless female around the park when he ought to be concentrating on matters of state.

And she supposed she really *should* be grateful for the way he was handling his need to thank her. She most certainly did not want to risk anyone overhearing anything that pertained to the events that had occurred on the terrace either.

Nor the ones that had propelled her out there.

'I apologise if I have misconstrued your, um, behaviour,' she said. 'But you need not have given it another thought. And I still don't see why...'

'If you would just keep your tongue between your teeth for five seconds, I might have a chance of explaining.'

There was a tightness about his lips that spoke of temper being firmly reined in. A few minutes ago, she would have been glad to see that she was nettling him.

But not now, for she was beginning to suspect she might have misjudged him. And deliberately chalked up a list of crimes to his account, of which, if she were honest with herself, it was Richard who was guilty.

It had started when he'd come out on to the terrace just when she'd most needed to be alone. As she'd dived behind the planters, she'd banged her knee and roundly cursed him. And then, recalling the look he'd had on his face when he'd arrived at the ball, she'd promptly decided he was exactly like Richard. From then on, resentment had steadily built up, when to be truthful, she really did not know anything about this man's character at all.

It was about time she gave him a chance to explain himself. So she made a show of closing her mouth and turned her face to look up at him, wide-eyed and attentive.

A slight relaxation about his mouth showed her that he had taken note of her literal obedience.

'You made an enemy of Miss Waverley that night,' he said. 'And since you came to my defence, I felt I owed it to you to warn you. If she can find any way to do you harm, be assured, she will do it.'

'Oh, is that all?' Henrietta relaxed and leaned back against the back of the bench seat.

'Do not take my warning lightly, Miss Gibson,' he said. 'Miss Waverley is a most determined young woman. Well, you saw it with your own eyes.' Eyes that were an incongruously bright shade of blue. He'd been thinking of her, ever since that night, in shades of autumn, because, he supposed, of her windswept hair and the way her temper had blown itself out, leaving the atmosphere behind it scoured clean. Her eyes therefore should have been brown. Brown as a conker. It was typical of her that they should not conform to his assumptions. Whenever he felt as though he had her classified, she did or said something to set him guessing all over again.

But not Miss Waverley. The Miss Waverleys of this world were entirely predictable.

'She will go to any lengths in pursuit of her ambition. I would not like to see that single-minded determination turned upon you, for harm.'

'There is nothing further she can do to me,' Henrietta replied gloomily.

Miss Waverley had already done her worst. Without even knowing it.

Henrietta had not been in the ballroom ten minutes before she had seen Richard. In spite of warning her that he had no intention of squiring her to any balls during her sojourn in town, there he was, all decked out in the most splendid style. His coat fit his broad shoulders to perfection. The knee breeches and silk stockings clung

Never Trust a Rake

faithfully to the muscular form of his calves and thighs. He had turned, smiled in recognition, and crossed the floor to where she was standing.

Her heart had banged against her ribs. Was this the moment? The moment when he would tell her she had never looked so pretty, and why had he ever thought dancing was a tedious waste of time and energy? There was nothing he would enjoy more than taking her in his arms...

Instead, he'd said how surprised he was to see her. 'The Twinings a bit above your aunt's touch, ain't they? Now, don't be disappointed if nobody much asks you to dance, Hen. People here set more store by appearances than they do in the country.'

'But you will dance with me, won't you?'

'Me!' He had pulled a face. 'Whatever gives you that idea! Beastly waste of time, if you ask me.'

'Yes, but you did tell Hubert you would look out for me while I was in town.'

He had frowned and stroked his chin. 'Aye. I did give Hubert my word. Tell you what I'll do,' he said, his perplexed expression clearing, 'I'll escort you in to supper. But I can't hang about jawing with you now, because some fellows are waiting for me in the card room. But I will see you later, at supper, and that's a promise,' he had said, backing away swiftly.

So swiftly, he had collided with Miss Waverley, who happened to be walking past.

'I say, dashed sorry!' he'd said, leaping back and landing on Henrietta's foot. She had tried not to yelp, for she detested cowardice in any form. Besides she'd taken far greater knocks from her boisterous brothers and their friends, growing up.

Afterwards, she wished she had made more of a fuss.

'Hope I didn't alarm you, Miss...' he said, while Miss Waverley had looked him up and down, coldly.

'So clumsy of me...' he'd blustered. Then he bowed. 'Allow me to make amends. Fetch you a drink.'

He had not offered to fetch *her* a drink, Henrietta had seethed. He'd said he had more important things to do than dance attendance on her. But when Miss Waverley had smiled at him, a tide of red had swept up from under his collar. When *she* had held out her hand and cooed that of course she forgave him, that a glass of lemonade would be wonderful, because wasn't it hot in here, and dancing made her sooo thirsty...

And he had dashed off to do *her* bidding.

As if that hadn't been bad enough, not twenty minutes later, from her seat on the sidelines with the other wallflowers, Henrietta had seen him take Miss Waverley on to the dance floor with an expression of besotted admiration on his face.

That was when she'd seen what a colossal fool she'd made of herself. She had followed Richard to town, thinking she could make him notice her. She had gone to stay with people who'd been strangers until she'd walked into their house, spent a small fortune at various modistes and outfitters, endured all kinds of painful procedures in the name of feminine beauty—and it had all been a complete waste of time. He simply did not see her as a woman. But he'd only had to take one look at the beautiful Miss Waverely to fall prostrate at *her* feet!

As she had watched them skipping down the set together, she had felt her heart breaking. At least, there was a pain, a very real pain in the region where she knew that organ beat. And her eyes began to smart. Bursting into tears in a ballroom was the very last thing any lady should do, but she was very much afraid she would not be able to hold her emotions in check if she sat there, watching Richard dance with another woman when he would not even condescend to *escort* her anywhere! Or waste his precious time talking, when he could have been in the card room with his *friends*.

Not that he even appeared to remember his

prior commitment to them any more. His entire being was focused on Miss Waverley.

Swiftly, before anyone could notice her emotional state, she'd dashed from the ballroom, running she knew not where, pulling open doors and slamming them behind her, in an effort to drown out the noise of the orchestra, whose cheerful strains seemed to mock her.

Somehow she had ended up outside. But she could still hear the music *they* were dancing to. She had gone to the windows that threw light on to the stone flags, even though she knew that if she looked inside, she would see them…still together, uncaring that she was out here, in the cold and damp, a sheet of glass between what she wanted and where she actually was in life.

She had let the tears flow then, but only once she was completely certain that nobody could see her.

Once she'd had her cry, and pulled herself together, she had planned to go back and act as though nothing was the matter. The very last thing she wanted was to have anyone know that she was suffering from unrequited love. It sounded so pathetic. If she had come across a girl crying because the man she had set her heart on was dancing with another, prettier girl, she would have no sympathy for her whatsoever. She would counsel this fictitious love-lorn girl to have a bit of pride. Show some backbone. Dry her eyes and go back with her head high, and dance the rest of the night away as though she had not a care in the world.

Perversely, the notion that she was betraying all her own principles over Richard made her tears start to flow afresh. How could she let him affect her like this? She despised herself for running after a man. But most of all, she despised herself for her total, abject failure at being feminine. It wasn't enough to put on an expensive gown and have her hair styled. She didn't have anything like the...*allure* of a Mildred, or a Miss Twining, let alone a Miss Waverley.

It was just as she had reached her lowest ebb that *he* had sauntered out on to the terrace. Lord Deben.

And she'd seen that if there was one thing worse than bursting into tears in a crowded ballroom, it would be being caught weeping, alone, by a man like him. She'd recoiled, earlier, from the way his hooded eyes had swept round the entire assembly with barely concealed contempt. She'd had no intention of handing him an excuse to sneer at her, personally, just when she was least able to deal with it.

And yet, now she cast her mind back, there had been one moment, when he'd turned that jaded face up to the rain, as though he needed to wash something away, when she'd wondered if he was facing some sorrow as great as her own. But then he'd pulled out his watch and turned to what little light there was. It had been enough to throw his harsh features into stark relief. She did not think she had ever seen a man who looked more jaded, or weary, or so very, very hard.

The brief pang of sympathy that had made her wonder what sorrow could have driven him out here in the rain, as well, withered and died. She was just thankful he had not noticed her. A man like that would never understand why she would run outside and weep over the notion her heart was broken. On the contrary, he would very likely laugh at her.

'Miss Gibson,' he now said firmly. 'Will you kindly pay attention?'

'I beg your pardon,' she said contritely. 'I was miles away.'

'I noticed,' he snarled. He had not only noticed, but been incensed by her inattention. He was used to people hanging on his every word. Particularly females.

'I can only assume you were re-living whatever it was Miss Waverley has done to make you believe there is nothing further she can do, but believe me, you are wrong.'

'I am wrong, but you are right, is that what

you mean? And do not presume you know what I was thinking about.'

'It was not difficult. You have a very expressive face. I watched every emotion flit across its surface. Yearning, despair, anger, and then came a resolute lifting of your chin that told me you refuse to let her win.'

'It was not...nothing like...' she sputtered.

'Then you have not had your heart bruised? You have not decided that only a perfect ninny would go into a decline?'

She winced as he flung her own words back at her.

'I may have said more than I should have, about matters which are quite private and personal...' She had not told anyone about Richard and, if she had her way, she would keep the whole sorry episode secret to her dying day. 'But that does not give you the right to taunt me...'

'Taunt you?' He shot her a sharp look. She looked upset. And his irritation at her preoccupation with other matters, when she ought to have been paying him attention, promptly subsided.

'Far from it. I admire your fighting spirit. If anyone tries to knock you down, you come out fighting, do you not? In just the same way that you erupted from behind your plant pots, taking up the cudgels on my behalf when you thought the odds were stacked against me.'

Which nobody had ever done before.

And though she was now giving a shrug of her shoulders, as though it was nothing, she had not denied that she had felt some kind of...empathy towards him and had wanted to help.

It gave him a most peculiar sensation. He ought, most properly, to have taken offence at her presumption he was in any way in need of anyone's assistance. But he wasn't offended in the least. Whenever he looked at her, when she wasn't annoying him, that was, he couldn't quite stem a feeling of warmth towards the only person who had ever, disinterestedly, attempted to stand up for him.

'And now I fear that the odds might be unfairly stacked against you. I repay my debts, Miss Gibson. I shall be your ally.'

She blinked up at him in surprise.

'Miss Waverley will try to harm you if she can,' he explained. 'She is the kind of person who would have no compunction about using her social advantages to prevent you from achieving whatever it was you hoped to achieve by coming to town for a Season.'

Henrietta let out a bitter laugh.

Lord Deben glanced at her sharply. 'You remarked that there was nothing *further* she could do. Has she already exacted some form of revenge? Damn! I had not thought she would move so swiftly.'

'No. You do not understand…'

And he would not understand if she explained it, not a man like him. He might say he would be her ally, but this was the same man who'd just told her he could stand back and watch a woman *commit social suicide* rather than do the gentlemanly thing.

'Please, just accept the fact that there is nothing Miss Waverley can do that she has not already done. And I thank you for your concern, but I assure you that there is no need to prolong this…excursion.'

They were just approaching the turn before the exit.

Before they'd set out Lord Deben had decided to spare Miss Gibson only as much of his time as it would take to express his thanks, deliver the warning and offer his assistance. He'd assumed it would take him no longer than it would take to drive her just the once round the ring.

But instead of steering his vehicle through the gate, he commenced another circuit.

He was the one who would decide when this excursion was at an end, not the impudent, ungrateful…unfathomable Miss Gibson.

Chapter Four

'You went straight home that night,' he drawled, refusing to let her guess he could be motivated by anything more than mild curiosity. 'You have not shown your face at any of the events attended by the set of which she thinks herself the queen. Therefore, whatever she did, she did before you came to my rescue on the terrace.'

Queen? Oh, yes, that described Miss Waverley's attitude exactly. Henrietta had only observed her that one evening, but she had certainly regarded male homage as her due. And she seemed to have susceptible, country-born boys like Richard queuing up to pay it.

Her mouth twisted into a moue of disgust.

'Aha! I have hit the nail on the head. Pray do not bother to deny it. It was something Miss Waverley did that sent you outside to cry that night.'

She had never seen such a cynical smile as the one which curled his lordship's lips.

'And when you saw your chance to thrust a spoke in her wheel,' he said, his upper lip curling with contempt, 'you took it.'

She was just about to deny having done any such thing, when she recalled what she had thought, earlier, about her not wishing to let Miss Waverley get her claws into *another* poor, unsuspecting man.

She sat back, a frown pleating her brow. Had she really put a stop to Miss Waverley's attempt to compromise Lord Deben out of jealousy and spite? She was appalled to think she could act from such base motives.

Shaken, she attempted to replay the scene, with another woman in the place of Miss Waverley.

It was hard to be completely objective, because she had not been thinking, so much as reacting to events that night. On first recognising Miss Waverley, she had wondered why she had not noticed the music had ceased, for her presence outside must mean her dance with Richard was ended. And her eyes had then flown to the door through which she'd come, in horror. Surely she'd suffered enough for one night! She could not bear it if Richard were to follow Miss Waverley on to the terrace and she had to witness a nauseating display of lovemaking between them.

By the time she'd realised that nobody had followed Miss Waverley outside, the brazen hussy had already sidled up to Lord Deben and was trying to get him to respond to her.

With about as much success as *she'd* had with Richard. The man was just not interested. In fact, he had looked as though he was finding Miss Waverley's persistent attempts to interest him repellent. She had felt like cheering when he had reproved her for her behaviour.

Then, when the door had burst open and Miss Waverley's mama had come out a split second after the girl had flung herself into Lord Deben's arms, she had felt as angry as the earl had looked and had reacted on instinct. All her resentments had come to the boil and ejected her from her hiding place in a spume of righteous indignation.

'You are quite wrong about me.' For a moment, he had made her doubt herself. But, having carefully examined her motives, she had made a reassuring discovery.

'I would have acted the same, had I come across *any* woman attempting to trap a man into marriage, in such a beastly, underhanded way as that,' she said hotly. 'It was deplorable!'

He glanced at her keenly.

'I note that you do not deny that you were crying because of something she had done, though.'

How annoying of him to read her so well. And to look at her as though not only was she an open book, but also one that he found fairly contemptible. She drew herself up and attempted to look back at him with a level of contempt to match.

'I knew it,' he said with satisfaction. 'What did she do, steal away the man with whom you fancied yourself in love?'

Lord Deben was beyond annoying. He was hateful. She had known, from the sneer that was never far from his mouth, that he would mock anyone foolish enough to suffer from the softer emotions.

'F-fancied myself in love?' She tossed her head and attempted a laugh. 'Do not be ridiculous.'

The smile that lifted the corners of his mouth now was positively triumphant.

'I am not the one being ridiculous here.' He eyed her nodding ostrich plumes with open amusement. 'Though perhaps you can take consolation from the fact that a lot of girls of your age have their heads stuffed full of romantic nonsense,' he said patronisingly.

'My head is not—'

But he continued, regardless. 'And I knew, five seconds after becoming acquainted with

Miss Waverley, that she is used to having men fall at her feet.'

Yes, thought Henrietta gloomily. While her own head was stuffed full of romantic nonsense about ancient Greek heroes, the beautiful Miss Waverley was cutting a swathe through real-life, modern men.

She looked away from the mockery in Lord Deben's lazy brown eyes.

'She is welcome to them all,' she replied, her voice quivering with emotion. 'If a man can't see beyond her beautiful face, then they are idiots. A man who can be taken in by a cat like that is not the kind of man I would ever want to...well...' her voice faded to a whisper '...marry.'

'You should not,' he said firmly. 'Any man who can so easily switch his affections from you to a scheming jade like that is not worthy of your regard.'

She supposed he was trying to make her feel better, but his words only reminded her that she had never been certain of Richard's feelings towards her. He had never given her any indication he was interested in her, other than as his best friend's sister, until the previous Christmas, when he had grabbed hold of her, tugged her underneath a bunch of mistletoe and kissed her very thoroughly.

All her daydreams about him had stemmed

from that one, surprising interlude. Before then she had never considered him as much more than Hubert's impossibly handsome friend.

After that… She shrank down inside her furs in the faint hope they could somehow shield her from Lord Deben's penetrating gaze. After that, when he had not followed up on what she had seen as a declaration of intent, she had shamelessly pursued him, that was what she had done.

Well, that was all behind her now. She was not going to waste any more time over a man who was too stupid to see what was right under his nose. There was plenty to keep her amused in London: lectures, exhibitions and all sorts of interesting people to converse with. People with good brains, who put them to practical use in the world of commerce, rather than idly frittering away their inherited fortunes on frivolous pastimes.

But she couldn't help sighing. 'Well, Miss Waverley *is* exceptionally beautiful. And poised. She only has to smile on a man to dazzle him…'

Lord Deben did not like to see her looking suddenly so dejected. It did not seem right that she should compare herself unfavourably to a female of Miss Waverley's stamp. 'Well, she did not dazzle me,' he said firmly. 'I was singularly unimpressed by her.'

Yes, Henrietta reflected with some satisfaction. He'd had no trouble whatsoever in repulsing her.

Encouraged by the way she perked up, he continued, 'In fact, I would go so far as to say she is no more dazzling than you.' Her confidence had suffered a knock, so he would give it a well-deserved boost.

'What!'

When Henrietta turned a puzzled face towards him, she found herself on the receiving end of a long, hard stare.

'Not that I am saying that you are a real beauty. Just that you are by no means less capable of dazzling a man, should you put your mind to it.'

'Not a beauty...' she managed to gasp before her breath caught in a lump somewhere in her throat, making speech impossible.

'You only have to compare yourself with Miss Waverley to know I speak nothing but the truth. But let me tell you, as an expert on what makes a female attractive to a man, that you are not completely lacking in potential.'

'You mean by that, I suppose, that I am not a complete antidote?'

'Far from it.' He turned his lazy perusal over her face once more. 'You have a remarkably good complexion. No superfluous facial hair. A fine pair of expressive eyes and a set of good, straight teeth. As a connoisseur of beauty, I cannot help regretting that your nose is out of proportion to the rest of your features, but I see no reason why you could not, to use your own words, "dazzle" a man who is not so nice in his tastes.'

'You...' She clenched her fists, struggling to keep her temper. 'You are the rudest man I have ever met.'

'Not rude. Honest. But how typical of a female,' he said with a curl to his lip, 'to latch on to the one item, out of a whole catalogue of genuine compliments, which you can construe as an insult and take umbrage.'

'And how like a man to deliver a lacklustre compliment in such a way that no female with an ounce of pride could take it as anything *but* an insult!'

'Miss Gibson, I have just complimented you on your complexion, your eyes and your teeth, told you that with the right attitude you could successfully dazzle a susceptible male, and you fixate on the one flaw that you cannot deny you have.'

They were approaching the Cumberland Gate for the second time.

'Take me home,' she said. 'I demand that you take me home right this instant. And never, *ever* call on me again.'

Lord Deben looked down at her in disbelief.

Women sought him out. They fawned over him. They sent him languorous looks across heated ballrooms and slipped him notes to let him know where they could be found should he wish to avail himself of their charms.

They even waylaid him on terraces in the attempt to force him into marriage.

They did not tell him he was rude, dismiss him with a haughty toss of their head and demand to be taken home.

So naturally he steered his team right past the gate and commenced upon a third circuit of the park.

'This outing will end when I decide it will end,' he informed her curtly. 'And if I wish to call on you, who is to prevent me? Your aunt? She would not dare,' he drawled with contempt.

Henrietta could not believe what he was saying. At the start of this outing, he had informed her himself that he had no intention of wasting more of his precious time on her than was absolutely necessary.

'You are abominable,' she hissed. 'You no more wish to prolong this outing than I. Nor can I believe you have any intention of calling on me again. You just like throwing your weight around. You…you bully.'

'A bully, by definition, oppresses those weaker than himself for his own pleasure,' he snapped.

'At no time have I attempted to oppress you. No, and what is more, *everything* I have done in your regard has been for *your* benefit. And the longer I spend with you, the more convinced I become that you need somebody to watch over you. You do not appear to have any instinct for self-preservation at all. You say whatever comes into your head, without giving thought to the consequences, never mind the way you act. You leap into situations that are well beyond your comprehension, with a naïveté that is truly stunning.'

'You have only seen me act impulsively the once,' she retorted. 'And believe me, I regret interfering...' She faltered. 'No, no, actually...' she lifted her chin and looked at him defiantly '...no, I don't regret it. I cannot like Miss Waverley and I don't suppose I ever shall. But I wouldn't have been able to live with myself if you really had ruined her, not knowing that I'd witnessed the whole thing and could have stopped it if I'd acted.'

'What?'

'I think you heard me. But to make it even clearer for you, I admit I may have acted in a way you think was naïve and foolhardy, but at least my actions that night ended in good.'

'Ye gods, you sound like some kind of...Puritan. As though you were brought up to believe in some antiquated code of fair play that went out with the restoration of the monarchy.'

'I was brought up to tell the truth, and value honour and decency,' she said. 'There is nothing unusual in that.'

He laughed mirthlessly. 'Now that just goes to prove how naïve you really are. And how much you stand in need of a protector. I have lived far longer than you and moved in wider circles, and so far I have not met anyone else who would put such values above their own self-interest. If it wasn't for the fact you allowed your feelings about Miss Waverley to show enough to call her a cat, I would wash my hands of you entirely. For if there is one thing I cannot abide, it is a sanctimonious hypocrite.'

'I am not sanctimonious! Nor a hypocrite. I—'

'Very well,' he bit out. 'I absolve you of that sin. Sin,' he laughed bitterly. 'Who am I to absolve anyone of sin? Since, according to one who considers himself an authority on the subject, I am the most blackened sinner of this generation.'

'Are you?' She flushed guiltily at having the temerity to say such a thing, and hastily attempted to cover her blunder. 'I mean…I wonder that anyone dared to say it.'

'A vicar tends to think his pulpit gives him a certain measure of authority,' he said. 'And since the vicar in question also happened to be my brother, he felt no compunction in haranguing me in public for a change.'

For a change? She frowned. 'If he is in the habit of, um, *haranguing* you, what on earth made you go and sit in a church where he was preaching?'

'An idiotic notion that my presence at his first appearance in the parish where he went to take up his living might go some way to mending the breach between us.' Instead, he'd learned that the seeds of hatred his father had sown during their childhood had taken such deep root not even his brother's so-called Christianity was sufficient to make him forgive and forget. Will's face had been contorted with spite as he'd moralised about the sins of fornication and adultery, culminating with a look of total malice as he'd rounded off by proclaiming that the meek would inherit the earth.

Well, that was as may be, but one thing Will would not be inheriting—no, not even though he'd already managed to get his wife with child—was one inch of his father's property. *His* father's property. He'd always known he would have to marry and produce an heir, but reluctance to end up tied to a woman like his mother, in a relationship like the one his parents had endured, had made him drag his feet.

That woman! He might have had real siblings

if she'd had any sense of decency at all. If she'd even bothered to defend any of her brood from his father's malice, they might now be able to tolerate one another. Instead of which, the olive branch he'd extended to Will, by going to support him in his new parish, had been taken out of his hands and used as a weapon to beat him with.

Well, if it was war Will wanted, war he should have. He'd decided there and then that he *must* put aside his aversion to women in general, and wives in particular, and set up his nursery. One legitimate son, that was all he needed. One male child, sired indisputably by him.

The look on Lord Deben's face made Henrietta's heart go out to him, even as her hand went out to clutch at the handrail. His brother had evidently hurt him by denouncing his morals from the pulpit. Not that men ever admitted to being hurt. But it certainly explained why he'd whipped up his horses and was suddenly driving them at such a demonic pace.

She braced her feet against the footboard as he put his curricle through a gap that was so slender she was almost convinced he would lock wheels with one of the other carriages. When they made it through, with what looked like barely an inch to spare, and he urged his horses to even greater speed, she bit down on her lower lip and the craven urge to beg him to take care. He had already accused her of various defects in her character. She was not going to let him add the feminine one of timidity to the list and give him another excuse to sneer at her.

Besides, men needed a way to work through their feelings, since they would scorn to go away somewhere quiet and weep. She'd seen it often enough with her brothers. They went out and shot something, or got into a fight—or rode their horses at breakneck speed.

'You can wash your hands of me with a completely clear conscience,' she declared, surreptitiously taking a tighter hold on the handrail. In the event they did collide with anything, at least she might avoid the ignominy of being pitched on to the grass verge like a sack of grain.

'I do not consider that you owe me anything.'

'Well, that is just where you are wrong, Miss Gibson. I owe you more than you can imagine.' His search for a wife would not have prospered with the scandal Miss Waverley had almost unleashed upon him. Oh, he had no doubt that there would have been women still prepared to overlook what they would perceive as a lack of gentlemanly behaviour, but the encounter with Miss Waverley had taught him he would, indeed, rather shoot himself in the leg than shackle himself to one such. 'And for that reason, I have decided to help you.'

He smiled. In a way that made him look cruel.

She shivered. And admitted, 'I am not sure I like the sound of that.'

From the look on his face, whatever form this 'help' might take did not stem from any sense of altruism. He'd already told her he did not care what anyone thought of him, or might say of him. So, if he was planning anything, it was not because he wanted to help her, not really, but because in some way it would benefit him.

'Come, come, wouldn't you like to win your suitor back from Miss Waverley?'

'Not particularly.' She was not about to tell him that Richard had never, technically, been her suitor. But anyway, she was done with trying to get him to notice her. All it had accomplished was her humiliation.

'Well, even if that were true,' he said in a derisive tone, not taking his eyes from his team, 'I think you would enjoy taking the wind out of Miss Waverley's sails. And I certainly would. I have a strong aversion to letting people think they can manipulate me.'

She knew it! This was nothing to do with protecting her, or helping her. He was trying to use her to take his own revenge upon Miss Waverley.

'So do I,' she retorted. She was not going to let him use her, or involve her in any of his schemes.

'Well, then, let us discuss what is to be done.'

'No, you don't understand, I—'

'To begin with,' he cut in before she could even start explaining, 'I do not think the case is as hopeless as you seem to think.'

Amazingly, his dark mood seemed abruptly to have lifted. He'd slowed his horses to a steady trot and he was smiling—although the smile that played about his lips was so cruel that it sent a shiver down her spine. This was not a man to cross. How on earth had Miss Waverley thought she could get away with it? He was downright dangerous.

'Miss Waverley obviously does not want him herself, or she would not have set her sights on me. Perhaps, once she had snared him, she discovered he is not as wealthy or well connected as she had first supposed.'

Henrietta did not think it had been as calculated as all that. It just seemed to be in Miss Waverley's nature to want to make a conquest of every good-looking male who crossed her path. And Richard was more than just good looking, he was downright handsome. Far more so than Lord Deben, whose features were marred by being always set in a kind of sneer. Or twisted by whatever inner demons had made him take such risks with his team, and his carriage, not to mention his passenger, by setting such a pace.

It was a shame really, she mused, darting him

a swift glance, because if he didn't look so cross all the time, he might be very attractive. He had the full, sensual lips, and the lazy hooded eyes, that put her in mind of portraits she'd seen of Charles II.

Not that he would be foppish enough to sport ringlets, or disguise that fit, muscular body in yards of lace and velvet.

'That is half the battle,' he said, giving Henrietta a brief vision of him leading a cavalry charge against a solid square of soberly dressed roundheads, wearing just the expression he wore now.

'The other half is demonstrating that you are far superior to Miss Waverley, in every way. That you are a woman worth pursuing.'

She snorted. She could not help it. Richard would never pursue her. She was the one who'd done all the pursuing thus far.

'Come, come, Miss Gibson,' he said when she did not make him any answer apart from that derisive snort. 'Have you no pride? Would you not like to see him realise the error of his ways?'

'I have plenty of pride,' she retorted. The trouble was, it had already taken enough of a battering. 'Which is exactly why I will do nothing to attempt to make him change his mind.'

'But at least,' said Lord Deben, 'you are no longer attempting to deny that there *is* an admirer, that Miss Waverley *has* poached him and that you were so upset you ran out of a ballroom to hide behind a set of planters to weep your little heart out.'

He'd tricked her! He'd spoken of things she'd wanted to keep private in such a way that she'd inadvertently confirmed everything!

'Are you satisfied? Now that you've pried all my secrets from me?'

'Not yet,' he replied calmly, as though he was impervious to her mounting rage. 'But before I am done, we shall both be, I promise you.'

'I...I...' She clenched her fists. 'I have no idea what you are talking about.'

'It is really very simple. If I were to appear to find you fascinating, other men would want to discover what I see in you. If I swear that I think you are a diamond of the first water, you could have your pick of the rest of the herd, if you find you no longer wish to take up Miss Waverley's leavings.'

'Oh, for heavens' sake! I have never heard such arrogance in my whole life.'

'It is not arrogance, merely knowledge of human nature. Most people are like sheep, who follow mindlessly behind their natural leaders. Besides, you are from a good family and comfortably circumstanced. Once I have brought you to public notice and cleared up the misconception about your connection to the Ledbetters, there is no reason why you should not acquire a bevy of genuine suitors.'

Henrietta hated to admit it, but she could see exactly what he meant. She had often observed that a man with strong convictions could persuade others to follow their lead. And also that what several men liked, others would claim to as well, or risk being thought odd. His stratagem might actually work.

'No, really...' she began, but even to her own ears her voice lacked conviction. So she was not surprised by his answer.

'You are tempted, I can tell. Wouldn't you like,' he said, his voice lowering to a seductive tone, 'to outshine Miss Waverley? Would you not like to be the toast of the *ton*? Have your hand sought after? Your drawing room full of suitors?'

The toast of the *ton*.

That...that did sound tempting.

It wasn't that she wanted Richard any more, not really. But he had said such hurtful things. And, ignoble though it was, she would dearly love to show him she was more than just a country mouse. To prove that London was not too rackety for her, but, on the contrary, that she could become one of its leading lights. Just imagine what it would be like to have London society at her feet!

The thing was, Lord Deben moved in the very best circles, not on the fringes where Richard had worked so hard to secure a foothold. He was an earl, with the right to go wherever he pleased, not the son of a country squire who needed to watch every step he took, every friend he made, for fear of being laughed out of countenance.

For a few moments she indulged in a daydream of attending some glittering *ton* event, where she danced all night with a succession of earls and marquises. And Richard would be gnashing his teeth in the doorway, because they wouldn't let him in to tell her how much he regretted missing his chance with her. Miss Waverley would not have even been invited to the event either. Or, no, even better, she *would* be there, but sitting on the sidelines, ignored as she had once been ignored…

It was so tempting. She knew Lord Deben was not offering her this chance for her sake, but out of his own desire for revenge, yet if she played along…

But then she suddenly recalled her father telling her that if she could ever apply the word *temptation* to something she wanted to do, then she knew she oughtn't really to be doing it. And felt like Eve reaching out to take that shiny, delicious apple from the serpent.

'You…you are a devil,' she gasped.

He chuckled. 'Because I am tempting you to give in to a side of your nature you do not wish to admit you have?'

Oh, there was that word again.

'Yes,' she whispered, ashamed though she was to admit it.

'But you will do it.'

The glittering vision he'd shown her wavered and took a new form. The faces of the people in it were haughty and cruel. And she, by joining them and giving former friends like Richard the cold shoulder, of inflicting the same misery that she'd borne on Miss Waverley, made her as cruel and hard as they were.

She didn't want to become such a person.

She straightened her shoulders and lifted her chin. She would *not* become that sort of person.

'No,' she said firmly. Then, a little louder, 'No. It would not be right.'

'You are refusing my offer?'

'Most certainly.'

The ungrateful baggage. He had never exerted himself to such an extent for anyone else, or promised so much of his time to aid their cause.

It was Will all over again. Spurning the hand of friendship which he'd extended and spitting in his face.

His face shuttered. 'On your own head be it, then.'

'What do you mean?'

She frowned up at him, those ridiculous feathers bobbing in the breeze. She really had no idea. Over the next few days, society would beat a path to her door, whether she wanted them to or not.

There was nothing she could do to prevent it. Everyone had seen him driving an unknown female around the park not once, but three times, and all the while engaged in animated conversation. He had taken care not to acknowledge anyone, which would stoke their curiosity about her to fever pitch. Why, they would want to know, would such a renowned connoisseur of female beauty have paid so much attention to this rather vulgarly attired little nonentity?

They would want to know who she was, what her connection was to him and where she had come from. They would not leave her be until they had pried every last one of her secrets from her. She would very soon regret her stubborn refusal to make her a reigning queen of society. Then—oh, yes, then he would have this proud little Puritan crawling to him.

'You will find out. And when you do, don't forget that I offered my protection.'

When they reached the gates the next time he put his team straight through them and took the turn out on to Oxford Street.

Henrietta could see she had offended him by

turning him down, but really, after only these two encounters with him, she was sure it would be better never to tangle with him again. He was too autocratic. Too far out of her social sphere. Too clever and tempting, and worldly and, oh, altogether too much!

She bade farewell to that vision of a glittering ballroom and all those nobles who'd wanted her to dance with them. She was going home, to her dear aunt and uncle, to Mildred and Mr Crimmer. Back to the world of pantomimes at Covent Garden, and dinners in the homes of businessmen, and balls where she would dance with the sons of aldermen and merchants.

And when she went home to Much Wakering she would at least do so with a clear conscience.

Lord Deben remained silent with that expression of displeasure on his face all the way back to Bloomsbury. But when she alighted outside her aunt's house, to her surprise he tossed the reins to his tiger, sprang down and caught up with her before she'd set foot on the first step.

'Miss Gibson,' he said sharply.

She sighed. What now?

'You are such a simpleton,' he said, glancing down the street as though he was already itching to be away. 'You don't know what you are saying, to turn down my offer of assistance. And though you have made me very angry, I cannot leave things between us like this.' He wouldn't mind making her pay for her rudeness to him by leaving her to the mercy of the gossipmongers. But he did not want her to come to complete shipwreck. She was so naïve, and…and green, believing in goodness and decency, and telling the truth and shaming the devil.

He seized her hand and looked directly into her eyes, his expression, for once, neither mocking nor dismissive, but earnest.

'You came rushing to my help, that night on Miss Twining's terrace, even though I did not need it. I find,' he said with a perplexed frown, 'that I cannot turn my back on such a foolhardy, gallant gesture.'

More than half of his anger with her, he had realised during the drive back to Bloomsbury, was due to the fact she did not appreciate how rare it was for him to want to put himself out for anyone. The rest, well…

'I think,' he said, 'that in some ways we are very much alike. You have a good deal of pride. It is why you hid behind the plant pots to cry, rather than go running to your aunt. Why you spurn the offer of help from me, a man you hardly know, rather than admitting you stand in need of it.'

Chapter Five

It was two weeks before she saw him again.

She had been some twenty minutes in the house of Lord Danbury, where she'd been invited, much to her surprise, by his daughter Lady Susan Pettiffer. Her party had spent most of that time removing their coats and changing their shoes in the ladies' withdrawing room, greeting their host, and wandering through as many rooms as they could—on the pretext of seeing if there was anyone they knew—so that her aunt could examine how each and every room in the earl's sumptuous town house was decorated and furnished.

They had just secured a place on a sofa in one of the upstairs drawing rooms when the entire atmosphere became charged. It was a bit like the tingle she sometimes felt in the air when she was out walking on the hills and a thunderstorm was fast approaching. Then the ladies started discreetly preening and several of the men checked their neckcloths in the glass over the mantel, if they were near enough, and those who weren't began to speak in more ponderous tones.

Lord Deben had entered the room.

Her aunt gripped her wrist. Ever since he had taken her out for that drive, Aunt Ledbetter had been expecting him to call again. Or, at the very least, to send a posy. In vain had Henrietta assured her there had been nothing romantic about him showing interest in her. *'But you are just the sort of girl a man like that would like,'* she had said, over and over again. *'They live a lot in the country, the aristocracy.'*

'Please, do not refine too much upon the fact that he happens to be here tonight. He has probably forgotten all about me by now,' she turned to her aunt to say.

'Nonsense. He just has not noticed you yet,' replied her aunt.

'Don't wave, don't wave,' Henrietta hissed out of the corner of her mouth, when it looked as though her aunt was about to do just that. 'If he wants to pretend he has not seen us,' she muttered angrily, for how he could have failed to see them, when the sofa upon which they sat was in full view of the door through which he had just walked, she could not imagine, 'then he must not want to recognise us tonight.'

Her aunt subsided immediately. It was one thing for a member of the *ton* to call at one's house, quite another for that same aristocrat to deign to recognise one in public.

Henrietta flicked open her fan and plied it over her aunt's heated cheeks. The excitement of getting an invitation to a household such as this quite eclipsed the coup of getting her Mildred into a mere Miss Twining's come-out ball. Although, in a way, they owed that, too, to Julia. She had called, with Lady Susan in tow, only a day or so ago, to enquire whether she had quite recovered from whatever had afflicted her during her come-out ball. 'Because,' Julia had said disingenuously, 'I was beginning to fear it might be something serious, since I have not seen you anywhere since.' As they'd been leaving, Lady Susan had asked if she would be interested in attending what she described as 'a very informal rout'.

Aunt Ledbetter had very nearly expired from excitement on the spot.

'Shall I fetch you some lemonade, aunt?' There were so many more important people thronging the house that the footmen circulating with trays of refreshments had bypassed them several times. And she was only too willing to leave the room in which Lord Deben was holding court, to go in search of a waiter willing to serve them.

'No, dear, I need something considerably stronger,' said her aunt. 'Lemonade for Mildred, though.'

Henrietta snapped her fan shut and deliberately avoided looking in Lord Deben's direction. She hadn't liked the way he'd kept invading her thoughts over the past fortnight. She hadn't liked the way her spirits had lifted when she detected some sign that he might have been working on her behalf, in the background, in spite of the way they had parted. Although he'd probably, no, definitely had more important things to think about than a badly dressed, shrewish country miss. For in what other light could he regard her? When she looked back on the two occasions they had met, she realised that she had made a spectacle of herself both times. On that first occasion, her face had been all blotchy with tears, and, she'd discovered to her horror when she'd got home and caught a glimpse of herself in the mirror, there was more than a handful of dead ivy in her hair. The second time, she'd deliberately made herself look as vulgar as she possibly could, and, because she'd still been recovering from Richard, had been very far from gracious.

Shrewish, to be perfectly blunt. And whenever she tried to justify herself by reminding herself of all the rude things he'd said, too, her conscience pointed out that he had at least tried to rein in his temper. Several times. Only for her to provoke him into losing it again.

All the poor man wanted was to express his thanks in the only way he knew how—by offering her the chance at retribution. And she had thrown it all back in his face.

She especially did not like the fact that just now, when he'd walked into the room, she had reacted exactly the same as her aunt had done. The only difference between them was that her pride had kept her from showing it—that, and the fact that she would not for the world expose her aunt and cousin to ridicule by having a man like that snub them, if he should choose to do so.

It was bad enough that at the moment even the waiters would not deign to notice them.

If only she hadn't turned down his offer to make her the toast of the *ton*, if only she hadn't been so ungracious, so ungrateful, everything might have been so different.

So deep had she fallen into a spirit of self-chastisement that she very nearly walked right into the large male who stepped into her path.

'Lord Deben!'

How on earth he'd managed to intercept her,

she had no idea. Last time she had permitted herself to look at him he had been on the other side of the room.

'Miss Gibson,' he said, inclining his head in the slightest of bows. 'Trying to avoid me, perchance?' He spoke softly, his lips scarcely moving.

'N-no, not at all! I thought *you* were...' She felt her cheeks heat.

His lids lowered a fraction. A satisfied smile hovered briefly about his sensual mouth. 'I have merely been complying with your wishes. You made it very plain you wanted nothing further to do with me. I was not, especially, to pollute your family's drawing room with my sinfully tempting presence...'

Her cheeks grew hotter still. 'I was angry and upset. I spoke hastily. I was rude. And...' she lifted her chin and looked him full in the face '...I apologise.'

The smile stayed in place, but it no longer reached his eyes. It was almost as though he were disappointed in her.

'But then you have had your revenge upon me, haven't you?' she continued gloomily. 'So I suppose that makes us even.'

'I beg your pardon?'

'Oh, don't pretend you don't know exactly what I mean,' she snapped. She hated it when he put on that supercilious *how dare you speak like that to me?* look.

'When you said "On your own head be it," it was because you knew just what would happen after you took me out driving in the park. Ever since that afternoon, my aunt's drawing room has been besieged by the most dreadful people all wanting to know who I am and how we are related.'

The smile returned to his eyes.

'No doubt you quickly put them in their place. I only regret not having been there to witness their discomfiture at your masterly control of the cutting comment.'

'I did not make any cutting comments to anyone. I told you, they were in my aunt's drawing room. I simply explained...' she continued, encouraged by the fact that he was smiling, even if it was at her expense. For he looked like another man altogether when he smiled like that, with genuine amusement. Younger, and an awful lot more approachable. '...that I was two and twenty.'

'Which naturally put paid to the initial rumour that you must be my long-lost love child, conceived during my reckless youth.'

Her eyes widened. She had not thought he would speak quite so frankly. Although to be fair, she was the one who had started alluding to the scurrilous things that were being said about her.

'You heard that one as well?'

He nodded, gravely. 'For my part, I said that although I appreciated the compliment, even a man with my reputation with the ladies was unlikely to have begun my amatory career at the age of nine.'

'And speaking of your reputation,' she said darkly, 'I had no idea when I accepted your invitation to drive in the park that you had never done so before with a woman who is not your mistress.'

His smile vanished completely. 'Who told you that?'

'That you only take a mistress up beside you?'

He nodded grimly.

'I don't think I'd better tell you his name,' she said, suddenly fearful for the vengeance a man who could look so cold might take on the bacon-brained youth who'd let that piece of information slip. 'Besides, another of the…gentlemen present soon stopped that line of speculation by declaring that he wouldn't credit it unless he also heard that you had developed some kind of problem with your eyesight.'

'He said what?'

'Hearing failing now, too, hmmm? Perhaps

you ought to sit down. At your age, you need to start being careful.'

'At my age? I am hardly into my thirties, you impudent…' He took her by the arm, steered her out of the room and up to a buffet, manned by a brace of footmen who had so far been ignoring her with masterly aplomb. With a few terse words, he arranged for them to take a tray of refreshments to her aunt and cousin, then whisked her into a small recess beyond the end of the last sideboard.

'You will inform me, if you please, the name of the man who insulted you in your drawing room…'

'But why?' She opened her eyes wide, in mock surprise. 'He only echoed what you yourself said in the park.'

'Nothing of the sort. I made a list of your best features, in an attempt to persuade you that you had as much chance of dazzling a man as Miss Waverly, should you care to…'

'Well, it doesn't matter anyway, because Mr Crimmer soon settled his hash.'

'Who is Mr Crimmer?' His eyes narrowed on her intently. 'Is he the suitor you were crying over at Miss Twining's?'

'Oh, no. He's not *my* suitor at all. It was when Lord… I mean, the man who had said your eyesight must be deteriorating said that he could have understood it if it had been Mildred up beside you, because she was a…I think his exact words were *a game pullet*, that Mr Crimmer, who is in love with my cousin Mildred, you know, lifted him off his chair by his lapels, bundled him out of the house and threw him down the front steps.'

She paused, peeping up at him cheekily over the top of her languidly waving fan. Her eyes were brimful of laughter.

She was not angry about the incident. If anything, he would have said she was vastly amused by the antics of the boors who had invaded her aunt's house. He leaned back against the wall and folded his arms across his chest.

'Pray continue,' he drawled. 'I simply cannot wait to hear what happened next.'

It was, he realised, completely true. He was affecting boredom, but he did not think he had enjoyed a conversation with any other female half so much during the entire two weeks he had been deliberately avoiding her. Not that he'd had anything that could accurately have been described as a conversation. He had definitely attempted to start several, with various young ladies who could lay claim to both impeccable lineage and trim figures, but they always petered out into a sequence of 'yes, my lord' and 'no, my lord' and 'oh, if you say so, then I am sure you must be right, my lord'. It had been like consuming a constant diet of bread and milk.

Running into Henrietta Gibson was like suddenly finding a pot of mustard on hand, to lend a piquancy to the unremittingly bland dishes he'd been obliged to sample of late.

'Well, the man who'd called Mildred a game pullet was rather annoyed to be treated with such disrespect by a mere cit,' Henrietta continued, 'and informed Mr Crimmer of the fact in the most robust terms. And Mr Crimmer replied that a real gentleman would never speak of a lady with such disrespect, to which that man replied that Mildred was no lady, only a tradesman's daughter.'

'You heard all this?'

'Oh, yes. Though I had to throw up the sash in the front room and lean out, because the front steps were a bit crowded with all the other, erm, gentlemen who had come with the man who'd called Mildred a name he oughtn't. And I had the pleasure of seeing Mr Crimmer plant a nice flush hit that sent the so-called gentleman reeling right out into the road. After that, though,' she said with a moue of disappointment, 'it descended into the kind of scrap that little boys of about eight get into.'

He raised one eyebrow again. He had never,

ever heard a female of good birth use boxing cant as though it were perfectly natural.

'Oh, you know the kind of thing,' she replied, completely misinterpreting the cause of that raised eyebrow. 'Kicking and grappling, and flailing arms without anyone really doing the other any damage.'

'No science,' he said, to see if she really understood what she was saying.

'None whatever,' she said with a rueful shake of the head. 'Although the other spectators appeared to enjoy it tremendously. There was a great deal of wagering going on.'

'May I ask what your aunt was doing while this impromptu mill was taking place on her front doorstep and you were hanging out of the window cheering on your champion?'

'I was *not* cheering,' she said, adopting a haughty demeanour. 'And he was not *my* champion. And as for my aunt, well,' she said, the laughter returning to her eyes, 'she thought about having the vapours, I think, but only for about a minute or two, because nobody was taking any notice of her. And she is a very practical person, too. So once she had got over the shock of having her drawing room taken over by a pack of yahoos, she sent the butler to fetch some of the male servants from the houses round and about, to make them all go away.'

So she had read the works of Dean Swift. Of course she had, with a father like hers. And the way she was chattering away now, taking his own knowledge of literature for granted, showed that she was well used to holding conversations that assumed all participants had a high level of education.

He'd been correct to tell her that with a few tips from him, she could learn to dazzle a man. Even without the benefit of his tuition, tonight, she was quite captivating. The way she was smiling at him, for instance, inviting him to share her amusement, was well nigh irresistible. He would defy any man not to smile back.

He would swear she was nowhere near so unappealing as he recalled, either. While she chattered on he surreptitiously scanned her outfit. The dress she was wearing tonight complemented both her colouring and her slender form. The accessories were not the least bit vulgar, so that anyone who didn't know better would never dream she was being sponsored for this Season by a cit. But he rather thought it was the sparkle in her eyes that made her look so very different from the last times he'd seen her.

In fact, if she could but learn to keep a rein on her temper, she could very easily become a hit, without him having to make people think she

had some hidden fascination which so far only
he had discerned.

'Why, then, have I not heard of this riot?' It
was time he made some contribution to the conversation. 'Because if the thing escalated into a
public brawl, involving the male servants of several houses and a pack of...*yahoos*...'

'Oh, it didn't come to that. Fortunately Mr
Crimmer's foot slipped on a cobble and he went
down with his opponent on top of him. He was
stunned for a few moments. Or he might just
have been winded, I suppose, because...well, let
us say that his opponent is no lightweight.' She
sparkled up at him.

He laughed outright at the picture she had just
painted. And it struck him how very rarely he
laughed, genuinely laughed, with amusement.
Very few people shared his sense of humour.
Or suspected he even had one. Miss Gibson, he
realised, had looked right past the outer shell,
which was all most people wanted to see, and
reached right to the man he...not the man he
was, or even the man he wanted to be, but perhaps the man he might have been had things
been different.

'But anyway, before he recovered the power
of speech, the yahoo claimed it as a victory and
went away, taking his friends with him.'

'In short,' he said, inspecting his fingertips

with an air of feigned innocence, 'far from exacting any kind of revenge, I have furnished you with no end of entertainment.'

'You... I...' She shut her mouth with a snap. 'I absolutely refuse to allow you to goad me into losing my temper with you again,' she said resolutely. 'Because you did, at least, warn me what it would be like. And it has all ended rather well for Mildred and Mr Crimmer, at least.'

'Good God,' he said with disgust. 'Are you really the kind of person who detects silver linings within even the darkest clouds? Not only have you completely outdated notions of morality, but it now appears that you also suffer from an incurable case of optimism.'

'Oh, well,' she said airily, 'if you do not wish to hear the end of the tale, then naturally, I shall not bore you any longer.' She made as if to leave the alcove.

'Oh, no, you don't.' He seized her arm, just above the elbow, and turned her back. 'You know full well that there is much more I want to hear. Oh, not about this Crimmer person, or your pretty little hen-witted cousin Mildred. It is obvious that once he leapt to her defence she has now cast him in the role of hero and his suit will prosper. No, what interests me is how you managed to wring social victory from what might have so easily been a crushing defeat.'

She pretended not to understand him.

'I want to know,' he persisted, 'how you got an invitation to this house, of all houses. Lord Danbury has a reputation for being very exclusive. Just being seen here will do your credit no end of good.'

'Well, it all stems from that incident, you know. Because after that, my aunt became far more discerning about who she would permit into her drawing room. Nobody gets in just because they have a title, any more. A visitor has to have some valid reason, apart from vulgar curiosity, before Warnes will allow them past the hall. Which meant that those wishing to have their curiosity satisfied had to send their sisters, or cousins, or aunts to ferret out what information they could.'

'And yet you still did not apply to me for aid? My God, once the tabbies get their claws into you, it can be far worse than anything a boorish young fop can achieve.'

'I did not think I needed to apply to you for aid. I thought you had already sent it.' She gave him a speculative look. She couldn't quite understand why she had hoped that in spite of the way they'd parted, the visit from his godmother had been a sign that he was still watching out for her, from afar. 'I...I thought you might have spoken to Lady Dalrymple and asked her to intercede.'

'Indeed?'

Henrietta's heart sank a little. She had forgotten the vast social gulf that existed between them for a few moments, but now he had erected the barriers again, with that one lazily drawled word, that repressive lift to one eyebrow.

'Well, yes. I am sorry, it is just that she is your godmother and she was there at Miss Twining's ball...'

'And she is as eaten up with curiosity as any of them. Perhaps more, given her relationship to me.'

'Well, however it came about, she did a great deal of good. Because she declared, straight off, that she'd come to scotch the rumour that I was a vulgar nonentity, thrusting my way in where I didn't belong.'

'I can almost hear her saying it.'

Henrietta giggled. 'I should think you might have done. She has a very carrying voice, does she not? Nobody who was in the drawing room the afternoon she called round could have failed to hear a single word of her conversation with me about my maternal grandmother and how they were such bosom bows, and how appalled she was not to have seen me at any of the kind of gatherings where Lavinia's granddaughter ought to have been invited.'

He smiled with satisfaction. His godmother

was one of those persons who knew everyone and everyone's antecedents to at least three generations, and thoroughly enjoyed showing off the extent of her knowledge.

'Did she restrict herself to merely mentioning your *maternal* antecedents?'

Henrietta shook her head.

'My father's connection to the Duke of Harrowgate came up very early on. Nor did she leave out my Uncle Ledbetter's lineage, which she followed by lecturing us all, at length, about the difference between the middle classes, who may truly be called vulgar mushrooms who push themselves up from nowhere, and younger sons of good families who are obliged to take up a profession. And since then, the invitations to, well, to be frank, rather *tonnish* events such as this have begun to trickle in.'

It had only been after Lady Dalrymple's visit that Julia Twining had called again, which was what had made her take both her repeated protestations of friendship, and her concern about her health, with a large pinch of salt.

'I am only surprised,' he sneered, 'that nobody has yet started a rumour that you and I are on the verge of matrimony. Given that her appearance in your drawing room will have dealt the fatal blow to speculation that any kind of scandal could be brewing between us.'

'Oh, dear, would people really…?' She whisked her fan shut and tapped it absentmindedly in the palm of her other hand. Poor Lord Deben must be regretting his association with her even more. The last thing he wanted was to have his name connected to any innocent, eligible female. He disliked the entire notion of marriage so much that he'd told her he would rather shoot himself in the leg than enter into one.

'No, no, I'm quite sure nobody suspects anything of that nature,' she said, a rather worried frown puckering her brow. 'A-at least…' She glanced about the room, looking rather alarmed. 'Perhaps we ought not to be standing apart in this corner, in this…intimate fashion.'

It felt as though she had forcibly thrust him into a stuffy room and slammed the door on him, while he'd been enjoying taking a walk on a particularly fresh and bracing October day.

'Do you dislike the notion so very much?'

His whole being swelled with indignation. Just because those bucks had let slip a few indisputable facts, and he'd admitted that even his own brother had publicly condemned his licentious lifestyle, the little Puritan was recoiling from the prospect of her name being linked with his.

How dare she? He was a *good* marriage prospect. Any other woman would be thrilled, not look as though she'd just inadvertently trodden in something unpleasant.

But instead of turning on his heel, and putting her out of his mind, the thought that was uppermost in Lord Deben's mind was a burning desire to force her to recant.

'Me?' Goodness, but he looked cross. He was probably regretting talking to her so freely now and coming to stand in this rather private little recess. Oh dear, but she hoped he did not now suspect *she* was trying to entrap him, too. She had better put him straight, at once.

'No! I mean, I had not thought about it at all. And I wouldn't.'

She could not believe that women would actually try to entrap a man who'd rather shoot himself in the leg than settle down to marital fidelity. Were they mad? Although perhaps they didn't know as much about him as she did.

'Why? Because you consider me an irredeemable rake?'

Well, he was one. She knew that now. The bucks who'd swarmed into her aunt's house had been incredibly indiscreet, letting slip all sorts of unsavoury facts about him. She hadn't been able to believe how coarse their conversation had been. It demonstrated not only a lowness of mind, but also an insulting disregard for her sensibilities. They were so keen to discuss the

latest exploits of the Devilish Lord Deben, that
they'd reminded her of a pack of baying hounds,
chasing down a poor unfortunate hare.

It had been years, they'd revealed, since he'd
kept a mistress in the conventional sense. Since
they'd seen him take one of them driving in the
park. They'd been slavering to guess what this
queer start of his might mean. Was he changing
his tactics once more? For, after he'd severed
connections to the last of his high flyers, he'd
methodically worked his way through the willing
married ladies of the *ton*. When he'd sampled all
the most beautiful, he'd cut a swathe through the
wanton widows. Had he now decided to pursue
unmarried girls of questionable birth for sport?
After all, everyone knew how easily he grew
bored, once he'd made a conquest. His *affaires*,
apparently, never lasted very long.

Yes, they concluded, he would have far more
sport attempting to seduce respectable virgins.
He must be looking for a challenge to pique his
jaded appetite. A virgin was bound to attempt
to hang on to her virtue for as long as possible.

Only the fat young lord had voiced a protest,
so blackened was Lord Deben's reputation. And
then only to point out that if it were the case,
surely he would at least start on a *pretty* girl.

Her cheeks heated, half with chagrin at not
being thought pretty enough to warrant seduc-

tion, and half with guilt at knowing far too much about the man who stood so close to her. She ought not to know such things about him. Or about any man.

'I beg your pardon. It is not my business to comment upon your behaviour. I...I think I had better return to my aunt,' she said, lowering her eyes.

'Yes, run back to the safety of a crowded room,' he sneered. 'You do not want your spotless reputation sullied by loitering too long in my presence.'

She glanced up at him in confusion. For a few moments she had felt as though she could say anything to him and he would understand. It had been an age since she had just been able to talk freely like this. Not since she'd left the all-male household in Much Wakering. Her aunt and Mildred set such store by only discussing acceptable topics that it had felt wonderful to let down her guard and just say whatever came into her head.

But of course he wasn't one of her brothers. Or a man she had known all her life. He was practically a stranger.

'You are correct, of course,' she said woodenly. The one thing she did know about him was that he was a rake. No, make that two things. He was a rake and an earl. And she was a nobody. 'A woman's reputation is a fragile thing.'

'Which you believe I am quite capable of casually destroying.'

'No!' Very well, she knew three things about him. The nonsense those bucks had spouted was so very far from the truth it was laughable. He had no intention of seducing her. His reasons for taking her out for a drive were completely honourable.

No, she corrected herself. She could not claim that anything Lord Deben did would be *completely* honourable, not in the way she meant it. He'd tempted her to take a course that she considered most *dis*honourable. But he had not suggested it to make sport of her, or ruin her. In his own way, he had extended the hand of friendship to her.

'Not on purpose, anyway. I am quite sure that I have nothing to fear from you.' He did *not* pursue innocent girls. 'But don't forget, I have already been subjected to a deluge of unpleasant gossip just because you singled me out for attention the once.'

She looked up at him again and what he saw in her eyes struck him like a blow over the heart.

Not on purpose, she had said, and she had meant it.

She trusted him.

And if she felt it was wiser to keep away from him, she did so with regret. It was all there in those eyes that were as transparent as the sky on a cloudless day.

'I could put a stop to all the unpleasant gossip,' he said, 'by allowing it to be known that I do intend to make you my wife. And then, if I appear to pursue you, they will be falling over themselves to become your friends.'

Even as he uttered the words, it occurred to him that he could do worse than really marry Miss Gibson. At least she would not bore him. He would not wish to limit his intercourse with her to the bedroom. She would be a charming companion. The prospect of marrying her was so very appealing that when she laughed it was all he could do not to flinch.

'Oh, heavens. You cannot really think that anyone would believe I am the kind of girl who would really tempt a man of your…well…' She felt herself blushing as she thought of some of the remarks the yahoos had made about his love life. 'Your…experience, shall we say? If you ever do decide to marry, they will expect you to pick someone…exceptional. She will be beautiful, at the very least. Probably wealthy, too, and with far better connections than mine.'

A wonderful feeling came over him as he saw that he had absolutely no need to make her recant. It was her own powers of attraction she was calling into question, not the entire concept of marrying him.

With any other woman, he would have wondered if she was fishing for compliments. But Miss Gibson was honest. Brutally honest, at times. So he could just take her remark at face value.

God, what a novel experience that was!

Another thing she had said he could take at face value…what was it she'd said, earlier? She had never considered the thought of marrying him. She really had not. There had been no speculative gleam in her eye when he'd taken her out driving. There was no coquettishness about her now. No, Miss Gibson was treating him as though he was her friend.

'Come, now. In the spirit of our friendship, what say you we have a little fun at the expense of all those yahoos,' he said, ruthlessly using her own terminology to bring her round to his way of thinking. She was not ready to think of him in terms of marriage. But he could soon change her mind, had he unlimited access to her. There had never yet been a woman he could not bring to eat out of his hand.

'I have already told you that you are eminently marriageable. And now that my godmother has made your connections known, people will be ready to believe in our courtship. Next to scandal, it is the one thing people love to think they can see brewing.'

She shook her head. 'I have already told you, I have no interest in playing such games. Though,' she admitted, 'I am flattered that you think I could figure as the kind of woman you might lose your heart to.'

'Are you?'

'Yes,' she admitted with a delightful blush. And then ruined it all by adding, 'Because even an ignorant girl from the country like me can see what a coup it would be, socially, to get an offer from a man of your rank and wealth.'

A coup. Socially. Had ever a man been so neatly put in his place?

And there was he thinking she'd actually started to like him.

His disappointment was out of all proportion to the slap she'd administered, particularly since she'd not done it deliberately.

'Then you had better,' he said coldly, 'return to your aunt, had you not, Miss Gibson?'

He watched her scurry away, like a mouse relieved to have escaped the paws of the kitchen cat. And he pretended the same indifference as would the kitchen cat, balked of its legitimate prey.

But behind his lazily hooded eyes his mind was racing. There had to be some way of making her change her mind about marrying him. He just had to discover what that might be. He would have to observe her closely, surreptitiously if necd be. Until, like a hunter stalking its prey, he would find the optimum moment to pounce.

And take her.

Chapter Six

'Miss Gibson!'

Henrietta faltered to a stop at the malice evident in the speaker's tone, turned, and saw Miss Waverley emerge from the doorway from where she must have been watching her tête-à-tête with Lord Deben.

'I might have known you would seize this opportunity to corner Lord Deben and thrust yourself upon his notice yet again.'

'It was rather the opposite,' retorted Henrietta, recalling how Lord Deben had accosted her on her way to the refreshment room.

'You would say that, you brazen hussy,' hissed Miss Waverley, bearing down upon her. 'I know what you are about. But it won't work.' She raked Henrietta with a contemptuous look. 'You are making a spectacle of yourself by pursuing him like this. Lady Susan only invited you here so that we could all watch you trotting after him, like some lovesick puppy. So that we could all laugh at you.'

She did laugh then and it was one of the most unpleasant sounds Henrietta had ever heard.

'He is not really interested in you,' she said. 'How could he be? You are just an ugly…nobody. He is very choosy about the females he permits into his bed, you know. They all have to be titled, for a start, and incredibly beautiful. And accomplished, too.'

'Then,' said Henrietta quietly, 'that certainly rules you out, does it not?'

'You impudent little…vulgar mushroom!' As Miss Waverley's face contorted with fury it occurred to Henrietta that she must not have heard about the way Lady Dalrymple had gone to such lengths to prove she was most emphatically not a mushroom of any variety.

Or if she had, she'd chosen not to believe it.

'I could have you thrown out of this house for daring to speak to me like that.'

Henrietta very much doubted it, but Miss Waverley did not give her an opportunity to speak, so determined was she to give vent to the frustrated spite that had clearly been building up

Never Trust a Rake

while she waited for just such an opportunity as this.

'But I shan't bother. You are not worth bothering with,' she said, almost as though she was repeating something another person had dinned into her. 'And Lady Susan may have taken you up, temporarily, the way she often does with odd people who capture her fancy...'

Strangely, although she'd been able to discount everything else Miss Waverley had said so far, recognising it as an outpouring of spite, the remark about Lady Susan struck home, for she'd been suspicious of her motives from the start.

'There won't be any dancing,' Lady Susan had informed her when she'd told her about this evening. 'Just the opportunity to mingle with interesting people and indulge in stimulating conversation. My father has read your father's treatise on the potential uses of de-phlogisticated air,' she'd said, leaning slightly forwards as though about to deliver a confidence. 'He was most impressed. And for my part, I am just longing to having one female amongst my acquaintance with whom I can hold an intelligent conversation. There are precious few in town this season.'

Henrietta had not missed the way Lady Susan's eyes had flickered briefly towards Julia, who had been sipping a cup of tea and staring vacantly at nothing in particular. And had decided on the spot she did not like her. Not at all.

And yet it still hurt, somehow, to realise that everyone would now regard her as one of the 'odd' people that sometimes caught Lady Susan's fancy. As odd as some of the other guests present tonight. The wild-haired poetess who'd been pointed out to her in one of the receiving rooms, for instance, or the penniless inventors, grubby artists and belligerent self-made men one would not normally see at a *ton* event, but who were tonight rubbing shoulders with peers and politicians.

And Lord Danbury, forcing himself to be polite to people he only tolerated in his house because they amused his daughter.

It made her feel a bit like one of those performing monkeys in a travelling circus. Especially when Miss Waverley added, 'But once the novelty has worn off, she will drop you again and you will sink back into obscurity where you belong.'

Like those performing monkeys, shut back in their cages once the show was over.

With that, Miss Waverley lifted her skirts and swirled away, leaving Henrietta standing stock still in the corridor. She was rather shaken by that display of venom, which was, in her view, completely out of proportion. Miss Waverley, she mused as she pulled herself together and set out for the drawing room where she'd left her aunt and cousin, must be all about in her head. For one thing, had Henrietta not intervened, she would have been at the centre of the most almighty scandal. Though she was not to know that. She had no idea what kind of a man she'd attempted to manipulate. That she'd done the equivalent of poking her hand through the bars of a lion's cage.

And as for predicting that she would sink back into obscurity—well! If the members of the *ton* were all like Miss Waverley, and those yahoos who'd invaded her drawing room and flung insults left, right and centre, then the sooner they lost interest in her the better. She had only accepted the invitation here tonight because she'd seen it would mean so much to her aunt and cousin. And they, she observed from the doorway, were now enjoying themselves immensely. Not only had Lord Deben convinced the waiters to serve them, but in the short time she'd been out of the room, Mildred had managed to acquire a brace of admirers. One of them was leaning over the back of the sofa and trying to murmur in her ear, and the other, who had pulled up a spindly chair to her side, was shooting him dagger looks.

Neither of them were in earnest, she didn't

suppose, and anyway, Mildred had learned a salutary lesson the afternoon of the brawl. Men of this class did not take women of her class seriously. They might flirt with her, but behind all the flattery lurked a contempt for her background that would prevent any but the most desperate fortune hunter from offering her anything more than *carte blanche*. Whereas Mr Crimmer, for all that he was cursed with a stutter and a fatal tendency to blush, had more than proved the strength of his feelings with his fists.

She took her place on the sofa on the far side of her aunt from Mildred, so as not to interrupt her light-hearted flirtation, and flicked open her fan. How soon would they be able to go home? And how soon after that would she be able to return to Much Wakering, and the very obscurity Miss Waverley had taunted her with as though it would be some kind of punishment? She sighed. Although she wrote regularly to her father, it seemed an age since she had seen him.

Perhaps he would come up to town for a meeting, or a lecture. He often took off at a moment's notice, after having read an advertisement in the paper.

Her hand slowed and stilled, as she imagined him going to one of his meetings, and unexpectedly hearing her name bandied about in the way Miss Waverley had just described, for Miss Wa-

verley was never going to let the matter drop. She
was so angry about having her plan to entrap
Lord Deben thwarted that she would most likely
take every chance she got to blacken Henrietta's
name. And she was so popular with the men that
she would never lack an audience.

A cold sensation gnawed at the pit of her
stomach. She did not care for herself, but her
father would be terribly upset to find he'd pitched
her into such an uncomfortable situation.

Not to mention her brothers. When they returned home on leave, what would it do to them
to find their sister talked about in that horrid
way?

Oh, they would understand without having to
be told how it was that their absent-minded father had come to send her to stay with the Ledbetters, which was what had led to the general
assumption that she had a background in trade,
but it would not make their chagrin on her behalf any the less. And even though Lady Dalrymple had enlightened some people, there were
others, like Miss Waverley, who would prefer to
believe the worst.

But it wasn't that, so much, which would
worry her whole family. It was the nature of
her entanglement with Lord Deben. She had
done absolutely nothing wrong, but Miss Wa-

verley was sure to make it sound just as bad as it could be.

It was a kind of poetic justice. Because she had rashly pursued Richard up to London, she was going to be branded as the kind of girl who chased after *all* men. She felt a bit sick. By pushing her father into hastily arranging what he thought was a Season for her, she might well have dragged her entire family into the mire.

She could still hear the drone of Mildred's two admirers buzzing in her ears, and see gorgeously apparelled people milling about the room, but she felt strangely detached from them all, guilt roiling through her like a poisonous miasma so thick that it practically blotted them all out.

Until Lord Deben strolled across the part of the room into which she was staring sightlessly.

Giving her a faint ray of hope. People were going to gossip about her, now, whatever she did. And that being the case, she would much rather they did so because she had become, mysteriously, the toast of the *ton*, than a byword for vulgarity.

She was *not* giving in to base temptation. She was *not* doing this because she wanted to put Miss Waverley's nose out of joint. She was *not* thinking of how often it would mean she would have to spend time in Lord Deben's stimulating company. It would just be far better for her

male relatives to believe she'd had a successful
Season, than pain them by becoming a laughing stock.

Rising to her feet, she walked across the room
to Lord Deben's side and, when he did not at
first notice her hovering on the fringes of the
crowd that had gathered round him, she reached
through the throng and tugged at his sleeve.

A matron put up her lorgnettes and stared at
her frostily. One of the men nudged another and
they both smirked.

Lord Deben eyed the little hand that had just
creased the immaculate sleeve of his coat, and
then, slowly, followed the line of her arm to her
face.

'Miss Gibson,' he said.

For one terrible moment, she thought she
might just have committed social suicide. If
he chose to snub her now, she really would be
finished. Silently, with all her will-power, she
begged him to help her. And after what felt like
an eternity, but was probably only a second or
two, his face broke into a charming smile.

'My dear, I completely forgot. You are quite
right to remind me.' He took her hand and pulled
her into the charmed circle. 'You will excuse us,
gentlemen? Ladies? Only I did give my word
that...' He trailed off, pulling his watch out of
his pocket and examining it. 'And I am already

overdue. We were so deep in conversation,' he said to Henrietta, 'that I quite forgot the time.'

He tucked her hand firmly into the crook of his arm and gave it a reassuring pat. The others moved aside as he led her out of the door and along a corridor. After only a few paces, he opened another door, peered inside, then pushed her into a deserted room, shutting the door firmly behind them and turning the key in the lock.

'Thank you.' She breathed a sigh of relief. A brace of candlesticks stood upon the mantel over the empty grate, so that although the room was not very inviting, at least they were not in complete darkness.

'Did you doubt me?' He folded his arms and leaned back against the door. 'I gave you my word that should you apply to me for aid, I would be there.'

But he'd never really thought she would come to him so quickly. His heart was only just returning to its regular rhythm, after the surge of jubilation that had set it pounding when she'd pleaded with him, mutely, to help her. It went some way to compensating him for having made the first move this evening. He'd still been rather annoyed with himself for doing so when two weeks earlier he'd sworn that the next time they spoke it would be because *she* had come to *him*.

And yet the moment he'd seen her, feigning indifference, he'd been compelled to confront her, even going to the lengths of barring her way when she would have left the room.

'Yes, that is why I came straight to you. It was only that I was not sure you would understand.'

'My dear, you would not approach me, push through a crowd who fancy themselves the most important people in the land, and tug on my coat sleeve unless it was a dire emergency.'

Which was why he had not been able to resist making her wait for his response. For a few moments, he'd had the supreme satisfaction of having her exactly where he wanted her—metaphorically, if not literally, on her knees before him—and it had been so sweet a feeling that he'd prolonged it as long as he could. It had been just punishment for the damage she'd unwittingly caused his pride.

'The most important people in the land? Oh, dear!'

'They only think they are,' he said with contempt. 'But never mind the conversation you interrupted. I am far more interested in learning what has occurred to induce you to abandon that fierce pride of yours and come to me as a supplicant. Not that I object, you understand.'

'Sometimes,' she said, observing the smugness of the smile that curved his lips as he referred to her as a supplicant, 'I really, really, dislike you.'

He took one step sideways. 'The key is in the lock. You may turn it and leave, if you so wish.'

'You aggravating man,' she seethed. 'You know very well I'm not going anywhere. Do you have to make it so hard for me?'

'Make what hard?' His smile was positively predatory now.

She glowered at him.

'To tell you that I have changed my mind. That if you would be so kind, I should like to take you up on your offer.'

'My offer?' His smile froze.

'To make me the toast of the *ton*,' she snapped. 'They are all going to gossip about me. I cannot stop it now. And at least if you...I don't know... do whatever it is you had in mind to make them think I'm...fascinating...then at least my brothers won't be ashamed to own me.'

A strange look came over his face. 'You are doing this for your brothers?'

She'd done something very like this before. When Lady Chigwell had been berating her, she'd borne it all with weary indifference. It had only been when the old harridan had cast aspersions on her family that she had flung up her chin and answered back.

Because she loved them.

Love was the key that he'd been searching for. If she believed she was in love with him, he would have it all. Her compliance to his wish she should marry him and, most of all, her loyalty. He didn't know why he hadn't seen it before. But now he had, he couldn't see her marrying anyone unless she fancied herself in love with him.

And once she'd made the commitment, she would remain loyal to the bitter end. No matter what she thought of him once she knew him well enough to realise he was not the kind of person anyone could really love, she would remain loyal. He might have mocked her for that streak of Puritanism she so frequently displayed, but that very morality would spare him many of the distasteful aspects of marriage that had made him avoid it for so long. She would not be the kind of woman to take a lover the moment she'd presented him with an heir. On the contrary, any children she bore would undoubtedly be his.

Just think of that. Having two or even three sons that were indisputably legitimate. It was far more than he'd ever dared to hope for. But with Henrietta as his wife...

He sucked in a deep breath as he imagined married life, with Henrietta Gibson as his countess.

Their marriage would not be in the least bit *fashionable*. She would be unfashionably loyal, unfashionably faithful and, most likely, with her open, honest nature, probably given to unfashionable displays of affection in public. Which would be a tad irritating, particularly as people would mock her.

Still, he had never imagined marriage would be without problems, and at least having a wife who was a bit gauche in public was far preferable to enduring one who played the whore.

He made a decision. Not only would he not reprimand her, should she be demonstrative towards him in public, he would actually defend her. It would be a shame to crush those traits of honesty and openness that made her unique. Any affection she felt for him initially would wither away and die eventually anyway, but he could at least not do anything to hasten her disillusionment. By the time she realised that love was a fairy tale, that it had no place in the real world, they might have reached a state of understanding which would enable them to at least present a united front to their children. He would do whatever it took to ensure that his own offspring would not become casualties of the kind of bitter war that had raged between his own parents.

All these thoughts flashed through his mind in less time than it took him to breathe in and out a couple of times.

That was all the time it took to decide that

he would have Miss Gibson at his side, and on his side, no matter what he had to do to ensure he won her.

Completely oblivious to the fact that Lord Deben was undergoing something of an epiphany, Henrietta had turned away and flung herself on to a convenient sofa.

'For Hubert and Horatio, to be precise. When they come home on leave I don't want them to hear the kind of gossip that Miss Waverley says will go round if I just sit back and do nothing. Oh, how I wish I'd never come to town. In doing so I've already let Humphrey and Horace down. I should have been at home when they had their school holidays. Mrs Cook is a very capable housekeeper, and very kind in her own way, but one cannot expect her to play cricket with them.'

She slumped forwards and buried her face in her hands. 'I've made such a mull of it all.'

Her despair over not being present during her brothers' school holidays only proved that he'd just made the right decision. Miss Gibson would make an exemplary mother. He could just see her playing cricket with his own sons on the East Lawn, not caring about ruining the turf. And more than that, he could see her protecting all the children he would get upon her with the ferocity of a tigress guarding her cubs. Unlike his own mother who, once she'd whelped, had scarcely looked over her shoulder as she returned to her relentless pursuit of selfish pleasures.

A lesser man might have blurted it all out, there and then, perhaps claiming to have been struck by a *coup de foudre*. His upper lip curled in contempt as he considered the outcome of speaking such fustian to Miss Gibson while she was so upset and angry. Particularly since some of her anger was directed at him. She resented having to apply to him for aid. Especially since, now he came to consider it, he had not been all that gracious about it.

And then, something about the term *coup de foudre* niggled at the back of his mind. Hadn't he, on that drive round the park, warned her that he was not the kind of man who would suffer from that complaint? He had.

In fact, he had been less than tactful with Miss Gibson on several occasions. And brutally honest about his views on love and romance.

He would have the devil of a job getting her to believe he was now receptive to the whole idea of love, within marriage, especially as he only expected her to be the one 'falling in love'. He could just picture how it would go, should he commence a courtship after the accepted mode. If he presented her with posies, started making pretty speeches, or gave her respectful yet meaningful glances across the set as they danced with each other, she would simply laugh at him. Frustrate him at every turn. In short, make him look like a fool.

There followed what he found a slightly awkward pause as it occurred to him that he could not have made a worse start with his intended bride.

To cover the awkwardness, and to give her something to think about while he grappled with a solution to the dilemma he'd caused himself, he said, 'Your parents gave you all names beginning with the letter *H*?'

If he appeared to be interested in the family she held so dear, that might at least start to smooth her ruffled feathers.

She looked up at him sharply. 'That has nothing to do with anything.'

'On the contrary,' he said, making a swift recovery and making damned sure he would not let her glimpse his true state of mind, 'I utterly refuse to do anything at all until you have divulged the reason behind such an eccentric example of parenting.'

'It was a bit of a joke between my father and mother, if you must know,' she said mulishly. 'Since their names both started with the letter *G*, they decided the next generation must all take the next letter of the alphabet.'

They had agreed on the names of their children between themselves. A pang of yearning shot through him. What would it be like to hang over a cradle, and discuss with his wife the naming of each and every one of the children she bore him? His own father had decreed that his name should be Jonathon Henry and had not cared what his mother chose to name any of the successive siblings that she periodically deposited in the family nursery.

He squeezed his eyes shut. He was letting his imagination run away with him. He could not start filling his nursery until he got Miss Gibson to accept a proposal of marriage from him and, judging by her present demeanour and what he already knew of her, she was not going to seize upon it with the delight he might expect from any other female present in town this Season.

He opened his eyes and regarded her slumped posture thoughtfully. For one thing, she had just told him she didn't particularly like him. Unlike the other débutantes he'd been discreetly interviewing for the position, rank did not mean anything to her. Then there was the mysterious suitor who'd abandoned her for Miss Waverley's surface charm. She might still have some lingering feelings for him. She'd claimed she had come to him because she did not want to disappoint her brothers, but he would wager it was more complicated than that. He could not leave the mysterious swain out of the equation.

But nor could he risk allowing her to slip through his fingers.

Then it hit him.

There was a way, just one way, he could definitely get her to accept a marriage proposal—and that would be if he asked her precisely one minute after taking her virginity.

For once she'd yielded to him, sexually, she was the kind of woman who would salve her conscience by telling herself she'd only succumbed because she was in love with him. She wouldn't be, of course, but that was immaterial. He did not need her to really love him, only to believe she did.

His blood stirred. The moment he started to think in terms of bedding her he couldn't help noticing what wonderfully clear skin she had. Her cheeks were soft as rose petals. And the upper slopes of her breasts, just visible above the modest neckline of her gown, looked so luscious he was already salivating at the prospect of closing his lips around them.

He took a deep breath, reminding himself he needed to keep a clear head. Though he was pleased she aroused the lust necessary to make her an acceptable bed partner, most of the desire he felt towards her had very little to do with the physical. Not that it was sentimental in nature. No, he was not such a fool that he would permit mawkish sentiment to cloud his judgement. It was just that there were so many things about her that made the prospect of marriage entirely... palatable.

As he eyed her dejected form an intensity came to his eyes, like that of a hawk hovering over its prey. For all her protestations of dislike, for all her rigidly held morals, she was not immune to him. He'd caught the occasional glimmer of appreciation in her eyes as she examined his face, or the set of his shoulders, or the skill with which he handled the ribbons. And if he wasn't mistaken, she had deliberately set out to make him laugh in the recounting of the tale of Crimmer and the yahoos. She'd wanted to impress him, at least, if not to enchant him.

Which was a start.

He wouldn't mind wagering that during the entire two weeks he had held aloof, she had been thinking about him, too, for she'd as good as admitted she'd wanted him to have been the one to send Lady Dalrymple to clear her name.

And she had not returned the handkerchief he'd pressed upon her, the first night they'd met. If she was completely indifferent to him, she would have had it laundered and returned via one of her wealthy uncle's footmen.

Yes, she was susceptible.

So, the only question remaining was how best to embark upon her seduction. In some ways it was a pity he'd already put the notion in her head that he was only going to pretend to find her fascinating. It was another reason why he'd seen it would be damned difficult to make her believe he was in earnest when he began to pursue her.

On the other hand, it would give him opportunities to sneak beneath her guard which she would never yield to a real suitor. All he needed was a plausible explanation for why he would push her beyond the bounds of what she would consider acceptable behaviour from a make-believe suitor.

All kinds of interesting possibilities occurred to him...

It felt like getting back on to familiar, firm ground after wading through a patch of quicksand. Because, even though she would no doubt make a spirited attempt to preserve her virtue, he had complete confidence that he could breach her walls. She was such an innocent she would not have a hope of maintaining a lengthy resistance to the range and sophistication of weapons he could wield. He knew how to lure a woman so stealthily that she thought she was the one doing the enticing. How to tease, and arouse, and tor-

ture a woman with sensual delights until she was
begging him for the mercy of release.

And not once, in his entire amatory career,
had any woman ever objected to his methods,
or his technique. Even the married ones purred
that he was a tiger in bed. And when he ended
an affair, they had all, without exception, let him
know they would welcome him back.

Though, he frowned, none of them had been
cut from the same cloth as Miss Gibson. Nor was
his interest in her merely sexual and temporary.
What he wanted from Miss Gibson was something entirely new. In some indefinable way, he
wanted more from her than just her body.

But taking possession of her body was where
he was going to start.

'Well,' she said impatiently, after he'd been
staring at her in complete silence for some minutes, 'are you going to keep your promise, or
not?'

'Oho, Miss Gibson, that sounds like a challenge.' He stalked towards her, but instead of taking a seat beside her, he bent and took her hands,
tugging her to her feet. 'Turn around,' he said,
letting go of her hands.

'What? Why?'

'Just do it,' he said, affecting irritation. 'I need
to see what material I have to work with.'

Shooting him just one look loaded with resentment, she turned, then plumped herself back down on the sofa and crossed her arms.

'Completely graceless.' He sighed. 'And far too thin to be fashionable,' though hers was not the pared-down, weakened frame that poets described as ethereal. She had the whipcord leanness of a girl who led an energetic lifestyle—playing cricket with her brothers, for one thing.

'The quickest way to make you fashionable would be to procure you vouchers for Almack's. And attend myself...' He had never set foot in the marriage mart before, and to do so now would be such singular behaviour that everyone would understand his intent. People were already beginning to speculate about his sudden interest in débutantes. When he began to devote himself entirely to Miss Gibson everyone but she would understand that he'd got her in his sights. It would afford her the kind of protection he would never otherwise be able to provide. Though his own treatment of her from now on must be utterly ruthless, he would make damned sure nobody else dared to so much as look at her sideways.

She was going to be his wife. His countess. Everyone needed to understand that and accord her due respect.

'If people suspect you are about to become the next Countess of Deben, they will be falling over themselves to win your goodwill,' he predicted.

It was just typical of her that instead of taking the lure he'd dropped into the conversation, about the potential for gaining a title, she wrinkled her nose, and said, 'Almack's? Don't be ridiculous.'

'Ridiculous?' Why would she consider going to Almack's ridiculous? Did she care so little for the superficial glamour of the society in which he moved that she would eschew the highest honour it could bestow on a girl with limited connections?

It would, he saw, take a very, very long time before Miss Gibson ever began to bore him. She was like no other female he'd ever encountered. Every time he thought he'd begun to grasp the essence of her, she'd surprise him all over again. But never in a bad way.

She was, in fact, just like his favourite season of the year, when summer began to ebb away, but winter did not yet hold his estates in the grip of its frosty fingers. When he could never tell, on waking, whether the day would be balmy as June, heavy with fog, or ripped to shreds by a bracing gale. When the undulating hills would flush with a last glorious burst of colour, as though each tree had absorbed every sunset and dawn that had tinted the summer skies, only to flaunt them in defiance of the approaching season of dormancy.

'In what way? Do you not believe I am capable of procuring you vouchers, perchance? Oh, ye of little faith. I am in possession of a certain piece of information for which Lady Jersey would give her eye teeth…'

'It isn't that,' she said with a touch of impatience. 'I don't care how many people offer to procure me vouchers to Almack's, I shan't go, and that's that.'

'I share your reluctance to set foot in anywhere so stuffy, but, Miss Gibson…'

'No,' she repeated firmly. 'It's all very well to talk about social advancement, and Aunt Ledbetter agreeing not to stand in my way, but I shall not turn my back on her and my cousin. I will not go anywhere that they will not be received, too. And you know very well they would never admit Mildred.'

'Ah,' he said. 'It sounds as though you are referring to a conversation you have already had, so I can only surmise that Lady Dalrymple has already offered to use her influence to promote you.'

She nodded.

'But only if you play down the fact that the people with whom you are currently residing are not quite the thing.'

She nodded again, glumly.

He clucked his tongue. 'How foolish of her

to suggest you should turn your back upon your relatives in order to feather your own nest.'

She looked up at him sharply. 'You do understand, then?'

'Of course.' He gave an insouciant shrug. 'You are too fiercely loyal to anyone you consider family to do anything so shabby. I only wish I'd been there to hear your reply,' he said, a gleam of appreciation in his eyes. 'Hampered as you were by the fact that you were, no doubt, in your aunt's drawing room at the time.'

'And,' she pointed out, 'by my own innate good manners. Heavens, your godmother had just offered to go out of her way to bring me into style. I would never, ever want to offend someone who'd just done that.'

He raised one eyebrow. 'Anyone but me, you mean. After all, have I not just offered to do the same?'

'Oh, you are different,' she said, slamming her hand down on the arm of the sofa.

'Am I?'

'You know very well you are. This is all just a game to you. So stop pretending to take offence,' she said, folding her arms and glaring up at him. 'And concentrate on coming up with some other solution.'

He planted his hands on his hips and examined her, head tilted to one side. He did his best to look stern, but no matter how hard he tried he could not quite prevent a smile from playing about his lips. He was *glad* she'd turned down his offer to procure vouchers for Almack's. Delighted with the reasons she'd done so. And thoroughly enjoying the spirited way she was sparring with him.

'It would have been quite a sacrifice, you ungrateful wretch,' he said with mock reproof, 'getting me to attend Almack's. Any of the lady patronesses would have been thrilled to think they'd seen me finally brought to heel.'

'Well, you shan't need to make that sacrifice now,' she pointed out.

He shook his head ruefully. 'No, instead I shall be obliged to pursue you through the lower echelons of society.'

'But...how will that answer?'

'You goose. Once people discover that I am prepared to go anywhere that you attend in the hopes of making you smile upon me, you will get invited everywhere. All you will have to do is ignore any invitation that does not include your chaperon and companion. Before long, the more astute hostess will understand what she needs to do to get you, and therefore me, to attend her party.'

Her face lit up.

'Oh, how clever of you. Yes, that would answer.'

He had never thought that a woman's smile could have such an exhilarating effect upon him.

Though it was simultaneously rather sobering to reflect that if she knew what he was planning for her, she would shrink from him.

But he was not going to let minor matters like scruples hold him back, not now. Miss Gibson was going to marry him and he would do whatever it took to get her to the altar. Even if it meant deceiving her.

'In part,' he said gravely. He made as if to sit on the sofa beside her. Henrietta shifted slightly to give him room, her eyes fixed on his with open curiosity. Another pang of something like remorse shot through him.

Again, he thrust it aside.

'At the risk of you accusing me of being rude, Miss Gibson, I have to remind you of the one factor which may give the lie to our little game.' He took her hands in his, without breaking eye contact. 'My reputation.'

'Y-your reputation? As a rake, you mean? Y-yes, I know that you do not normally pursue innocents…'

He shook his head. 'Even among those who could never have been described as innocent have I ever had to *pursue* any female. At the most, all I have ever had to do is drop a few subtle hints. If the woman in question did not respond, I saw no reason to persist. After all, there have always been plenty who were willing to pursue me. Thus, I have been able to avail myself of the ones who are…'

'The most beautiful!' She tried to draw her hands away, but he held on to them firmly.

'It is not that you are not beautiful, Miss Gibson. I have already told you that you have many good features. Clear skin, speaking eyes and a perfectly acceptable mouth. Your problem, my dear, is, as you yourself have already pointed out, that you do not have what you call the "charisma" to attract the notice of a man such as myself. Though I would call it allure. Feminine allure. That elusive factor which draws men to some females like moths to a candle flame.'

She frowned. 'You aren't going to suggest I suddenly start apeing all those girls who flutter their eyelashes at men and say how clever they are, and agree with whatever nonsense they spout?' She wrinkled her nose in disgust. 'Even if I restricted my fluttering and fawning to you, I don't think I could be very convincing…'

She faltered as he began to chuckle.

'God, no! You must remain your own, refreshingly honest self at all times. Only a more feminine version of yourself.'

'How can I become more feminine? You aren't going to advise me to wear low-cut gowns and paint my face, I hope?'

'That would be to make you look desperate,' he replied drily. 'As though you are out to snare any man who will throw the handkerchief your way. No, what I plan to do is make you aware of yourself as a woman. Only when you understand and embrace your own sexuality will other men understand what it is that attracts me to you.'

'Embrace my s-s—' She tugged her hands free, a tide of red sweeping over her cheeks. 'What,' she said primly, 'exactly, are you suggesting?'

'Do not look at me like that,' he said frostily. 'Do you think I intend to ravish you upon this sofa?'

'N-no, but—'

'No buts, Miss Gibson. Either you trust me to turn you into the kind of woman who can have a man panting after her with one glance, or you do not.'

He could teach her how to have a man panting after her with one glance? Was that even possible?

Yes. Yes, it was. Hadn't she seen Miss Waverley bewitching Richard? And even Mildred had the mysterious power to draw men to her side, and keep them fascinated, even whilst holding them at arm's length. She had thought it was simply that she was beautiful. But Lord Deben was saying there was more to it than that.

'Do you trust me, Miss Gibson?'

She looked into his stern features. If she said she didn't trust him, he would get up and walk out, she could tell.

'If I didn't trust you, I wouldn't be sitting here in this room, on the sofa with you, with the door locked,' she pointed out. 'I just don't really understand how...'

'I know you don't understand. That is why you must trust me. Let me teach you about your body and the power it has.'

'Teach me about my body? How will that help?'

'You really have no idea, do you?' His eyes, which could sometimes look as hard as polished jet, softened to something she felt she could drown in.

'If you were more aware of yourself as a woman, the power to attract a man's notice would flow naturally from that.'

'I don't know what you mean.' Why was it becoming so difficult to draw breath? 'Of course I am aware that I'm a woman.'

He shook his head, almost pityingly. 'No. Miss Gibson, though you inhabit the body of a fully grown woman, you are still, in many ways, just a little girl.'

'I am not!'

'Oh, but you are. You wield none of the weapons that other women employ upon the battlefield of the ballroom. You walk and talk more like a man than a gently bred female of two and twenty summers.'

He laid one finger upon her lips when she opened her mouth to make an objection.

'And, my dear, it is quite obvious to every experienced male that nobody has ever kissed those innocent lips.'

'Oh, but they have. I mean, they did. I mean, of course I have been kissed!'

'Not to any great effect,' he said with a slight sneer. 'It was obviously a fumbling boy, not a man that kissed you, or you would not appear so untouched.'

Untouched? Richard's kiss had flummoxed her so much she had chased after him all the way to London.

'Whereas,' he was continuing, silkily, 'if I were to kiss you, you would never be the same again.'

'You are the most arrogant man I have ever met!'

'No. Just truthful. If I were to kiss you, I would take great care to ensure you would never be able to look at a man's lips in quite the same way again. When you next spoke to a man, any man, you would not be able to help wondering if his lips could wreak the magic that mine did. Your eyes would linger on them, speculatively. And he would know that you were summing him up. Know that you were wondering what it would be like to kiss him. And then he would want, above all things, to show you.'

Magic? He was declaring that his lips would work some kind of magic upon her? And yet, it appeared, the magic was already beginning to work because as he spoke, she found it impossible to tear her eyes from his mouth. And wonder what was so special about it that one touch would change her into someone who could draw men to her like moths to a flame.

Of course, he had a vast amount of experience.

And he did have a reputation for being so very good at carnal things that any lady who'd been fortunate enough to attract his attention wanted it again. And suddenly it was not just his mouth she was thinking about, but his whole body, naked, in a rumpled bed, where he was rendering some faceless female delirious with desire.

He smiled, a lazy, sensuous smile that did funny things to her insides and made her heart race. Or had it been racing like this for some minutes already?

'Exactly so,' he purred softly. 'You are wondering what my lips will feel like. So, naturally, I wish to oblige you.'

'How can you tell what I'm thinking?' Her voice came out in a horrified squeak. Goodness, if he knew she'd just been picturing him naked, she would never be able to look him in the face again.

'It is the way you are looking at my mouth, Miss Gibson. With curiosity. And longing. And, best of all, with invitation.'

'I...I wasn't...'

'Oh, but you were.'

He frowned. 'At this point in the proceedings, with any other man but me, you would pull up the drawbridge and retreat behind it, since you do not wish to appear fast.'

'P-pull up the drawbridge?'

'Last chance, Miss Gibson. Stop me now, or I will kiss you. And I promise you, if I do that, you will never be the same again.'

Chapter Seven

She wasn't the same already. She had never, ever, thought about what a man would look like naked, in bed. Or felt her lips tingle with expectancy. Nor had her heart raced like this while she was sitting completely still. And all he'd done so far was *talk* about kissing.

Heavens, no wonder women were queuing up for the privilege of taking him as a lover.

'Do you wish to continue?'

'Wh-what?'

'With your lesson. Do you wish me to take it to its conclusion?'

Lesson. She blinked.

And although there was still a pool of lethargy where her knees had previously been, most of the haze cleared from her mind at his curt reminder that this was not real.

Not for him, anyway. He considered her a pupil, very much in need of tutoring in the arts of which he was a skilled practitioner.

It was a good job he'd recalled her to reality. It would never do to start thinking there was anything *romantic* about what was going to happen next. She'd read far too much into a kiss before—and look where that had ended up.

She must think of this merely as a practical demonstration from a master craftsman to his apprentice.

'I cannot think of anyone better qualified to teach me about kissing,' she said tartly, 'than you, Lord Deben.'

And with that, she shut her eyes, tilted her head back and puckered up her lips.

'Miss Gibson...' he chuckled '...you are the most absurd creature.'

Well, that dealt with any last lingering shreds of girlish excitement she had not so far managed to squash. She opened her eyes and glared up into his mocking face.

It was all very well accepting she was ignorant and in need of tuition, but that did not mean she would sit back and tamely let him mock her.

'That's it,' she snapped. 'I have changed my mind.'

When she made as if to get up he reacted astonishingly swiftly, seizing her about the waist and pulling her back down. Then he took hold of her chin with his free hand.

'Don't fly into the boughs because I laughed,' he said sternly. 'You should not have pushed your mouth into that absurd little shape. It made you look ridiculous. Never do it again.'

'How dare you speak to me like that!'

'I dare because you asked me to teach you how to be more feminine, sweet tempest,' he pointed out.

It was strange he should have spoken of a tempest, because it really did feel as if some kind of tempest was raging through her. It was making her breathless. Her heart was pounding against her ribcage. But it wasn't, at least not all of it, the product of outrage at his high-handed attitude towards her. A good deal of it stemmed from the determined way he was holding her captive, which was having the peculiar effect of making her want to sink into his strong embrace rather than make any attempt to struggle free of the confines of those muscular arms.

'You should let your lips relax,' he instructed her. 'Perhaps part them a little for me. Moisten them, if you wish.'

He licked his own, then, as if demonstrating what she ought to do.

She couldn't have torn her eyes from his mouth if her life had depended on it.

'R-relax,' she stammered.

He smiled and gently caressed her lower jaw with his gloved hand. A flash of something very like electricity struck her midriff as he angled her head into a position of his own choosing.

'By all means close your eyes, if you wish.'

He was lowering his head towards her. Any second now...

'I find that absence of sight heightens the other senses.'

Immediately, she screwed her eyes tightly shut. Though it wasn't about heightening her senses, since hers were pretty over-stimulated already, so much as hiding. She did not want him looking into her eyes when they kissed, in case he saw...

What? That she had never felt like this? Could never have imagined feeling like this? That, in short, he was right, damn him? That just having a man of his reputation holding her so close was making her all soft and melting and more aware of her femininity than she had ever dreamed possible?

Particularly since he was so hard and demanding, and masculine.

She swallowed.

And felt his breath, hot against her cheek. Then he nuzzled her ear. And breathed in, deep and slow, just as though he was... What was he doing? Smelling her? Why would he want to do that? Although, hadn't he said something about heightening the other senses? And it was very… affecting, having him just breathe in and out like that, as though he was inhaling her very essence.

She couldn't help being extremely aware of the scent of him, too. It was incredibly inti-mate—yes that was the word, intimate—to be so close to a man that she could identify the unique smell of the shaving soap he'd used, overlying freshly laundered linen and what she suspected was just him. Spice and musk. Masculinity.

Oh, bother the man. What was he waiting for? Why did he have to make such a meal of it? Why could he not just get on with it?

His hand went to the nape of her neck. His fingers speared upwards, into her hair, massag-ing her scalp. He nudged at her jaw line with his nose, as though he wanted her to tilt her head back still further.

And because it felt rather as though her spine was melting, she had no problem with letting her head loll against the back of the sofa.

He buried his face in her neck.

'Oh!' He was *still* not kissing her. Instead, he was very gently nipping along the length of her neck. And now not only her spine, but every sin-gle bone in her body was melting.

He lapped at the little hollow beneath her collarbone with his tongue. And it occurred to her, shockingly, that he would only have to lower his head a fraction more, nudge aside her bodice and his mouth could gain access to her nipples. Which certainly needed something. They had gone so hard and tight they were almost painful. And that hot, wet tongue would be incredibly soothing.

She whimpered.

He lifted his head, briefly. She did not open her eyes, but somehow she knew he was examining the effects of his handiwork. Or should that be teethiwork? For he was only employing his hands to keep her in place. Which was a jolly good thing. Because, when he started suckling at the juncture of her neck and her shoulder, she went so limp she would have slid right off the sofa and melted into a pool on the floor without them to anchor her in place.

'Ooohhhh,' she moaned breathily. The skin of his face was slightly bristly, although he'd looked clean shaven. It rasped in contrast to his tongue, which lapped, and his lips, which brushed petal soft.

'Mmmhhm,' he growled into her neck just below her ear. The sound sent vibrations through every nerve ending in her body, sending a message to the juncture of her thighs, where a completely delicious sensation was building. It was getting harder and harder to keep still. Her hips seemed to have developed a mind of their own.

She shuddered. And squirmed. And wondered what to do with her hands. If she let them have their way they would tear off her gloves so her greedy fingers could plunge into the thickness of Lord Deben's black curls. Then she would push his head back down to her breasts, which were getting desperate for the attentions of that clever, wicked mouth.

Mouth. So far he had not gone anywhere near her mouth. He was teasing her. Tormenting her. Goading her to grab him by the ears and pull his face to hers so that she could know, at last, what it would feel like to be kissed by an experienced man.

So she clenched her hands into fists and rammed them into the sofa cushions, lest she gave way to this sensual torment and reveal how very desperate he was making her.

'Miss Gibson.'

'Hmmhh?'

'Here endeth the first lesson.'

'Wh-what?' She opened her eyes, to find him looking down at her.

A horridly satisfied, smug look on his face.

Somehow she managed to sit up and push him away, though it took a few more seconds before she could gather her scattered wits enough to speak.

'Thank you.' Was that her voice? It sounded so hoarse and breathy at the same time. As though she had been running. Gracious heavens. Her legs most definitely felt as though she'd been running. All weak and trembly. Like a newborn lamb's.

'That was most…edifying,' she croaked.

'Indeed it was. And now for the second lesson.'

'The second?' Oh, no. She was not ready for any more of that sort of thing. Whatever had she been thinking, to ask a rake to teach her about seduction? What was it she'd thought about Miss Waverley—that she'd done the equivalent of poking her hand through the bars of a lion's cage? Well, she had just opened the gate, walked right in and practically offered herself up to him for dinner.

And just look at him! All cool and calm and collected. Not a hair out of place. Not a wrinkle in his coat.

The contrast between them brought her quite suddenly, and bewilderingly, close to the brink of tears.

'When you leave this room,' he said quite sternly, 'I want you to think about your waist, as you walk.'

'My waist?'

'Yes. If you think about your waist, as you walk, you will find your hips will sway, naturally. And men will watch you with interest. If you see one you like the look of, catch his eye.'

Oh, how very lowering. But at least his brutal reminder that he was only doing this to give her the ability to attract *other* men dealt with her fleeting emotional lapse. Had she not warned herself not to read anything romantic into this... this episode on the sofa?

'Then look at his mouth,' he said. 'You know the potential for pleasure a man's mouth can bring to your body now. Consider, will the touch of this man's lips make your breasts tingle? Will the heat of his breath on your cheek send shivers of desire down your spine? Will his hands work your reins with skill, or will he fumble?'

Dear God, he'd known she felt like that?

Of course he did. He'd been with dozens of women. Scores of them, probably. And she had been making little mewing noises, and gyrating about, so it must have been obvious that his lips had been every bit as potent as he'd boasted. Chagrined, she averted her face.

He took her chin in his strong fingers and turned her back, so that she had no choice but to meet his dark and penetrating gaze.

'Your face is so open,' he said more gently.

'No man could help but respond, without even perhaps knowing why. And then, Miss Gibson, you must lower your gaze and blush. Which you are doing very prettily, by the way.'

She tossed her head, freeing herself from his grip.

'Hmmm,' he mused. 'That look won't do. You ought rather to flick open your fan and cool your heated cheeks. Then look back at your prey over your shoulder as you walk away. I guarantee you will catch him watching your neat little behind.'

Dammit, but the fellow would have his tongue hanging out. Might she succumb to what she thought were real advances from some other man who would be bound to want her once he saw past the rather unprepossessing exterior?

What the hell had he started?

Hot jealousy at the thought of her responding to this faceless rival, as she'd just responded to him, scalded his guts and made them twist into a tortured knot. He should have been prepared for this. This, after all, was what had poisoned his parents' marriage and made him so determined to avoid the unholy institution. He'd had his suspicions that he would be like his father, unable to tolerate a 'fashionable' marriage.

He got up and strode to the door, unlocking it with swift, impatient movements. He'd chosen Miss Gibson precisely because he did not believe she was capable of being 'fashionable' in the way that his mother had been. She placed too high a value on loyalty. On keeping her word. If she vowed in a church, before God, to keep only to one man so long as she lived, then that was exactly what she would do.

The fact that she'd just responded to him so sweetly, with such an intoxicating blend of passion and surprise, did not mean she was ready to experiment with another man. That display of chagrin, afterwards, was proof of it. She was such a little Puritan, she'd felt guilty.

He must concentrate on feeling flattered that he'd made such rapid progress with her seduction, rather than allowing groundless fears to spoil this marriage before he'd even embarked on it. Henrietta Gibson, he repeated to himself under his breath, would *not* permit any other man the same liberties he'd just taken with her.

But in any case, he wasn't going to give any other man the chance to cut him out.

'If you would be so good as to furnish me with a list of your engagements,' he bit out, 'I shall endeavour to find you, within the next day or so, and you can report your progress.'

Pride demanded that he mention their next meeting as though the timing of it was a matter of indifference to him. But in his heart he already knew he would find her *tomorrow*, wherever she was, and move the seduction on swiftly. Before she knew what was happening, she would be so deeply enmeshed in the sensual web he would weave around her that there would be no escape.

Once she'd told him of as many of her engagements as she could bring to mind, Henrietta peered past him into the corridor, making absolutely sure the coast was clear before leaving.

Think about her waist? How could she think about her waist, and swaying her hips, when all that filled her brain was the sudden coldness with which he'd dismissed her? One moment she could almost have imagined tenderness in his eyes. The next it was as though he couldn't wait to be rid of her.

Yet, as she made her way back to the drawing room where she'd left her aunt and Mildred, she realised that she did not have to make any effort whatever to think about her body. It was still thrumming with the after-effects of her encounter with Lord Deben. She was drifting along the corridors in a kind of daze. She'd never *drifted* anywhere in her life. She was more likely to walk briskly, since she was generally so busy. There was always so much to occupy both her time, and her mind, in running Shoebury Manor for her father and seeing to the needs of all four of her brothers, that it would be a sinful waste of both to just *drift*.

However, it would be a useful accomplishment to cultivate while she was in town. It was probably a prerequisite to joining the ranks of the sort of women men found fascinating.

But the moment she tried to pin down exactly what it was that was making her legs incapable of proceeding in a business-like manner, they went all gangly and awkward.

Oh, bother it. She felt like a child trying to capture a bubble. The moment she touched upon the truth it disappeared in a disappointing spray of its component parts. She could *classify* her present state of being, by comparing herself to a harp-string, recently plucked, and still vibrating from the touch of the musician's hand, but she could not, by effort of will, replicate the condition.

Though it was not entirely accurate to compare herself to a harp-string, anyway, because it had not been Lord Deben's hands that had reduced her to this state, but his mouth. And that little sound he'd made, just beneath her ear.

Oh, heavens, but just the thought of that utterly masculine growl of pleasure made her legs go all languid again.

She drifted the rest of the way to her destination where she dropped down gratefully on to the sofa next to Aunt Ledbetter. She unfurled her fan. And as she waved it languidly before her heated cheeks, her mind began to clear a little.

That growl Lord Deben had made—it *had* been a sound of pleasure. She had not imagined it.

A sound of pleasure. No, more than that. He'd sounded like a man about to feast on some delicious confection, after having been deprived of any sustenance at all for some considerable time.

She fanned herself more briskly as it occurred to her that though he might have appeared cool and calm and collected, he had not been completely unmoved by their encounter.

A small smile tugged at the corner of her mouth. Even if it had been for only one fleeting moment, Lord Deben, a man renowned for only deigning to take the most beautiful women as lovers, had really been enjoying himself. With her.

Take that, Miss Waverley! He never kissed you. Nor wanted to, no matter how hard you tried to entice him.

Oh dear. It was very ignoble of her, but she just couldn't help feeling positively jubilant. It wouldn't matter if she never became the toast of the *ton*, now. Just knowing that she'd made an impact on a man who looked so hard that nothing could melt him was her own, personal and very secret triumph. Something she could hug to herself and examine at leisure.

Richard might not think she had what it took to survive in *sophisticated* society, but she had just had an intimate encounter with a notorious rake and emerged unscathed. If you didn't count the wobbly legs.

Not only that, but she'd also, somehow, managed to make just the tiniest impact on him. Oh, she knew she could not possibly leave a lasting impression on a man that hard and world-weary. But for one moment, that moment when he'd made that very revealing little sound, she had most definitely found a chink in the cynicism which he wore like a coat of chainmail.

When her aunt decided it was time to leave she made a valiant attempt to drift to the waiting carriage. But a girl cannot drift when she's on the verge of a fit of the giggles. And the harder she tried to apply Lord Deben's admonition to think about her waist, the more ridiculous it became to think of herself as a siren. She was just plain, practical, rather tomboyish Miss Gibson. The possibility of her being able to lure some poor unsuspecting man to his doom with one sway of her hips struck her as being so absurd it was all she could do not to laugh out loud.

* * *

The trouble with becoming entangled with a rake, Henrietta discovered the next night as she was getting ready to go out, was that he planted such outrageous notions in her head that she could not help dwelling on them.

All that day, while out shopping, or paying social calls with her aunt and cousin, she had found herself watching the way men watched women and discovering to her shock that Lord Deben had been quite correct. A large number of them did, indeed, study a lady's behind if he thought he could get away with doing so.

She twisted her upper body to peer at her own behind in the mirror. She had never been all that bothered about her behind before. She relied on a maid to make sure everything was correctly fastened up and tidy back there. But now it seemed she had neglected an aspect of her appearance that not even her aunt had deemed all that important.

He'd told her it was 'neat'. She tugged the material of her gown so that it outlined her meagre curves, trying to see why he should describe it in such terms. There was not, she reflected, all that much of it. Perhaps that was what he had meant.

When he'd said it, she'd taken it as a compliment, but now she was not so sure. The men she had surreptitiously studied today had appeared to appreciate the behinds that had wobbled rather like silk-covered blancmanges just as much as the firmer ones.

No, she sighed, letting go of the folds of silk and gauze so that they draped naturally, there was no advantage in having a neat behind. He had merely been describing it, not complimenting it.

She studied her reflection in the normal way, face on, her spirits unaccountably depressed. She had begun to think that since Aunt Ledbetter had given her a hint about which styles and colours became her, she could claim to look...

She whirled away from the mirror in annoyance. Not even Richard had been tricked by her London finery. Just because she'd had a fleeting effect on Lord Deben, it did not mean she had suddenly become *alluring*. She was not a beauty and she never would be.

But at least tonight, at the Lutterworths' soirée, there would be nobody present she particularly wished to impress. The Lutterworths would not presume to invite Lord Deben into their home, palatial though it was.

And it was ridiculous to attempt to impress a man like Lord Deben anyway. She was honest enough with herself to admit that it had been he she'd been thinking about as she'd preened and posed in front of the mirror. And intelligent enough to know that any attempt she might make to impress him would only make him laugh at her.

Though she shied away from considering why she should care if he did laugh at her.

Instead, she concentrated on feeling grateful that she would have at least one evening free from him. Even if she could not stop thinking about him, at least she would not have to deal with his person—and the effect he had on her.

But even telling herself quite sternly to put him out of her mind had not quite worked, because the moment she spotted a sofa amongst the furniture gracing the Lutterworths' palatial dwelling, the entire episode with Lord Deben upon just such a useful article came flooding back with such force that her legs went all languid, her insides turned to mush and her progress across the room slowed to a sensuous drift.

At which point— 'Well done, Miss Gibson. You have the walk down pat already.'

'Lord Deben!' Henrietta could not believe he was standing in front of her just as she'd been remembering the incredible sensations that he'd produced by nibbling all the way down the entire length of her neck.

Nor could she believe that his first words to

her should be those of a schoolmaster praising a pupil.

'Wh-what are you doing here?'

'Seeking you out, naturally,' he said, sweeping her a mocking bow.

Her face was burning. She felt as though he'd caught her doing something reprehensible.

'No. No, I meant—that is, I never imagined when I told you I should be here tonight that the Lutterworths would have sent you an invitation.'

'Why should they not?'

'Well, because it just isn't done to invite a member of the peerage into your home when you've made your fortune from pickles.'

'You shall not slander Mr Lutterworth,' he replied gravely. 'He did not commit the social solecism of sending me an invitation.'

'You mean you just...walked in?'

He laid his hand over his heart. 'Alas, I fear I care nothing for the conventions. I have shamelessly used my rank as a kind of passport. Upon whichever door an earl knocks, you know, he will nearly always gain admittance.'

She'd managed to flick open her fan by now, with fingers that felt all thumbs, but no matter how diligently she employed it, it seemed only to drive the heat to other parts of her body. Which made her even more embarrassed.

Just then, a man whose face looked vaguely familiar approached them.

'Excuse me, Miss Gibson, but we are engaged for the first dance.'

He held out his hand expectantly.

When she made as though to go to him, Lord Deben took hold of her hand and tucked it into the crook of his arm. She was startled to see that his face, which had looked so relaxed only moments earlier, was now set in a cold harsh mask.

'I think you will find you are mistaken. Miss Gibson is engaged to me for the duration of the first set.'

Whatever protest the young man might have wanted to make was never uttered. With one last frustrated glance at Henrietta, her dance partner turned and scuttled away.

'Do you know, I rather think I had agreed to dance with him,' she said. 'And anyway, I most definitely had not made any arrangement whatsoever with you for any part of tonight. I had not expected to see you for days.'

'Whenever I am at any event you attend,' he returned coldly, 'you will make yourself available to me whenever I say so.'

'That's very high-handed of you. Besides, how am I supposed to dazzle dozens of men if you frighten them all off with one of those ferocious scowls of yours?'

'Was it ferocious?' He appeared surprised. Then he shrugged. 'A show of jealousy on my part will only serve to stoke curiosity to fever pitch,' he offered by way of explanation. 'Since I have never, ever displayed it before.'

No. He was renowned for growing bored with his conquests remarkably rapidly, she reflected as he snagged a glass of champagne from a passing waiter and presented it to her. She supposed she would become something of a rarity if he even managed to keep up the pretence of being interested in her for more than a fortnight.

'Now, let us sit on this convenient pair of chairs, in this recess, and discuss your progress, while we pretend to watch the dancing.'

The band had struck up. The people who had been forming sets for the opening dance were all bowing and curtsying to each other. She sank on to the chair Lord Deben had indicated and he took the one beside her.

'Oh, very well,' she said, taking a sip of champagne and watching the dancers. She didn't quite dare look straight at Lord Deben, while they were sitting so close, not after last night. And because the moment he'd materialised in front of her, her whole body had reacted almost as strongly as if he had done some of the things he'd done then. Her legs already felt as unsteady as they'd done by the time he'd finished with her, and all he'd done was say *'Miss Gibson'* in that molten-velvet voice.

'Dare I ask what you were thinking about, to make you start so guiltily when I greeted you just now?'

'I w— I d—' She shook her head vigorously. 'No, I c-cannot speak of it.'

With a smile, Lord Deben took her fan and plied it over her reddened cheeks.

'I guessed as much. For whatever it was gave you a similar look to the one you wore when you left my presence last night.'

A sudden horrid thought struck her. 'You don't suppose other people will be able to tell, just from looking at me, what we were doing in that locked room last night? Did anyone see us go in there? I w-wasn't thinking...'

'Do not worry. I have enough experience at that kind of subterfuge to be able to hide my tracks. People may suspect a level of flirtation between us, but nothing more, I assure you.'

Nothing more, because they knew he only took beautiful, sophisticated women for his lovers. He did not waste his time on plain, gauche débutantes. They would think, she realised in horror, when they saw her drifting about the room with a soppy expression on her face, that she'd completely lost her heart to Lord Deben. And they would pity her.

Or they might have done, had he not pursued her to such an unfashionable venue, and pushed his way in without an invitation, making it appear that the attraction was not merely on her side.

He had thought of everything.

'Thank you, my lord,' she said, truly grateful, now, that he had made it look as though he could not bear to spend a whole evening without catching just a glimpse of her. She would just, somehow, have to deal with the flutter in her chest and the languor of her knees, and the feeling that she was blushing all over.

He shrugged dismissively. 'Our intent is to set tongues wagging. Last night, you made a good start by walking up to me and daring to interrupt what those participating thought of as a serious discussion. Far from cutting you, as is my wont with impertinent creatures, I smiled, took your arm and went apart with you. Giving you such a marked sign of favour, in public, must have stoked the curiosity about us almost to fever pitch.'

'By that reckoning—' she frowned '—you need not have done all that kissing at all.'

He smiled, lazily. 'Would you prefer that I had not?'

Her cheeks, already heated, became blazing hot. She darted him a nervous glance, then took refuge in sipping her champagne whilst searching for a suitable reply.

He chuckled. 'I thought not. Nor do I regret it.' He leaned forwards and murmured in her ear, 'You are quite delicious, Miss Gibson. I am looking forward to tasting you again.'

Some of the champagne bubbles went up her nose and she started spluttering. Lord Deben swiftly produced a pristine white-silk handkerchief from somewhere and handed it to her, so that she could at least cover her mouth and chin with it while the coughing fit lasted.

'Not for some time, though,' he said, once she'd regained her composure. 'For the next few nights, our courtship will be carried out in full view of the public.'

'Will it? I mean, of course!' She dabbed at several spots of champagne that sprinkled her lap. 'We ought *never* to be private together. I was not intimating that I wished to do anything so very shocking, Lord Deben, I—'

He placed one gloved finger upon her lips, silencing her.

'Do not fear, little one. The next few times I make love to you, it shall be entirely verbal. We shall not need to withdraw behind locked doors.'

Chapter Eight

'M-make love to me? Verbally? I'm not sure I understand what you mean.'

As she glanced up at him warily, he reached out and twined one of her ringlets round his gloved finger.

'I can say how much I admire your hair, for example,' he said in a sultry voice before allowing it to fall back on to her neck.

Then she understood. The tone of his voice, combined with that gesture, was so stimulating that he might just as well have trailed that finger all the way down her throat.

'Which is the truth, by the way. I never pay compliments if I don't mean them. Which you know, don't you, my sweet?'

'D-do I?' Yes, actually, she supposed she did,

if that horrible outing to the park was anything
to go by. For had he not told her that he thought
her nose was too big for her to ever be considered a beauty? Not that it wasn't true. It was just
that he need not have mentioned it.

'Why do you look so cross?'

'I don't know,' she said mendaciously. She was
not going to admit that his brutal honesty still
rankled. 'It is just that my hair is nothing special. It's just brown.'

'It curls naturally, though. Which leads a man
to imagine it rioting across his pillow first thing
in the morning.'

She blushed fierily, but protested, 'You cannot possibly tell if my curls are natural. Let alone
know what they would look like when I wake up
in the morning.'

'On the contrary. By the end of the evening,
false curls unwind, particularly when the atmosphere is damp. But that night on the terrace,
that first night we met, yours were a positive
riot of energy.'

'My hair was a frizzy mess, you mean.'

He sat back, leaned one arm along the back
of her chair and tilted his head to one side as he
scrutinised her.

'Why do you always turn a compliment on its
head, so that it becomes a criticism? You should

accept flattery as your due, not squirm in your seat as though I have said something obscene.'

That was supposed to be flattery?

'I am just not used to receiving compliments, I suppose,' she admitted grudgingly.

'I cannot believe that no man has paid compliments to the glorious natural energy and lush bounty of your hair.'

Oh, that was much better. 'You really think my hair is glorious?' Immediately she wished she had not said that out loud, but she had not been able to help herself. At last, at last he'd said something unequivocally positive about her appearance.

'Well, nobody else has ever said so.' She frowned, robbed utterly of the pleasure of knowing he liked her hair. He might think it glorious, but her inability to respond as he thought she should was just one more proof that she was lacking as a woman.

'Are the men of Much Wakering blind?'

She darted him a shy glance and saw that he was looking completely baffled. Which, in its turn, baffled her.

'What do you mean?'

'How can you have reached your age without having had at least a dozen admirers?'

He thought she ought to have had admirers? That observation cheered her up no end.

'Well…' she mused, wondering if there really wasn't so very much wrong with her after all. 'I suppose…' now she came to consider it '…that I haven't really mixed with many men before. Not ones to whom I am not related, anyway. Except schoolboy friends of my brothers, or scholarly acquaintances of my father's. All of whom treated me as though I were either a sister, or an honorary niece.'

Until the night of that totally unexpected kiss from Richard under the mistletoe, which was even more of a puzzle, given his subsequent behaviour. She had not seen him once since the evening he'd met Miss Waverley, she reflected with resentment.

'But there must have been some sort of social life in the area. Surely you mixed with the better families in the county? Even attended the local assemblies?'

'Well, of course we went to dine with friends and attended informal parties of various sorts. But, no, I never went to assemblies.'

'Why is that? Is your father very strict?'

'Quite the reverse. He is an absolute darling,' she said with a fond smile. 'It is just, well, I never did learn how to dance. And so it would have been pointless attending assemblies, only to sit at the side, aching to join in and being quite unable to do so.'

'Yet you dance now.'

'Oh, yes. Aunt Ledbetter hired a dancing master as soon as I came to stay with her. Though I am sure, had I asked, my father would have arranged for me to have lessons himself. Only, somehow I never quite wanted him to think I was hankering for anything so frivolous. You know he is something of a scholar.'

He nodded.

'Well, he could see the point of going to dine with interesting people, where the conversation would be stimulating. Or inviting all sorts of people to dine with us, or even to stay with us. Scientists and explorers, and inventors. And those house parties were very lively, I can tell you. There were sometimes explosions at the dinner table when men whose theories ran counter to one another had been seated unwisely. And—' she smiled '—even the occasional, literal explosion in one of the outhouses when there happened to be a number of experimental scientists about. But there was never any suggestion anyone wanted to do anything so frivolous as dance.'

'Scientists and explorers,' he repeated, with disdain. 'Very pleasant company for a young girl, I should imagine.'

'They were very interesting people,' she retorted.

'But not given to noticing you enough to pay you any compliments.'

'Well, the ones who were young enough to be considered, um, eligible, were generally so wrapped up in their own pet theories that they thought of little else. Not that I ever wished to receive any attentions from any of them,' she said, wrinkling her nose as she mentally reviewed the parade of unkempt and self-absorbed geniuses she'd met over the years.

'Besides, I was far too busy acting as hostess and keeping things running smoothly to wish for that sort of distraction. You can have no notion how badly experimental scientists can upset the servants if there is nobody to listen to their complaints.'

'You acted as you father's hostess?'

She nodded. 'Of course.'

'From what age?'

'Well, Mama passed away when I was twelve. So, shortly after that, I suppose, when Papa began to recover enough to want to entertain again.'

'At twelve years old, in short, you took over the role that should have been that of an adult woman.'

'I don't know why you are looking so cross. Who else should have cared for my family, pray? Papa was distraught for some time, and if I had not reminded him to eat, or wash, I do not know what would have become of him. Then there were Humphrey and Horace to think of. Somebody had to take care of them.'

'And who took care of you?'

'I did not need anyone to take care of me. I was perfectly content to—' She stopped, an arrested look on her face. 'Oh. Oh. Do you know, I think that feeling useful actually helped me to deal with my own grief. But anyway,' she said with a shrug, 'it is not as if I was compelled into a situation I resented. And nobody denied me anything I really wanted. I could have gone to assemblies and such, or had dancing lessons, if I'd wanted. And you must know that the moment I raised the question of having a Season, Papa took the matter in hand immediately.'

She was not going to admit that she'd already come to the conclusion that had he put a bit more thought into it she might not have ended up staying with a family whose head was engaged in commerce.

'But he did not make those preparations for you without a reminder.'

She lifted her chin. 'I make no complaint. And if I do not, I'm sure you have no reason to make it sound as though I have been neglected, or overlooked in any way.'

'But your education *has* been sadly neglected,'

he said somewhat irritably. 'It sounds as though your childhood ceased the moment your mother died. Instead of learning how to be a young lady, you became a household drudge. I have heard you say that your younger brothers are at school, while your older ones have their own professions, I take it? But who has made sure that you have been educated as you should have been? Good God, they have gone out into the world so they must know that you are decidedly lacking in accomplishments.'

So, he thought her lacking in accomplishments, did he?

'It was not like that.'

'It was exactly like that. But at least now I can see exactly why you are so determined not to turn your back upon your socially inferior aunt. For the first time in your life, somebody has lavished care and affection upon you, instead of taking you utterly for granted.'

'That is a rather harsh assessment of my past,' she said, shaken. And it wasn't true! Her father had immediately put aside his own needs so that she could come to town and enjoy herself. And as soon as he'd heard about it, Hubert had done what he could, too, though he was so far away.

The fact that Julia Twining's friendship could be described as tepid, at best, was absolutely not Hubert's fault. Nor was it his fault that Richard had evidently thought he'd done his duty by coming to inspect the relatives she was staying with, and, once he'd decided they were perfectly respectable, returned to his own habitual pleasures without a backward glance.

'Do you have any idea how remarkable you are?'

'What?' She glanced up at him irritably. Whenever she felt as though there was something about her that he liked—such as her hair, for instance—he robbed her of all the pleasure she might have had in hearing it by immediately launching into a series of criticisms. This time they were of her upbringing. Which was what had resulted in her being so singularly *lacking in accomplishments*.

'I am not in the least bit remarkable,' she snapped. Had he not just said so?

'Oh, but you are. In fact, I would go so far as to say you are a treasure. Not many women would have cared for their family so uncomplainingly, nor come out of a youth like yours without getting twisted under the burden of accumulated resentment.'

'Resentment? What do you mean? I have nothing to feel resentful about.'

He thought she was a treasure?

He smiled ruefully. 'There are women who

fancy they have the right to feel resentful about their lot in life, with far less reason.'

'Well then, they must be very silly. Better to count your blessings than fancying yourself ill used all the time.' He thought she was a treasure. Her nose might be too big and she was lacking in feminine accomplishments, but not only did he think her hair glorious, but now he was saying there were aspects to her personality he admired, too.

'And I have plenty of blessings to count,' she continued, in exactly that frame of mind. 'I am healthy, have always been comfortably circumstanced and have had far more freedom than many other young ladies, from what I have observed since I came to town.'

Funny, but as she said it, the feeling of being weighed down, which she'd had ever since the night of Miss Twining's ball, finally slid from her shoulders like a cloak untied after coming indoors out of the rain. She really had been enjoying her stay in town, though it was in an entirely different way from what she'd expected. And much of it, now, was centred on this man.

She stole a glance at him, then found she could look her fill, since he was gazing across the room with an air of abstraction.

'How I wish,' he said, coming back to himself abruptly, 'that my own sisters would take a leaf out of your book. As girls they were forever complaining to me about one thing or another and now I dare say they treat their husbands to the same litany of imaginary woes.'

'You have married sisters?'

He nodded. 'Two. And a third who will be making a come out next year.'

He wondered whether it would be worth asking Gussie if she would invite Miss Gibson to one of the extravagant entertainments she was bound to be throwing this Season. Since she'd married Lord Carelyon their paths had crossed fairly frequently and she had never displayed the very blatant hostility that his other siblings did not bother to hide.

'Perhaps you will meet one of them, one day,' he said.

'Oh, no. There is no need. I mean, I really do not expect you to attempt to embroil your family in our...in this...' She blushed as she faltered to a halt. 'I am quite content with the invitations I am already receiving. There is so much to do in London. Balls and trips to the theatre and exhibitions and I don't know what. In fact, I am enjoying myself far more than I thought I would.'

And in a totally different way, too. Even though Lord Deben took away with his left hand what he gave with his right, the very fact that he found anything about her to praise was very heartening. More so, perhaps, because he did not scruple to point out the faults he perceived in her as well.

'You really like my hair?' She fingered the ringlet he'd toyed with earlier.

'Oh, yes. And your mouth, too.'

He bent his eyes upon it. His lids drooped. He shook his head.

'Not tonight. And definitely not here. But soon.'

The breath stuttered in her chest. They were back to speaking of kissing.

'So tell me,' he said, leaning closer, 'whether I may expect to see you at the theatre tomorrow night?'

'Yes, you will. Of course you will. I told you Uncle Ledbetter has hired a box, did I not?'

'I recall something of the sort. But who knows, you may have received so many invitations since we last spoke that your aunt has decided to take you instead to the Arlingtons' soirée, or the Lensboroughs' rout party.'

She shook her head. Heavens, but it was hard to breathe, let alone form rational thoughts, when he looked at her mouth like that...

'Oh!'

He was doing it to her. Looking at her mouth, in just the way he'd told her she was to look at a man's mouth, to let them know she was speculating.

'That is a very effective tool,' she said, in total awe of his skill. 'And a very practical demonstration of the kind of look I should be giving men.'

The sultry look died from his eyes.

'A salutary lesson,' he said, somewhat bewilderingly.

Then his face hardened.

'Time to cease, now, I think. You look sufficiently flustered by my love-making to stir up the gossips.'

She felt like a deflating balloon. For a moment she had forgotten this was all make-believe. She had felt as though she was just talking to a friend.

But a man like Lord Deben could never truly be her friend.

She forced herself to smile, and look about her in an interested way once he'd bowed and left her. Above all, she refused to allow her eyes to follow his progress through the room, like a *lovesick puppy*. Yet her fingers closed round the handkerchief he'd left lying in her lap. And when she thought nobody was looking, she stuffed it hastily into her reticule. Only then, her mouth firmed with determination, did she get to her own feet, and set off through the throng to seek out her aunt and Mildred, and the rest of their party.

The moment they entered their box at the theatre the next night, Henrietta scanned the auditorium to see if she could spot Lord Deben. He was standing, quite alone, in a box that was virtually opposite theirs, gazing down upon the crowd below with a decided air of disdain. He couldn't have been in a better position to *notice* her if he'd planned it. As she sat down, she wondered if he had. She could imagine him discovering where they were going to be sitting, by some nefarious means, and then making sure he would be able to watch her all night without having to go to the bother of craning his neck.

Well, she wasn't going to appear any less cool about their forthcoming assignation than he. She would not keep stealing glances at him, to see whether he was watching her, or whether he would acknowledge her across the theatre by bowing, or making some other sign of recognition.

But it was no use. Just knowing he was there and that he would be coming to their box during the first interval made it completely impossible to think about anything else. The harder she tried to avoid looking at him, the more aware of him she became. Though she kept her eyes riveted upon the stage, she was completely unable to follow the plot and, when the other occupants of her box burst out laughing, she was at a loss to comprehend whether it was due to something the actors had done on purpose, or the result of a joke Mr Crimmer had made about their performance.

Even when he did come, it was quite impossible to look at him directly, but only to dart him small glances. He greeted her uncle, and while he spent a few moments talking to him about the play she looked at his shoes, his evening stockings, and the way her uncle's cravat bobbed in and out as he talked. Then her eyes slid towards her aunt, who was gazing up at Lord Deben in awe, taking in, on the way, the set of his shoulders and the way his hair curled upon his coat collar.

And then he was taking her arm and she could only conclude that her aunt had granted him permission to take her for a walk along the corridor behind the boxes.

'Miss Gibson.'

She gave a start and looked up to find Lord Deben giving her a quixotic smile.

'Dare I ask,' he said, 'what you were thinking about so deeply? If I were a more sensitive man, I would think you were scarcely aware of me at all.'

'Oh. Lord Deben. I do apologise. I was just…'

'Wondering what you might say to enchant me tonight?'

'I most certainly was not.' She'd already worked out that any attempt to impress him would meet with derision. So there was no point in being anything other than herself.

'Most women would have made use of that opening to commence flirting with me. But you, Miss Gibson, you are a delight. I adore the fact that there is no artifice about you.'

'Do you?'

'Indeed I do. You need have no fear of telling me what has been occupying your mind, you know. There is nothing you can say that would shock me.'

'I can believe that,' she muttered darkly. 'However, there are things that no lady should discuss with a man.'

'Well, now I am really intrigued,' he said. 'Although I cannot, for the life of me, imagine you thinking about anything so improper you dare not let the subject pass your lips.'

She wished he had not spoken of lips. It made hers tingle with hope and recall what his had felt like against the skin of her neck.

'If there are improper thoughts in my head,' she said resentfully, 'it is entirely your fault for putting them there.'

'Now that sounds promising,' he said with a wicked gleam in his eyes. 'I do not think I shall be able to rest, now, until I know the nature of them.'

Oh dear. She should have known better than to attempt to fence with a man of his experience. She could not, would not admit that the mere sight of him was enough to make her weak at the knees. Or, worse, that thoughts of him filled her mind to the extent that from time to time, today, she had found herself scarcely able to flounder through the most routine of conversations. And most especially not that she was growing increasingly impatient to have him actually kiss her, mouth on mouth, breast to breast, thigh to thigh.

Just then, they passed a man lounging against the wall, ogling the passing ladies through his eyeglass, and inspiration struck her.

'Well, if you must know,' she said, absolving herself with the reminder that what she was about to say was true in a sense, 'it is what you said about...' her cheeks flushed and she lowered her voice '...*bottoms.*'

He burst out laughing. 'I never know what you are going to say from one moment to the next. Whether you are going to fly up into the boughs, or say something utterly outrageous.'

She flicked open her fan and worked it rapidly over her burning cheeks.

'D-dare I ask,' he managed to say once he'd controlled his mirth, 'in what context?'

'Well, you pointed out that men watched them. Ladies' ones, I mean. And so I found myself watching men do it. Like that man, there,' she said, nodding her head in the direction of the lecher with the eyeglass. 'But,' she said firmly, 'it does not seem to matter very much whether they are neat or untidy, or whether ladies sway their hips enticingly or not. Men look anyway.'

'Indeed we do. It is one of life's harmless little pleasures.'

She huffed. 'It might be harmless for men to look, but I'm beginning to think that attempting to make men look is not harmless at all. Why, I have seen *married* ladies sashaying round the room in such a way that nobody can doubt they are doing it on purpose to make men look. And the ones that do that have a tendency to smile in a rather naughty way at handsome gentlemen once they've caught their attention. And shoot them positively inviting looks over the tops of their fans,' she finished in disgust. 'Oh, no doubt you've seen it all before. But I never really thought about the way women go about attracting the notice of men before.'

'And it shocks you,' he observed.

'Yes, it does. It does not seem to me the way that married ladies ought to conduct themselves at all. I…I suppose that makes me seem very gauche to you, sir.'

'Say refreshing, rather.'

'Really?'

'Oh, yes. You are the only female I have ever met who says what she thinks. Most ladies do nothing but flirt with me. They speak on the surface about one topic, whilst underneath there is always a second meaning.'

She frowned. 'Even the married ones? With you?'

Of course they did. He was famous for having conducted affairs *only* with married women at one stage in his life. She hoped he would not take her remark as a criticism of his own behaviour. Of course, it was very reprehensible. But somehow she found the women who would betray their husbands more to blame than a single gentleman who took them up on their invitation.

'Yes. While their husbands are in the card room dealing with their boredom by gambling for ridiculous stakes, their wives get their thrills from seeking out new lovers. Say it.'

'Say what?'

'What you are thinking. I can see it written all over your face, so you might just as well ask why on earth they got married in the first place, if neither of them meant to remain faithful.'

'I don't need to now, do I?'

'Persons of my rank choose partners because they come from good stock. It is all about inheritance. Bloodlines. There is very rarely any affection between such a couple. At best they tolerate each other, whilst getting on with their own lives.'

'That's very sad.'

His mouth twisted into a cynical smile. 'It is the way of the world.'

'And why you have never married.' She felt his arm stiffen under her hand and shot him a nervous look. She should not have presumed to touch upon such a personal matter. He was frowning.

'So far,' he agreed. 'Though I shall have to marry, one day.'

His heart was beating rapidly. Not that she was ready to receive a proposal from him, not yet. Besides, he would never propose to a woman in such a public place, during the interval between one act and the next. But this was a golden opportunity to open the topic so that when he did propose, it would not come as a complete shock.

'I must have an heir, you see. I do have a younger brother, but lately I have begun to see that he is not a suitable person to succeed to the title, should I die childless.' His mouth twisted into a grimace of distaste. 'It is no secret. He is not my father's son.'

'Not your father's…' Henrietta's eyes widened.

'No. My mother was one of those ladies who did not take her marriage vows all that seriously, not once she'd done her duty in producing me. And although many men of my father's rank do not care, he did *not* regard her infidelities with complaisance. It led to such unpleasantness that it has rather soured me against the whole idea of entering the married state.'

'I am not surprised,' she murmured.

'However, I really cannot allow my own preferences to prevent me from doing my duty indefinitely. Just recently, I have begun to…'

'What?' He had remained broodingly silent for so long she'd begun to think he had regretted confiding in her.

But then he flashed her a grim smile and said, 'It is that damned poem, if you must know. The one about time's winged chariot thundering up behind a man. It has been haunting me ever since my friend Toby Warren's funeral. It was the unexpected nature of his death, I think, that shook me. One night I was drinking with him in my club, the next morning he was as dead as a doornail, for no apparent reason.'

'How dreadful.'

'It was, actually, because not a week earlier, we'd both attended Lord Levenhulme's funeral. Now *he* had fallen from his horse and broken his neck, which is the sort of stupid accident that might happen to any man. But for Toby to just... not wake up. It made me...'

'Realise that you cannot put off the inevitable.'

'Precisely so.'

Henrietta did not know what to say. And so they proceeded for a few paces in complete silence.

Until he sighed, and said, 'Do you have no advice for me? No pearls of wisdom?'

She shot him a startled look. 'I would not presume to give you advice.'

'Have I not just asked you to do exactly that?'

'Well, then,' she began, tentatively, 'it seems quite obvious to me what you should do.'

'Pray enlighten me, then.'

'You should look for a woman you like, who likes you back. And then perhaps having to marry her won't seem such a dreadful fate.'

'It is a start,' he conceded gravely. 'I shrink from embarking upon a lifelong relationship with a female for whom I can feel no affection. Nor would I wish to stay shackled to some poor creature who could feel none at all for me. As was the case with my mother. Although,' he said, shooting her a challenging look, '*like* is such a tepid word. I would have thought you would have recommended I looked for something stronger. Like, perchance, love.'

'Oh, no! I would never recommend you wait until you fall in love. I don't think you are capable of...' She trailed off, blushing.

Although that could not have gone better if he'd planned it—for he had to make her see that although he would not mind if she loved him, she must not expect him to love her back—for some reason he did not like to hear her say it with such conviction.

'You think me incapable of experiencing such a strong emotion? Or perhaps you meant to say, such a noble one?'

'N-no, I would never say anything so...'

'Impertinent?'

'I was going to say unkind. I just don't think, from what I have observed of your behaviour, that you are the kind of man to take any action, of any sort, without thinking about it carefully, and planning it down to the last detail. Falling in love is a very...impulsive thing to do. You cannot plan to do it. It just happens. Happens to you in such a way that you would feel...no longer in control. I do not think you would like that feeling. I think you would take care to avoid it.'

'In that you are correct,' he said. 'I would not

like it.' Well, it was better for her to understand him. 'And you are also correct in thinking that I shall not take a bride without studying her most carefully, and being absolutely sure she will be both a loyal wife to me and a loving mother to my children. Where do you suppose,' he said quizzically, 'I might find such a paragon?'

'I'm sure I have no idea,' she replied, although at least she did have more of an idea why he'd been so horrified by Miss Waverley's attempt to trap him. He would have to respect a woman a great deal before she could persuade him she was worth overcoming his reluctance to enter the married state. And Miss Waverley had forfeited his respect by revealing an aspect to her nature that he would never tolerate in a wife.

'No?' He smiled at her then, and shrugged his shoulders. 'Never mind.'

She couldn't quite understand why that insouciant shrug of his shoulders should make her feel so depressed. It wasn't as though she wanted Lord Deben to look upon her as a marital prospect.

It was just, well, it was not at all pleasant to discuss some imaginary female, the kind of woman who would tempt him to abandon his bachelor freedoms for, when he took it as read that she was not that woman.

He found her company amusing. She had

made him laugh on several occasions. She supposed she must represent quite a change from all the people who agreed with his every word.

But she was very far from being the kind of person who could handle marriage to a man of Lord Deben's stamp and they both knew it. Or he would not be able to talk to her about the kind of woman he *would* consider marrying, with such ease. And he would not be teaching her how to go about becoming seductive enough to attract that bevy of suitors he kept talking about.

Oh, no. Was he just using her to distract him from a task he found singularly unpleasant? The task of sizing up the current crop of eligible débutantes, and deciding which of them he could steel himself to feel a little affection for?

If that were the case…

And she'd begun to think he really liked her. That they shared something…

'Do you think we ought to return to our box now? My aunt and uncle will be wondering what has become of me.'

She was wondering what had become of her. She had no reason to feel as though he'd just plunged a knife into her heart. It wasn't as if she'd come to town looking for a husband. Not unless it was Richard.

Though now the thought of marrying him roused nothing but cold revulsion in her stomach.

Lord Deben dipped his head in acquiescence and they retraced their steps.

'Until tomorrow night,' he said just before ushering her through the door.

'At the Arlingtons',' she replied. He had correctly summed up society's reaction. The morning had seen a veritable flood of invitations arrive with the post. And while her aunt was thrilled that, at last, Henrietta would be moving in her natural milieu and carrying Mildred along in her wake, all she could think, now, was that it would be at such glittering gatherings where Lord Deben would find the woman who would meet all his requirements.

And that it wouldn't be her.

Chapter Nine

After a fortnight of having Lord Deben make love to her in public, Henrietta was beginning to feel a bit like a length of wet linen being put through a mangle. And he was the one turning the handle, smiling mockingly as he wrung her out. She could even see him hanging her out to dry once he'd tired of their association. He would say he had done what he had agreed—made her the toast of the *ton*. And she would have no excuse to make a complaint. He'd been honest with her from the start.

She was the one who had begun to change. Not, she huffed, staring out of the fogged-up carriage window as it waited in line to debouch her and her party outside the home of tonight's hostess, that anyone could blame her, surely? What girl could withstand the assiduous attentions of such an accomplished and handsome rake? The things he said, the smouldering way he looked at her as he said them, all had the effect of melting her insides. And causing her to drift about rooms several times a day, particularly when he was not there.

Because when he was present, she had to make sure he did not guess that his charm was making her weaken towards him. She had to hold him at arm's length, and pretend that it was all a game to her as well. It was what they had agreed. She had to stick to the agreement.

It was nothing to do with worrying that if he guessed her feelings for him were becoming increasingly wistful, he would stop playacting at being enamoured of her and would treat her with the same disdain he displayed for other ladies who'd foolishly fallen for his charm. According to the gossip.

Although, the last couple of nights, it had not been as hard to act nonchalantly with him as all that. Because she was growing increasingly annoyed with his ability to treat it as a game, when to her, it was becoming, dangerously, all too real.

'I am so glad,' said Aunt Ledbetter, as the coach lurched one place further up the queue, 'that the little misunderstanding about your place in society seems to have been rectified. No doubt you will soon attract the kind of suitors about whom I shall be pleased to inform your father.'

She pursed her lips and looked uncomfortable. 'I did not like to reprimand you at the time for walking up to Lord Deben in that bold manner the other week, but really, now that it seems as though society is opening its doors to you, I feel I must caution you to behave with a little more discretion. Especially with him. I know I permitted you to go out for a drive with his lordship, which may have led you to believe I approved of him, but since then I have heard such very disturbing things about him that...'

'You need not worry,' Henrietta replied quickly. 'I know that he is not going to offer me marriage.'

Though he was steeling himself to find *some-one* to marry and raise his heirs. She could see it being yet another reason why he'd been so keen to get her to agree to his plan to make her the toast of the *ton*. He wanted everyone to be too busy wondering what he was doing with her to notice his real motive for attending the kind of events he normally avoided like the plague.

Her aunt relaxed. 'Well, it does not appear to have done you any harm, which is the main thing. Indeed, the interest he has shown, coupled with Lady Dalrymple's visit to my drawing room, has had a most positive effect, to judge from all the invitations that have been arriving of late. So long as you do nothing, from now on, to cause any more speculation in *that* quarter, I am sure we will be able to see you happily settled before the Season is over. Now that my Mildred's future is secure, I shall have more time to devote to you.' Mr Crimmer had plucked up the courage to ask Mildred and, to his astonishment, she had accepted. 'It would be such a coup,' she said with a smile, 'to be able to fire off the pair of you!'

Henrietta returned her a thin smile, but was spared the necessity of making a sensible reply as their coach finally reached the head of the queue and they went through all the business of bundling skirts, reticules and shoe bags in one hand to leave the other free to take that of a footman as they alighted.

He would not be there yet. After the first few nights, she had learned not to expect him until it was almost time for supper. During which period he would monopolise her, scandalising her hosts and her aunt in about equal measure, then disappear into the night, leaving her, well, wrung out.

She fixed a polite smile on her face as they went through the ritual of greeting their hosts, changing from their outerwear, and making their way through the crowded corridors to the ballroom. Tonight she would not, she promised herself, look towards the door until the first two sets of country dances were finished.

At least she never lacked for dance partners these days. Though she could not recall the names of the young men who sought her hand from one event to the next.

It was a shame, really, because she was sure that some of the younger sons of good birth clustering around her were genuinely interested in her. Or rather, in her portion, which she had a sneaking suspicion Lady Dalrymple might have advertised.

In Lord Deben's eyes her fortune would not seem all that great. But for a young man obliged to make his own way in the world, it would be enough to make the difference between struggling to survive and moderate comfort.

Yet when he arrived, much later, it was as though she'd just been marking time through the earlier part of the evening. When he beckoned to her and indicated the pair of chairs he had secured on the edge of the supper room, she was halfway across the room before it occurred to her that she ought to have shown a little more restraint. Instead, to her disgust, she had just run to him like a spaniel trained to come to heel.

'You appear a little vexed tonight,' he said, handing her into her chair.

'Not vexed,' she denied hastily. 'Merely baffled.'

'Ah?'

'Yes,' she said, rapidly grasping at a topic she felt she could safely pursue with him tonight, for it would never do to tell him that he occupied far too much of her thoughts. That she chose her gowns with his approval in mind. That the evening had felt dull and flat until the moment he'd arrived.

'I had the most remarkable conversation with Lady Jesborough earlier during which she introduced me to her three unmarried daughters and said she hoped we would all become firm friends.'

'Why should it baffle you? I told you I would make you the toast of the *ton*,' he said, handing her a glass of champagne which he'd managed to procure from a passing waiter.

Although waiters did not pass by him. They were always very attentive.

'Yes,' she replied, furling her fan and placing it in her lap while she sipped at her drink. 'You did. But I did not think it would happen so soon. I thought it would take weeks. Yet every day more and more quite startling invitations arrive, and tonight, people came flocking round me the moment I walked through the door, just as though I was somebody interesting.'

'You are somebody interesting. Have I not told you how fascinating I find our conversations?'

'Oh, you, yes. I know you find me amusing. But that is only because I never mind what I say to you. When Lady Jesborough just complimented me on my gown, I only managed to stutter a few incoherent sentences about my aunt's modiste and how much better she is than the dressmaker in Much Wakering. I must have sounded like a perfect ninny. And yet she patted me on the cheek, and said I *would do very well*.'

'Did she? Hmmm. I had not thought she had such perception.'

'What do you mean?'

'Only that your success is assured. From now on, I don't doubt you will be receiving much more of the same sort of flattery. Not, you know, that she might have been completely insincere. The gown you are wearing tonight really does make you look utterly charming, in an innocent, unpolished way.'

Why could he not have stopped at *utterly charming*? But, no, he'd had to go on to qualify the praise by reminding her she was *unpolished*.

'I do wish you would not keep doing that,' she said.

He raised his eyebrow in silent question.

'Dig about for something about me that does

not meet with your disapproval, then toss it to me as though it is a compliment.'

He frowned. 'Miss Gibson, I thought we had dealt with your inability to accept compliments. I have said nothing I do not mean. Indeed, every time but one, when we have met, I have thought how very charming your dress has looked. I said nothing, because I did not wish to draw attention to your glaring descent into bad taste, by remarking on the change. But I do approve of your style. For one thing, your elegance lends credence to the rumours flying about that I am enamoured of you.'

'I cannot believe,' she said crossly, 'that people think you might really be developing a *tendre* for me, because of the way I dress.'

'Don't you? Surely you have not forgotten that they thought the very opposite, that day I took you for a drive in the park. You told me yourself that it would be quite impossible for me to take as a mistress any woman dressed as badly as you were that day.'

'They cannot think you wish to take me as your mistress?'

'Let us not worry about what anyone else thinks, Hen.'

'I have to worry about it. Just on the way here tonight my aunt warned me to beware of you. And don't call me Hen! I haven't even granted you permission to use my given name, never mind shorten it to such a revoltingly unflattering word.'

He tapped her on the nose. 'Then never again wear clothes that put me in mind of a chicken, my sweet. Really, with that nose, and all those gaudy colours, topped off with those red feathers, bobbing in the wind...'

'Now you really are treating me as though I were your mistress.' Or a doll, which he picked up and toyed with to distract him from the real business of his life. A doll that he would toss aside the moment he grew bored.

'That is what you do, is it not? Dress them up to suit your whims? Well, for your information I only wore that ridiculous get-up to teach you a lesson.'

'Ah,' he said, leaning back with a lazy, knowing smile. 'I suspected as much. At the time I was at a loss to comprehend why you were so cross with me that day. Perhaps you would care to enlighten me?'

'You snubbed my aunt. You were insufferably haughty, refusing to speak to any of the guests in her drawing room. And you positively crushed poor Mr Bentley for daring to mention how much he liked your horses.'

'And making yourself look ridiculous was supposed to punish me how?'

She glowered at him for a moment, before replying, 'I thought you would hate being seen about in public with a woman dressed in such vulgar style. Though now *I* know *you* better, I see it was foolish of me to think you could be swayed by anything that another person can say or do. You are so arrogant that you would think it absurd to take notice of beings you consider so very inferior to you.'

His face hardened.

'I do not know why you are in such an unreceptive mood tonight, Miss Gibson. My intention was merely to engage in a little light flirtation. Upon any other night I might have expected you to deal with my impertinence in criticising your dress sense, and teasing you with a slightly derogatory pet name, by putting me neatly in my place, as is your wont.'

Was she as bad as that? Yes, she rather thought she was. She couldn't think what came over her when she was with Lord Deben. Back home in Much Wakering, she'd hardly ever lost her temper. She stood up to her brothers when they were being particularly idiotic, it was true, but she managed to do so without acting like a harridan. Everyone said what a sunny nature she had.

But then she'd never had dealings with a person of Lord Deben's stamp before. In the whole of creation, there could not be a more infuriating male. She'd been on tenterhooks all night, waiting for him, but did he care? No. This was all a game to him. He was enjoying making fools of other members of the *ton*. He'd only picked her for the game because doing so was guaranteed to put Miss Waverley's nose out of joint. He had no compunction about using her to prevent people knowing he really was thinking about taking a wife. And the worst of it was she was *letting* him use her.

Where was her self-respect?

'For some reason, tonight, your sense of humour seems to be entirely absent. Why is that, Hen? Has something occurred to distress you?'

'You don't think sitting there mocking me might have distressed me? Or ignoring my wishes about using that revolting abbreviation of my name?'

She snatched up her fan and got to her feet. 'I refuse to sit here and let you use me so ill one moment longer.' She turned and slammed her empty glass down on the window ledge behind their chairs.

When she turned he was startled to see tears of rage and humiliation in her eyes.

He, too, got to his feet. 'I had intended only to tease, not to mock,' he said grimly. 'I forgot that you are not skilled in the arts of flirtation.'

'Flirtation? You call it flirtation, to say I look

like a chicken?' She was glaring at him, her chest heaving with every breath she took, her fists clenching. 'And what would you have said next, pray? That it must have been fate to have me so aptly named? To go on to making jokes about ruffling my feathers, or getting broody, or—'

'None of those things. My word, but you are sensitive about your nose.'

She could have screamed with vexation. He was missing the point entirely. It was not the derogatory name, which she'd borne with fortitude for years. All her brothers' friends went through phases of using it on her. Most of them with a rough sort of affection.

It was the patronising way he refused to take anything about her seriously.

It was the fact that he was at the very centre of her existence, while she was only on the periphery of his.

The way he was holding her in the palm of his hand, without even noticing.

Because he didn't really care.

Whereas she...

Her breath hitched in her chest as the awful truth struck her.

'I can only assume,' he continued with a measuring look which reinforced her feeling that he regarded her as an experiment in progress, 'that somebody in your past has teased you about it in such an unkind manner that you now have something of an issue with it. Miss Gibson, I have told you before, your nose is nowhere near large enough to detract from the attraction of your other features. It does preclude you from being described as a beauty, perhaps, but that is all.'

'That. Is. All?'

How could he be standing there, calmly discussing the shape of her nose, when she'd just had a shattering revelation? She'd fallen in love with him. *That* was why she spent not just the early stages of a ball, but entire days marking time until she could see and speak to him again. Why she only felt fully alive when she was with him. Why her heart soared when he paid her compliments and plunged when she reminded herself he did not mean them. It was why she was so absurdly sensitive to every nuance of his voice and watched his face avidly, hoping to detect some softening, some sign of genuine emotion in his eyes. Nor could she recall the last time she had slept without waking at some point in the night, reliving those feverish moments on the sofa in the locked room at Lady Susan's.

Richard's kiss had not given her a single sleepless night. She'd been surprised when he'd kissed her. Too surprised to react to it physically in any way at all. She had been flattered, more than anything, when she'd worked out exactly what it was that had been pressing into her belly by the time he'd finished. And when he'd returned to London without making a declaration, she rather thought it was pique that had made her decide she wasn't going to be left behind, for another whole Season, while he went off enjoying himself without her. It hadn't seemed fair of him to assume she would still be there waiting for him when he'd tired of living the high life.

It had all gone on in her head.

Any emotions she'd felt for Richard were more of a girlish infatuation than anything. In fact, it had been more of a snatching at the hope of love. It was the difference between a little girl playing with a doll and a real mother with a live baby in her arms. One was pretence, play-acting, and more than a little bit of hope for something she was not really ready for.

But this—this entanglement with Lord Deben—was grown-up, messy, painful and all too real.

'Don't, whatever you do, attempt to speak until you have your anger under better control...' he warned her.

'Or what?' Oh, him and his precious self-control! For two pins she would...she would... well, she didn't know what she wanted to do. She was so furious with him for being so utterly calm and rational when her whole world felt as though it had just tilted on its axis.

How could she have let this happen?

And then her own words came back to mock her. *You don't plan to fall in love. It just happens.*

Was there anything worse than falling victim to something you'd only just warned someone else about?

Yes. That person discovering you'd done it. So she would have to take jolly good care he never guessed.

'Afraid I might try to peck you?' In lieu of finding anything sensible to say, she found herself going back to the chicken analogy. 'Even humble, ordinary farmyard chickens can defend themselves, you know.' Which she was going to have to take great care to do. 'In fact, they can be downright scary if you get on the wrong side of them.'

'I am sure they can,' he said. 'Which is why men set such store by their fighting cocks...'

Her face went scarlet. 'How dare you turn an innocent remark about chickens into something so...vulgar?'

Damn. He'd forgotten she had brothers. Apparently she was used to hearing epithets he would have thought her ears too innocent to recognise. 'I was not being vulgar,' he protested. He would never deliberately lead any conversation with her down such a dark alley. That kind of vulgar talk was the prelude to equally vulgar, not to say tasteless, couplings.

He'd only meant to say that he respected her opinion. What maggot in her brain had her taking everything he said the wrong way tonight? 'And it is unjust of you to fly into the boughs with me over a perfectly innocuous remark...'

He was about to tell her that he now regarded the strength and prominence of her nose as indications of her character. That, in fact, he thought she would look quite nondescript without it. That he'd grown downright fond of it.

But her uncertain temper made him hesitate while he formulated the words. And when he was ready to speak, he found himself saying, 'There is no saying anything to you tonight. You really should learn to master that temper of yours...'

'And you should learn not to be so...'

'So determined to have the last word?' He reached out to run one finger down her face. 'You won't do so, however, because...'

With a little cry of vexation she lashed out at him with the hand that held her fan. The flimsy weapon splintered against his forearm. In utter shock that she should have reacted so dramatically, in such a public arena, she dropped the shattered bits of wood and paper on the floor, turned on her heels and ran to seek out her aunt.

* * *

'Now I know I told you not to encourage him, my dear,' said Aunt Ledbetter, on the way home, 'but you really need not have carried out my advice quite so strenuously, even if he was making improper advances. Which was bound to happen eventually, with a man of his stamp,' she finished repressively.

'I know and I am sorry to have caused you embarrassment,' she said meekly, hanging her head. 'But nobody makes me as cross as he does. It seems that every time I meet him I act in a way that I know I should not. Yet I cannot seem to help myself. First, I—'

'Threw together that dreadful ensemble, to make him regret ordering you to go out for a drive with him.' Her aunt nodded sagaciously.

'You knew?'

'Well, your taste was a little bit on the dull side when first you came to town, but you have always known what colours match, at least. Wearing a fox fur with a mulberry pelisse could only have been a deliberate decision to look as dreadful as you could. And, having observed the interaction between the pair of you since then, I can only conclude that...' She paused, her face puckering into a troubled frown.

'That what?'

'Why, that unfortunately you appear to have fallen head over heels in love with the man.'

'Oh dear. Is it that obvious?' And how come everyone else had seen it before she had? Miss Waverley had accused her ages ago of trotting after him like a lovesick spaniel. But it had only been tonight that she'd castigated herself for behaving like a particularly well-trained dog of that specific breed.

'Then it is true,' her aunt continued in a worried voice. 'I suppose I should have done something about it sooner, but then I have never seen anyone truly struck by the *coup de foudre* before. In fact, I thought it only happened in romance novels. So at first, when your reaction to him seemed to be doing you so much good, I was simply pleased for you.'

'Doing me good?'

'Yes. When you first came to town you were a little unsure of yourself. Instead of blossoming, you began to look downright moped. I was beginning to worry you would ask to return to Much Wakering. And then, all of a sudden, Lord Deben put a sparkle in your eyes. I know, on that first day, that it was from anger, but I thought at the time it was better to see you fire up like that than to see you dwindling from day to day into a shadow of the girl you ought to be.'

'Now you see, that is what I don't understand.

He makes me so angry! Surely, if I really do love him, I should be feeling…I don't know…sweet. And a bit soppy and melting when I see him.'

'That would only be the case if he returned your feelings, my dear.'

'Which he doesn't, does he?' When her aunt remained silent, Henrietta sighed.

'It is mortifying. I hardly ever stop thinking about him, whereas he seems to regard me as an amusing diversion. It was that which made me lose my temper with him so badly tonight.'

From the shadowy corner of the coach she heard her aunt sigh.

'I should have taken steps before it came to this. I am sorry that I did not fully appreciate what was happening between you. It was only when you reacted to him with such passion, in public, tonight that I saw how very deeply your feelings run. But I should have seen.' She clucked her tongue. 'Wherever we go, you scan the room to see if he is there. When he is present, your eyes follow him, with your heart in them. When he beckons, you fly to him like a little homing pigeon. But the most telling thing of all is the way you have become aware of yourself as a woman.'

'I have…aware of myself…?' She could feel her cheeks heating. Though it was exactly what they had been aiming at, she asked, somewhat defensively, 'What do you mean?'

'It is all perfectly natural, my dear. When you fall in love, your whole body comes alive when the object of your affection is within sight.'

'Oh, no...' she groaned '...I never knew. I never guessed...not before tonight.'

Her aunt leaned across the seat and patted her hand.

'I can hardly criticise you for falling for him, when he has been at such pains to charm you. Rakes are very charming. It is their stock in trade.'

'He has not been charming at all,' Henrietta protested. 'Every time we talk, we...sort of fence with each other.' Even the time he'd kissed her, it had been a contest of sorts.

'That is the way he has chosen to fascinate you. Just be thankful he did not choose another way.'

Oh, if only her aunt knew! That kiss had been so tantalising that she was waiting with mounting frustration for the night when he might deign to whisk her away to some secluded spot and kiss her on the mouth.

'At least you can walk away from him with your reputation intact, now that you realise what he is about.'

Her spirits plummeted. 'After the way we

parted tonight, I don't suppose he will bother with me any more.'

'That would be for the best. You have several very eligible suitors dancing attendance upon you, after all. Mr Waring, for instance—what do you think of him?'

Henrietta supposed he must be one of those younger sons who'd taken to seeking her out as a dance partner.

'I am sorry,' she said with a shake of her head, 'but I cannot even bring his face to mind. There is no point in discussing him. No point in discussing anyone, for the present. In fact, I wonder if perhaps I should just withdraw from all this,' she said, waving her hand vaguely in the direction of the fashionable neighbourhood through which they were driving. 'I was quite content before he, that is, Lady Dalrymple, inter— intervened.'

'Absolutely not! I have already accepted several invitations which I have no intention of letting slip through my fingers. Besides, if you withdraw from public so quickly after that little incident, it will only make people think the worst. You are just going to have to weather it out.'

Henrietta grimaced. She had agreed to go along with Lord Deben's plan in the first place because she worried about what effect her Season in London would have on the rest of her family.

'I suppose you are right. I shall attend all the events you wish me to attend, of course.'

'That's the spirit. And when you encounter Lord Deben the next time, you must exercise some restraint. If he should approach you, you must just be polite. Nothing more.'

'Polite,' she echoed. Would she be able to manage polite? She had been so used to speaking her mind with him that it would be very hard to draw back and treat him just as though he was anyone.

But she would try. She had to try. She was already far too tangled up with him, emotionally. Perhaps this would be the way to break free of the insidious hold he had over her. If she kept on behaving politely and with distance, perhaps eventually she would start feeling polite and distant, too.

'You do realise,' he said two evenings later, ambushing her as she exited from the ladies' retiring room, 'that this show of coldness on your part will only make me even more determined to storm your citadel?'

'I beg your pardon?'

Being cool and polite only had so much effect on Lord Deben. He had blithely ignored her show of hostility on the first night after the fan-breaking incident, saying he knew she hadn't meant it. He'd infuriated her further by saying he didn't mind the fact she had such a temper. That she had, at least, the virtue of not being boringly predictable.

She had listened with mounting anger at his patronising tone, thanked him *politely*, dropped a curtsy and beat a hasty retreat back to her aunt's side.

'I have been used to having women fling themselves at me,' he said, sidestepping to block her progress down the corridor when she would have evaded him. 'I have had my pick of them. Your very spirited resistance to what everyone is saying was an improper advance has apparently fired my blood. Now I must have you.'

'Stop it,' she snapped. Not only did he sound as though he was repeating the lines of one of the villains from a Covent Garden melodrama, but behind him she had just spotted two girls, who'd been about to avail themselves of the facilities, suddenly pretend they needed to adjust their hair in the mirror first.

'People are watching.'

'We want them to watch, don't we?'

'Not any more, no,' she said wearily. It was impossible to hold him at arm's length while he still thought she was playing the game. She needed to stop it, now, before she got really hurt.

'You have been generous to devote so much of your time to me,' she said firmly. 'Particularly considering how ungracious I was about your offer to start with, but...' It was too dangerous to continue. She rather suspected that, having experienced Lord Deben's brand of lovemaking, she would never want any other man to touch her that way. He'd told her to watch other men's lips and imagine what they would feel like upon her, but the only man's lips she wanted to look at were his. Nor could she imagine anyone else being able to provoke such a response as the wild thrill that had gone through her on Lady Susan's sofa.

Who was she ever likely to meet with half the experience, the charm, the attraction of a Lord Deben anyway?

Not that she could tell him why she wanted to end it. It would be mortifying to have to admit she was afraid she had fallen in love with him.

'There is no need to continue. We have achieved our intended result.'

His face closed up.

'So, now that I have made you a social success, you intend to toss me aside? I have served my purpose and now you have no further use for me?'

'No! It is not like that.'

He inhaled sharply and bowed his head.

The dread of losing her made it feel as though he'd swallowed a rock.

It would all be much simpler if only they lived in an earlier age. An age where a man of his rank could just carry a maiden off to his castle and imprison her deep within his fortress. But it wasn't the middle ages. This was the age of reason. He'd already seen that he would have to go about capturing in quite another way—with cunning and stealth, and subtlety. And that most potent weapon of all, the power he wielded over her body.

He'd thought he'd been making steady progress. But now, for some obscure reason, she'd shied just when he thought she was ready to take the final hurdle.

Before he raised his head, and looked at her again, he was careful to wipe all expression from his face.

'If you have any consideration for me at all,' he said firmly, 'you will not end our...agreement in this way.'

'Why not?'

'I have my reasons. Perhaps you can put it down to pride. Perhaps I do not wish people to think that you have rebuffed me so very finally. Do not forget, our entire relationship has been carried out in full view.'

She'd not thought he cared what anyone thought of him. But in this matter, perhaps it was different. He had a reputation for being irresistible to women. It would dent his pride to have been found completely resistible to one such unprepossessing female, particularly since he'd gone so very far out of his usual milieu in order to appear to pursue her.

'Very well,' she said. 'You may choose the method of ending this charade. But please do not drag it out for much longer.'

'Oh, no,' he said, giving her an ironic bow. 'You may be sure I shall bring it to a swift conclusion.' He stepped to one side. 'I, too, am growing impatient with things as they are.'

She knew it. She'd known he had no real interest in her. The pain she felt as she walked away from him was so severe she wondered she could still draw breath.

Her only consolation was that she'd been the first one to declare the end must come. He had no idea that the thought of breaking with him was tearing her apart.

It didn't make the pain go away.

Chapter Ten

By the next afternoon, Henrietta was managing to breathe remarkably steadily again. She'd scarcely slept the night before, nor been able to consume a single mouthful of food all day, but breathing—yes, she'd regained the ability to do that.

She'd even been able to make herself presentable, come downstairs, and take part in her aunt's At Home. At least, she'd sat and given the appearance of listening to whoever happened to be speaking to her and inserted one or two comments that didn't seem to have been wildly irrelevant, to judge from the way they were received.

It would get much easier to pretend she was not in pain once Lord Deben had done whatever it was he'd decided to do to bring down the

curtain on their performance. Then at least she
wouldn't feel as if she was on an execution block,
waiting for the axe to fall. The connection would
have been severed and she could commence the
process of getting over him.

Although, she reflected, absently rubbing at
her neck, getting back to anything like normal,
after the association with Lord Deben had come
to an end, might well prove as difficult as recovering from decapitation.

Her full attention was brought back to the
present by Warnes announcing, 'Lady Carelyon.'

Henrietta's eyes flew across the room to stare
at the glamorous, redheaded young woman entering her aunt's drawing room.

As Lady Carelyon greeted her aunt, Henrietta examined every detail of her dress, demeanour and physique avidly. She looked as though
she was about the same age as Henrietta. Pe-
tite, and very pretty, although when she turned
and advanced towards Henrietta, her hands out-
stretched, she found something about the way
she was smiling rather chilling.

'My dear Miss Gibson,' she said, taking her
by the hands and giving them a brief squeeze. 'I
do hope you do not mind me being so forward,
but I just could not wait for an introduction to the
woman who has become famous for giving my
arrogant brother such a public set-down.'

'You...you are Lord Deben's sister?'

The redhead made a moue and nodded. 'I know, I look nothing like him. And I hope I *am* nothing like him either.' She gave a theatrical shudder. 'The cold-hearted brute.'

It was all Henrietta could do not to gasp. She would never speak so of any of her own brothers to a perfect stranger. Not even if they were in the middle of one of their infrequent squabbles. Especially not at an At Home where everyone present could hear. It was not as if Lady Carelyon was troubling to keep her voice down, either. Why, it was almost as if she *wanted* everyone to know how much she disliked her brother.

'Oh, dear, I have shocked you,' said Lady Carelyon, pulling her down so that they would sit next to each other on the sofa. 'But it is so rare to hear of any female, not related to him, who is immune to his surface charm that I was sure we should be firm friends.'

'Oh, well, I...'

'And I am positively scandalised by this latest display of vice on his part,' she said as she drew off her gloves.

'Vice?'

Lady Carelyon took her hands again, in a gesture of sympathy which was completely at odds with the malicious gleam in her feline green eyes. 'Perhaps nobody has warned you yet that he is a hardened rake. But it is obvious to those who know him well that Deben has clearly grown bored with seducing other men's wives, now, and has progressed to attempting the virtue of innocent damsels such as yourself.'

Henrietta gasped. What a horrid thing to say! It was bad enough that those dreadful men who'd invaded this drawing room at first had put such a vile interpretation upon their association. But this was his sister. Surely she knew him better than that?

The gleam in Lady Carelyon's eyes intensified. 'I can see that I have shocked you by speaking so plainly, but somebody had to give you a warning. And I suspected you would only heed that warning if it came from such a one as I. The word is that you are a girl of much spirit. If anyone less closely related to him than I had dared to speak so, you would have sent them to the rightabout, would you not? But you won't be angry with me, will you?' She tipped her head to one side and widened her eyes, like a little girl pleading for a treat from the sweetshop.

'You are already standing firm, according to the story that reached my ears. Yes, you have begun to take steps to repulse attentions that are becoming unsavoury to you. And I say, good for you,' she said, patting Henrietta's hand in an odiously patronising way. Just as though she were a matron of forty, not a slip of a thing scarcely older than herself.

'And now I come to the main purpose of my visit,' she said, giving Henrietta what she thought was a very sly look. 'Once he realises you are never going to permit him to ruin you, he will be furious. For you will have made him look like a fool. And he will want his revenge. When that time comes,' she said, leaning forwards and lowering her voice, 'you will stand in need of friends, my girl. Or he will find some way to grind you beneath his boot heel.'

No, he would not! He wasn't like that. Even if Lady Carelyon was correct in thinking he was attempting to seduce her and had failed, he would never be as vindictive as she was suggesting. She only had to think of the way he'd dealt with Miss Waverley. He'd wanted to punish her, yes, but not to destroy her. And anyway, he wasn't trying to seduce her. How could anyone believe it of him?

Or that if he did wish to seduce innocent virgins, he would choose her, of all people?

'You find that hard to believe?'

Henrietta's face must be revealing what she was thinking. She'd never been any good at the gambling games her older brothers tried to teach her, because she lacked the ability to act as though she wasn't excited when she held a winning hand. Or hide her disappointment when the deal had not favoured her.

'But then he has never permitted you to see the man he really is beneath all that surface charm. As his sister, though, I can tell you exactly what he is like when crossed. He was over-indulged from the moment of his birth,' she said with evident bitterness. 'Everything he could possibly want was given to him, at the snap of his fingers. And he has grown up to think that everyone else exists only for the purpose of providing him with amusement. He believes that everyone is beneath him and makes sure we all know our place.'

Henrietta cringed. She'd thought that very thing once or twice herself. He didn't take her seriously. He did think his way was the only way.

'It started when he was a child,' Lady Carelyon continued. 'If ever we chanced upon him at Farleigh Hall, any of his brothers and sisters that is, we had to bow to him. Nor were we permitted to speak unless he deigned to start a conversation.'

'Well, I don't suppose it was his fault...'

'Oh, no, not then. *That* was all Papa's doing, of course. He wanted us to know exactly how highly he prized his heir, whilst relegating the rest of us to the sidelines. I am not exaggerating.' She tossed her head, making her copper ringlets bounce theatrically. 'Jonathon lived in a separate wing from the rest of us. Had his own staff, too. The aim was, I think, to prevent him from being contaminated. Not that it worked. Papa might have kept the spare children away from his precious heir, but he forgot to forbid the servants from mingling below stairs. Consequently he took the measles at the same time as the rest of us,' she said with glee. 'Don't you find that hilarious?'

No. She though it was terrible. Poor lonely little boy, kept so rigorously apart from his siblings. How miserable he must have been, laid up with the measles and nobody to keep him company. Did that explain the wistful look she thought she'd glimpsed on his face when she'd been talking about her brothers?

The lonely little boy had certainly grown into a lonely man. She'd glimpsed it on the terrace that night, when he'd believed himself unobserved. He'd very soon covered it all up with the mask of cynical boredom he always affected when he was in company. But how else could he have dealt with the dreadful isolation of his childhood, except by telling himself, over and over again, that he didn't care?

'How awful,' she murmured, wanting to weep for him. No wonder he'd armoured himself so thoroughly. How else would anyone deal

with having his every attempt to demonstrate
family unity rebuffed? He'd told her how one
brother had responded when he'd gone to hear
him preach. And now his sister… Oh, how could
she not see how unfair she was being?

'I am so glad you are taking heed,' said Lady
Carelyon, completely misinterpreting Henrietta's words. 'Because I have no doubt that if you
continue to resist him, eventually he will turn on
you. He will put it about that he has tired of the
chase, perhaps. Start to tell people that you are
not worth it. That it all began as a bet, or something. He will drag your name through the mud,
my dear, and when that begins, you will need
an ally. I am in the best position to defend your
reputation. So—' she flashed a smile that was a
parody of what one friend might give to another
'—we ought to begin to establish our friendship
at once. To that end, I have come to bring your
invitation to my dress ball next week, rather than
just sending it. And do you know what the most
humorous aspect of the situation is? He has actually asked me himself if I would take you up!'

She laughed—and Henrietta immediately re-
vised her opinion that Miss Waverley's laugh
was the most unpleasant sound she had ever
heard. It had not a tenth of the malice in it.

'He says that I must include your aunt.' She
sighed, looking around the drawing room with

disdain. 'And that pretty little cousin of yours—' she darted her a rather envious look '—from whom apparently you are inseparable. So sweet.' She grimaced as though she'd just consumed about a pound of fudge in one go and was feeling faintly nauseous.

'Well, so far I have heard they have behaved themselves prettily enough elsewhere and so I have told Carelyon. You need not worry you will meet with a snub in my house.'

Henrietta wasn't having any trouble breathing now. She was drawing in such huge, great indignant breaths that they were making her entire body quiver. What she was having trouble doing, however, was holding back the words she only wished she was at liberty to say to this patronising, spiteful, malicious, disloyal…cat!

Oh, if only she were not in her aunt's drawing room, she would…

She was pulled up short by a vision of Lord Deben, his sensuous mouth twitching with amusement at her quandary: to speak her mind or to mind her manners. To cause a scene in her aunt's drawing room or to allow his sister to get away with maligning him.

He would pretend he didn't care that his own sister was determined to think the worst of him. He would just shrug if he heard that she had been making such conjectures about him, in public.

But she could not pretend not to care.

'Thank you for doing me the honour of condescending to invite me to your home,' she said with frigid politeness. 'I shall, of course, have to consult with my aunt to see what events we are already committed to.'

Lady Carelyon's eyes flashed with annoyance, though she kept a smile pinned firmly to her lips as she replied, 'How terribly correct of you. Not that I imagine you will have anything on that evening that could possibly prevent her from wishing to gain the entrée into *my* set.'

'Don't you?' Henrietta rather thought that if the dress ball clashed with an event being thrown by a real friend of her aunt's, or a useful business contact of her uncle's, then they would be sending their apologies. They had no need of the patronage of such as Lord and Lady Carelyon. And she would rather walk a mile barefoot than to appear on friendly terms with anyone who so obviously hated her own brother.

And now, bother it, she wished she had not already spoken to Lord Deben about ending their involvement. If they weren't careful, this spiteful cat would think it was her doing. She would gloat. She couldn't bear the thought of doing anything to cause somebody to be able to gloat over Lord Deben's discomfort.

Even before Lady Carelyon left, Henrietta

could feel the beginnings of a headache nagging at the base of her skull. Why, oh, why had she ever embarked on this ridiculous charade? She was getting more deeply entangled day by day. Even trying to end it was fraught with problems.

But she was bound to see Lord Deben tonight. They must find an opportunity to talk and come up with a way to break free of each other that left him with his pride intact. For he was the one who would be staying in town and would have to deal with any gossip that might ensue. Eventually, she would return to Much Wakering, where people would only marvel that she had captured the attention of such a notorious rake at all.

Which was something that still frankly puzzled her. He need not have had anything further to do with her, after he'd thanked her for attempting to rescue him from Miss Waverley's machinations.

Especially because he had not needed her to do any such thing. He'd told her he would never have been pressured into marriage, yet he had behaved as though he believed he owed her something. Had said that was why he had taken such pains to find her and thank her.

The puzzle occupied her thoughts almost as much as did the means of ending their strange entanglement throughout the rest of the day.

Hadn't he said something about her saving him from a fate worse than death? She'd been so cross—and without reason, too—that she had not been paying as much attention as she ought to have done. But it nagged at her now. Why should he have said anything about her saving him, if he had not intended to marry Miss Waverley at all?

The tension at the base of her skull drew so tight that just before they went upstairs to get ready, her aunt actually asked if she was sure she was well enough to attend the Swaffhams' ball.

'You look rather pale. And you have hardly eaten anything all day. I fear you may be sickening for something.'

'I had a slight headache earlier,' she prevaricated. She could not stay at home. She had to see Lord Deben. Had to speak to him. 'But it is nothing, truly.'

'Another one? Oh dear. I suppose it is almost time for your monthlies,' her aunt concluded.

Face on fire, Henrietta did not attempt to deny it. Nor did she make any objections when her aunt sent her very own maid, Maudy, to rub lavender water into her temples. Although she did think it might have done her more good had the girl rubbed it into the base of her neck, where the tension was reaching screaming point. She did not know what to do. About anything. That was the problem.

She just wanted to lay it all down at Lord Deben's feet.

Though there would, of course, be a great deal of evening to endure before she was able to do so. The dances with the nameless young men, the false compliments from society ladies who followed the fashion by being seen talking to the right people. And perhaps, tonight, the gleeful speculation about whether Lady Carelyon's assumptions might have some basis, if those who'd been present when she'd made them had managed to disseminate the story.

The night dragged as slowly as she'd foreseen, each minute seeming like an hour, each dance a major feat of endurance. She had just about given up hope of seeing him at all when he came strolling across the ballroom towards her, greeting a favoured few with an appearance of tolerance, or pretending not to see others he considered beneath his notice.

'I wonder,' he said when he eventually reached her side, 'what sort of mood you are in tonight? Dare I ask if I may sit beside you?'

'I do not know why you bother,' she complained as he sat, without having waited for her response, 'since you meant to sit there no matter what I might have said.'

He inclined his upper body towards her. 'How else am I to discover what it is that has made you appear so very unhappy tonight? Are you perchance having second thoughts about bringing our charade to an end?'

'Well, yes,' she began.

He smiled. 'Ah, you find that you have grown so accustomed to having me at your beck and call that you would rather not forgo the pleasure.'

'It is not that…'

'You have discovered, then,' he said, his smile broadening to something that was very nearly a smirk, 'that you have fallen so violently in love with me that you wish to cast caution to the winds and admit that you cannot live without me.'

'Don't be absurd,' she said, shrinking into herself. Dear lord, he couldn't possibly have guessed how she felt about him, could he? She knew it wasn't easy to disguise what she was thinking, most of the time, but she'd been so careful not to gaze up at him with spaniel eyes, or simper or sigh, nor any of the things she'd seen other girls do to indicate they found the gentleman with whom they were talking utterly irresistible.

He heaved a great sigh, as though she'd wounded him. And when she knew that having her fall in love with him must be the very last thing he'd want, it made her want to hit him.

'It is your sister,' she snapped. 'She paid me a visit this afternoon and congratulated me, in a very loud voice, for resisting your vile attempts to seduce me. Apparently you are now such a hardened rake that committing adultery on a regular basis has grown too tame. You are now embarking on a career of seducing and abandoning innocent girls.'

'And?'

'Well, isn't it obvious? If you stop pursuing me now, after that little incident...'

'Where you broke your fan over my arm and ran to your aunt as though I'd made an indecent suggestion...'

She coloured up. 'Yes. I admit it is all my fault that people should have started to think such vile things about you. S-so we can't just stop now. Or people will think...'

'That your maidenly reluctance has spiked my jaded palate,' he finished for her, a curl to his lip.

'I know. I'm so terribly sorry. I wouldn't for the world have people believing such a horrid thing about you.'

The cynical expression leached from his face. Eyes fully open, he stared at her.

'All this concern, the pallor in your face, your agitation, your change of mind regarding our arrangement, it all stems from a desire to protect *my* reputation?'

'Yes. You see...'

He flung back his head and laughed.

She firmed her mouth and turned her head away. The headache, which had been building all day, was now making her entire skull feel too tight. She wanted to go home.

'No, now, Miss Gibson, please do not take offence,' he said. 'It is just that my reputation is already so blackened, that the notion of anyone trying to defend it is beyond priceless.'

'Yes. I quite see,' she said, getting unsteadily to her feet. 'If you will excuse me, Lord Deben, I shall remove my quite-unnecessary presence from your vicinity, your life, and no doubt within a very short space of time, your memory...'

He leapt to his feet and seized her wrist, all traces of humour vanished. 'Your presence in my life is far from unnecessary. You may not believe it, Miss Gibson, but...'

But how was he to finish that sentence? She'd never been further from being receptive to a declaration. He'd given her the perfect opportunity to tell him if she was softening towards him and she'd said he was being absurd. If he told her that he only wished to stop the charade because he wanted them to have a real relationship, that in fact he wanted to marry her, in the mood she was in, she'd turn him down flat.

Well, he wasn't going to give her the chance to humiliate him with a refusal. No woman would bring him to his knees. He had his own methods of getting what he wanted, which would be much more effective than making a formal proposal.

'I find myself regretting ending things between us before I have finished your training,' he said smoothly. 'You were proving such an apt pupil, too.'

'I was not,' she denied hotly. 'Anyway, there hasn't been any training...'

'Ah, yes, there has. But it has perhaps been too subtle for you to notice. You melted under my kisses like butter left out in the sun, that night,' he said, leaning in close. 'Since then, I have taught your body to respond merely to the feel of my breath against the places I laid my mouth. I am arousing you, right now, just by murmuring into your ear. Your breathing has gone shallow. Your nipples have gone hard.'

'It isn't true,' she protested, her shock at the accuracy of his statement making her take such a hasty step back that she cannoned into the chair she'd just been sitting on.

'Oh, but it is. You want me. You are positively aching for me to kiss you. Really kiss you. On the mouth. I would wager you want my hands on your body, too.'

'S-stop it!'

'Oh, there is no need to be angry. I want you, too. Have I not already told you that I want to taste you again?'

'But you won't. You cannot. We are ending this, this…'

'But what better way to end it, than with a farewell kiss? The kiss we have both been waiting for? Panting for?'

'I am…not. I…panting? No!'

He smiled down at her, mockingly. 'I did not take you for a coward. Or a liar.'

'I am neither!'

'Then prove it. Go out through the doors at the end of the ballroom. You will find yourself on a terrace. Should you walk to your right, you will find a series of French doors. Enter at the fourth set and you will be in a small study, which is rarely used. I shall be waiting for you there, having gone by an entirely different route.'

She glared up at him, not sure just what it was about that outrageous statement that made her the most angry. The accusation that she was panting for him, which was true. But to say so to her face…how dare he? It made her feel so… naked. He knew her so well. The reactions she'd tried so hard to hide. He'd known all about them, all the time.

Then there was the horrid suspicion that to know the layout of the house so well that he could tell her exactly how to reach the spot he'd designated for a secret assignation meant he must have used that room for trysts in the past.

'You will have a long wait,' she said, her chest heaving with emotion.

'Good,' he murmured, a gleam of appreciation in his eye.

'What do you mean, good?' He did not want her after all? He had been just teasing her? Or testing her? Oh, why was the man so hard to understand?

'I mean that your demeanour now has everyone convinced that the most recent rumour is true. They are all watching us—no, don't look round. Keep your indignant little face turned towards me. Yes, that's it. Let them think I am a satyr,' he said, his mouth curving into a smile so wicked it was almost a leer. 'Do you think I care?'

Oh. He had not been lying about wanting her, then. She felt almost giddy with relief. For a moment. But then she remembered Lady Carelyon's nasty suspicions about him.

'But then your sister will have triumphed. It is not right.'

'I have not been so fortunate in my siblings as you have been in yours. I have never succeeded in making any of them relinquish the resentments brought about by the injustice they suffered in their childhood, no matter what I do. So to hell with them all.'

His features were still fixed in that satyr look, but she could see what looked like torment burning in the black depths of his eyes.

'Just grant me one last request before we part,' he grated. 'Let me kiss you. Let me taste your innocence, your freshness, your purity. Just once. Is that too much to ask of you?'

Her whole being strained towards him. He was so alone, so unloved. And all so unjustly. The things his siblings had suffered in his childhood were not his fault. Why should he have to pay for them?

And, oh, how she wanted to know what it would be like to kiss him. Just once.

'Leave now,' he drawled, lasciviously. 'Flounce out of the room and go out on to the terrace.'

'I don't think I know how to flounce.'

'March out with your nose in the air and your back ramrod straight then, the picture of outraged innocence. It will serve the purpose just as well.'

'You mean, to confirm that horrid story your own sister is putting about?'

He folded his arms across his chest and smiled at her—a smile so completely without mirth that it made her want to weep.

'Tears will do, I suppose,' he said, reaching out as though to catch one that was forming on her eyelashes. 'A woman's last resort,' he said with a mocking sneer.

That was too much for Henrietta. She was almost weeping for him, yet he could still mock her. He admitted he wanted to kiss her, yet it was only to sample her freshness, as though she was some sort of exotic fruit.

She was almost breaking her heart over him and he was donning his suit of chainmail again. She wanted to beat her fists against his chest. Wail and tear her hair.

But of course she did no such thing. Grappling with the strings of her reticule for a handkerchief, she stumbled away from him, half-blinded by tears of mortification, and sorrow, and confusion. How she managed to find her way out on to the terrace she had no idea.

It was by sheer coincidence that she stumbled through the French doors where she made her way to the parapet, and leaned on it, blindly staring out over the dimly lit gravel walks below.

Or was it? After only a very few moments

she realised he'd pointed her in this direction before giving her that final taunt. The whole affair mattered so little to him that even when she was almost in tears, he remained cool enough to manipulate her. Of all the devious, conniving, overbearing men...

Yet this was the man she loved. How could she? She pressed the handkerchief to her eyes, inhaling the calming scent of lavender with which it had been soaked.

He was probably making his way to the little room of which he'd spoken right now. With a swagger to his walk and a smug little smile hovering over those sensual lips. So sure that she'd come to him like a...what was it her aunt had said? Like a little homing pigeon, that was it!

Well, that smile would soon falter when he waited, and waited, and she didn't go at all. That would show him!

But were there not enough people in his life already who reacted to his faults by treating him as though that was all there was of him? Did she really want to join their ranks?

Did she want to leave him with the impression she didn't care? Or that she held her own pride more dear than his feelings? Feelings that he would deny he had, but, oh, she'd glimpsed the hurt in his eyes before he'd disguised it under the mockery.

And how could he ever believe in the existence of love, unless somebody was prepared to show some to him?

Not that she dared hope that being true to the love she felt for him would make much of an impact on that scarred and hardened heart of his.

But *she* would know she'd been true. And maybe, one day, he would look back upon this time they'd shared and realise…

Her shoulders slumped. Realise what? That she was as susceptible to him as every other woman on earth? That she could no more resist his charm than all those legions of married women he'd conquered? That was all this was to him. Another conquest, of sorts. She was no more to him than an amusing little toy, which he could pick up and play with when he was particularly out of sorts, then discard when he had more important things to think about.

The way that all the men in her life regarded her. She sucked in a sharp breath, shocked in the same way she'd been once on leaping into a spring-fed pond one hot summer's day and finding the water so cold it took her breath away. Those discussions she'd had about her family with Lord Deben had made her see her whole past in a different light. She'd always adored her older brothers, but they *had* gone out into the world and *were* advancing their own careers,

with scarcely a thought for her. Oh, Hubert may
have written and asked Richard to keep an eye
on her during this Season, but look what good
that had done.

And as for her father—well, he lived for his
books. His studies. He did love her, in his own
way. But the very fact that he'd made such a mull
of arranging for her London Season only went
to prove how little effort he'd expended on it.
She'd seen him writing dozens of letters, to every
known collector in the country, when spurred to
acquire a rare geological specimen. She was sure
there were any number of relatives he could have
written to concerning her Season, some of whom
would perhaps even have been able to arrange a
court presentation. Instead, she suspected he'd
inserted a paragraph into a letter he'd already
been composing to the Ledbetters with whom
he met up fairly frequently on his own trips to
town, for her Uncle Ledbetter was one of those
men who had contacts everywhere. He kept an
eye open for when rare books, or newly discovered mineral samples, were coming on sale and
notified her father. He would send the adver-
tisements for lectures by obscure scientists who
rarely ventured outdoors from their experimen-
tations. Had her father assumed he would have
the kind of contacts that would launch a girl into
society? Or had it not even occurred to him that

her requirements for a Season in London were nothing like those of a scholar?

Further along the terrace, she heard the snick of a door latch. She glanced over her shoulder and saw a door open, just an inch.

Lord Deben was waiting for her.

She jerked her attention back to the garden, her breathing shallow, her heart pounding in her chest.

If she went to him, he would kiss her. Kiss her in the way she'd been dreaming of for what felt like for ever.

It was wrong, totally wrong to be alone with a man like him, knowing he intended to act with impropriety. He'd spoken of putting his hands on her body.

She peeped over her shoulder again.

If she went in there, she would be admitting he had conquered her. That she could not resist the temptation of knowing what it would be like to have him kiss her.

Not that anybody else would know. He was so experienced in carrying on clandestine intrigues that he would make quite sure of that. He'd staged that final scene in the ballroom so that everyone would think it was their final farewell. So that this parting would be their secret— theirs and nobody else's.

She turned round fully, though she still leaned

back against the balustrade, her fingers clinging to the copingstone as though it were the last
bulwark of respectability. But her mind was already racing ahead.

Since nothing could come of their relationship, since it had to end, she didn't see why she
shouldn't have at least one memory to take back
to Much Wakering with her. One memory of
doing exactly as she pleased, without worrying
what impact it would have on everyone else.

One sweet memory of a real kiss, from a man
like no other. She would hug it to herself. Bring
it out and examine it during the long lonely days
of her spinsterhood, because there would never
be anybody to measure up to Lord Deben. And
why should she settle for second-best?

She was halfway across the terrace before
she'd even noticed that she'd pushed herself
away from the balustrade. Her feet were carrying her across the uneven flags as though Lord
Deben were pulling her towards him with in-
visible cords.

She hesitated, her hand on the latch.

One kiss, that was all this would be. A farewell kiss.

She didn't see why she should deny herself

just that one treat, no matter how wicked anyone else might say it was.

She took a deep breath, lifted her chin and
crossed the threshold.

Chapter Eleven

'You came,' said Lord Deben, gruffly, reaching round her to lock the terrace door.

She could not see his face clearly, for the room was lit only by one candle, set upon the mantelpiece. But she'd heard something in his voice that made her heart leap. Eagerness. Relief? No, not that. It couldn't possibly matter to him all that much whether she had come to him or not. That was just wishful thinking.

Nevertheless, she yielded to the temptation to lay her forehead against his chest as he yanked the curtains closed to prevent anyone from being able to see in, for the action ended with his arms closing about her. For a moment, it felt almost like a real lover's embrace.

And when he said, 'I am glad', and dropped

a brief kiss on the crown of her head she almost dared to snake her arms about his waist and hug him.

Hug him? What was she thinking? He would not welcome a show of affection. He did not believe there was something uniquely precious about this moment. It was not affection he wanted from her. It was something darker. And twisted. Something comprised of myriad layers she had not a hope of ever penetrating.

She was out of her depth with this complex, embittered man.

And yet if she was, if she floundered, somehow she knew he would not let her drown. She couldn't love him if she hadn't detected, beneath all that armoured cynicism, glimpses of something that would never be completely corrupted. Something that called to her.

It was only when she stirred in his arms that he realised that he was holding her so hard she could probably scarcely breathe. It took an effort for him to be able to relax his grip. He hadn't dared hope she would really work up enough courage to come to him like this. He'd paced the floor at nights, since sleep eluded him, knowing his entire future depended on this final throw of the dice.

But now she was here. And it would be here,

in this room, if all went according to plan, he would bind her to him for ever.

She looked up into his face. 'I don't want you to think...' she began, but he stopped her by placing one finger over her lips.

She had come, that was the main thing. He had no wish to hear her justifying her reasons for being here.

'Not another word,' he said. 'I already know that though you do not wish to associate with me in public any more, you are still curious about what it would be like to be kissed by a notorious rake.'

His face looked so harsh, his words sounded so bitter. He'd managed to make it sound as though she was somehow insulting him by coming here. And it wasn't like that. Not at all. She would not be here if he were any other man. And even though it would make no difference to him, she still wanted him to understand.

She took a breath to protest, but before she could even begin to explain, he'd swooped down and pressed his mouth over hers.

And all rational thought fled. They were pressed hard together, along the entire length of their bodies. He'd clamped one arm round her waist, while his other hand had gone to the back of her neck, to hold her in place while his mouth took possession of hers.

It was heaven. Almost. Because he was only doing this to stop her speaking her mind. And she'd hoped for so much more than anger. And if this was their one and only kiss...

She whimpered.

'Forgive me,' he said, breaking off. 'That was not very adroit of me, was it? It would be much more comfortable on the sofa,' he said, altering his hold so that he was beside her, the arm round her waist now guiding her across the room.

She was so relieved it was not to be their only kiss that she said nothing, merely allowed him to sit her down and position her exactly as he wanted. Next to him, with his arm round her shoulder, half-reclining against a bank of cushions conveniently arranged against one end.

'Better?'

No. She had preferred him all hot and apparently passionate to this cold, studied man who'd spent the time waiting for her arranging cushions.

'If this is to be our farewell,' he continued, in that cynical drawl she so detested, 'I must endeavour to make the occasion memorable for you, must I not?'

She would have been happy with another few moments in his arms, with his mouth pressed so hard to hers that it felt as though her neck would snap under the weight of his passion. She didn't want a performance, which was what this was. She could tell by the calm deliberation with which he was removing his gloves.

He'd regrouped, withdrawn and was now treating her with the same cool contempt he was said to employ on all his other women.

But then what could she expect? She'd destroyed whatever friendship she'd begun to hope might be blossoming between them by asking him to reveal this side of himself. By agreeing to this kiss, she'd made him see her in the same light he saw all those others.

And this was his way of saying farewell to her. By reducing her to just another conquest, just another woman whose curiosity about his prowess had got the better of her, any hurt she might inadvertently have caused him would pass more swiftly.

And she had hurt him. She hadn't meant to, but instead of standing with him and facing down the gossip his sister was setting in motion, she'd agreed to walk away. She'd agreed to let him play the villain of the piece.

It was almost as if he was bringing that performance into this room.

'No,' she whispered on a shiver of horror. 'I have changed my mind.'

'Too late,' he said coldly. 'You are locked in

here with me now. And I have no intention of letting you go until I'm done.'

'I have already kissed you,' she protested, one hand against his chest as he loomed over her. He seized her wrist and flung her arm up above her head as he used his body weight to bear her down amongst the cushions.

'No,' he said, his eyes glittering with what looked like suppressed rage. '*I* kissed *you*. You merely stood there, too surprised to make any response at all. Though now,' he drawled, 'you seem to be thinking of screaming for help.'

Henrietta was a bit afraid. He looked so cold and hard. The way he'd looked when Miss Waverley had tried to entrap him. But through that emotion rose others, just as surely as his body heat was seeping inexorably through the flimsy barrier of her dress and his waistcoat. One of them was sheer physical excitement. Being so close to him, with him so determined to behave outrageously, was the most intoxicating feeling she'd ever known.

But deeper even than her physical reaction was her love. Which told her that though he might play at being a villain, though he might be trying to frighten her a little, to punish her for hurting him, for taking the easy way out when she should have stood by him, he was not a villain at all. He would not have offered to suffer public censure so that she could walk away with a spotless reputation, if he was.

If anyone was being wicked here, it was her. Her reasons for being here were utterly selfish. And improper. And possibly a bit perverse. She was sure she ought not to feel so thrilled that he was pinning her down, intent on punishing her.

'I won't scream,' she said. Although to her guilty ears, her voice sounded almost like a purr.

'No?'

She shook her head. Cleared her throat. 'I can see, now, that I have made you angry with me, which is why you are being a bit brutish about the way you are going about this. But I have nobody to blame but myself. If I didn't want you to kiss me, the way an experienced man wants to kiss a woman, then I should not have come here.'

'You won't scream for help, no matter what I do?'

She shook her head again, then somehow found herself raising her free hand to cup his lean jaw.

Damn. He might have known he couldn't frighten her into conforming to the predictable pattern any other female would follow.

So that was the end of hoping for her indignant aunt to come bursting in to her rescue, preferably bringing one or two witnesses to confirm public speculation about his evil intent, which would have resulted in him offering to make reparation by marrying her. She would not have refused him on those terms. For some reason, she was particularly protective of his reputation.

Something like a short laugh escaped his throat. 'I should have known you would never do anything so missish,' he said, catching the hand she'd laid against his cheek and drawing it to his lips. 'It makes you irresistible.'

She looked sad. 'Please don't bother with insincere flattery. Not now. There's nobody here to listen.'

'When will you get it into your head that I am completely sincere? I have not said one word to you that I do not mean. And I never shall.'

He might resort to extreme lengths to bend her to his will, he might disappoint her in a thousand ways, but he would never lie to her.

Quickly, before the trusting look in her eyes could make him relent, he silenced whatever she was about to say by kissing her again.

Henrietta surrendered to the heated urgency of his mouth with a sigh of bliss. She stiffened in surprise when he took advantage of that sigh to thrust his tongue into her mouth, although it was not at all unpleasant to taste him in such an intimate way, as well as making her feel—well, not to put too fine a point on it, invaded, in a totally shocking and yet completely delicious way.

Lord, she wished she knew what to do with her hands. The rest of her body seemed miraculously to know exactly what to do. Instinct, she supposed. The totally natural reaction of a woman to the man she loved. Her heart was pounding, her bones were melting and that secret place between her legs was swelling and softening in preparation for the invasion that his tongue was mimicking in her mouth. Her body was completely uninhibited. Only her hands remained shy, buttoned up in gloves that would make the undoing of masculine attire a clumsy affair that would only be frustrated in the end by the inability to feel bare skin. Even if she plunged her fingers into his hair there would be a barrier of silk to mar the experience of sifting through the dark silken curls. Why had not she had the forethought to remove them, as he had?

Because on his side, it was not love at all. He might be kissing her with an urgency that felt like passion, but she'd seen the look in his eyes before he'd started the kiss. It had looked very like determination.

And a man in love should not have to steel himself to kiss the woman he was with.

A little sob rose up in her throat. When she tried to suppress it, it escaped as a frustrated whimper.

He gentled his kiss at once, nipping at her

lower lip with his teeth, then soothing it with his tongue as he withdrew it from her mouth.

Terrified he was going to end the kiss so soon, she flung her arms round his neck and pressed her mouth fervently against his, hoping to atone for her lack of experience with enthusiasm.

To her great relief, he made that low growling sound in his throat that meant he was pleased, and took over the kiss again, moving his lips gently across hers this time, alternately sucking her lower lip into his mouth, then her upper one, as though he was tasting and savouring her.

Only when she'd relaxed a little did he transfer his attention to her throat, nibbling his way down her neck, then back up to nuzzle and nip at her ear lobe. Almost delirious with pleasure, she let her head fall to one side to grant him better access.

And he nibbled all the way down her throat again until he'd dipped below her collarbone and was edging the bodice of her gown aside with his teeth.

This was the point where a good girl would have made some form of protest. But Henrietta had wondered last time what it would feel like to have his mouth on her breasts. Had spent night after frustrating night wondering whether she was not sufficiently feminine enough for him to want to explore any further.

Well, he definitely wanted to explore further now. His fingers were already dealing with the fastenings. So she stifled the small, almost token twinge of conscience by telling herself this would be her last chance to satisfy her curiosity in that regard.

Almost as though he knew she might balk at this step, Lord Deben draped one of his legs across hers, pinning her very effectively in place while he tugged the loosened material aside so that he could gain access to her breasts.

She shut her eyes. It didn't prevent him from looking at her breasts, but it was all she could do to deal with her sudden attack of shyness.

He dealt with it for her most effectively by covering one breast with the palm of his hand, whilst suckling on the other.

She gasped. Had she thought she was delirious with pleasure before? This was so much more. She wanted him never to stop. To that end, she took his head in her hands to hold him in place.

He gave another growl of approval. But then his hand moved away.

She was just about to voice her disappointment, when she realised he had only stopped ministering to her breast to devote attention to the rest of her body.

He'd told her she'd want his hands on her body, hadn't he? And she did. She did. It felt wonderful to have his hand sweep along her rib cage, caress the indentation of her waist, trace the swell of her hip. Especially as he kept right on licking and nipping at her breast. If he'd stopped doing that, she might have had to do something, like begging or pleading, but as it was, it was all completely perfect.

Except that for some reason, the better it got, the greater grew her need, until she was almost weeping with longing.

When he stopped, abruptly, suckling at her she almost did cry out.

Fortunately, he was only shifting position so that he could kiss her mouth again. In gratitude, she wrapped her arms round his neck again. The material of his waistcoat abrading her bared breasts felt so utterly right that she found herself arching herself against him to increase the friction.

She hadn't thought her body could experience more pleasure than he'd given her so far. And yet every new thing he was doing kept on stoking her higher and higher.

The feel of his hand on her hip was making her squirm under the barrier of his leg. As though he knew exactly what she needed, he moved his hand round to the apex of her thighs, at the same time as sliding his leg lower down hers.

When he pressed the heel of his hand against the exact spot where her desire was growing the strongest, she felt as though she was going to explode. She wanted to do something with her legs. They were pressed too tightly together. And she couldn't move them, to relieve her aching need, not only because Lord Deben's leg was holding them down, but also because her skirts were just too restricting.

She was almost beside herself with excitement. She'd heard the phrase before, but she'd never experienced it. Her whole body was writhing and yearning, just as though it wanted to be somewhere else, even when just here was the most enjoyable place it had ever been.

She needed…she needed… Oh, thank God, he was reaching down and sweeping those bothersome skirts out of the way. Now she could hook one of her legs over his, and turn towards him a little… No, he did not permit that. He pushed her on to her back again, though he rewarded the boldness of her left leg by caressing her bared thigh, then sliding his hand under her knee and bending her leg still further so that he could push his own between hers. Then somehow he'd managed to slide his hand up the inside of her thigh and he was pressing the heel of it against her feminine mound again.

But this time it was bare flesh to bare flesh.

And he didn't just stop at rubbing against her, but slid one finger inside her, then began to push it in and draw it out, mimicking the mating act. She gasped in shock. It was indecent. She was sure what he was doing to her was indecent, but her whole body was clamouring for more. She was aching with wanting. Trembling with it.

And a strange, compelling tension was building where he was so skilfully manipulating her with his fingers. She moaned and clung to his shoulders as he ground the heel of his hand against her once more.

They had gone too far now for her to protest that this was more than just the kiss she'd agreed to. All she could manage was another tortured moan as her hips bucked against the heel of his hand, which he was circling at the apex of her building pleasure. And though part of her was a little shocked at what she'd instinctively done, it had felt so right that she bucked again, more deliberately. And again. And he kept on pushing against her and thrusting into her. And then instinct took over completely. It was like being on a runaway horse, with no stirrups and no reins. All she could do was hang on to its mane until the beast itself decided to shudder to a halt.

Though she was the one who was shuddering. And pulsing. And something like lightning was striking from the place where she was bucking against his hand, streaking up her spine and radiating throughout her entire body. Only it wasn't over in a flash, but kept on pulsing and flaring, until she thought she would not be able to bear the exquisite radiance a moment longer.

Then she rather thought she might have screamed, but somehow Lord Deben had his mouth over hers and was swallowing the sound even as she uttered it.

And then, instead of a peal of thunder, a wave of total bliss followed in the wake of the lingering lightning, rolling her over and over and washing her up on the shore where she lay gasping for breath.

Now was the time to bring all his planning to fruition. They didn't call it *the little death* for nothing. She lay sprawled amidst the cushions, panting, her arms limp at her sides, thighs lax, lips parted, her eyelids lowered as though she didn't have the strength to open them fully. She was barely capable of even voicing a protest, let alone making a move to defend herself.

He could have his breeches open and be inside her before she was even aware of what he was doing. And then it would be too late. The brief pain of losing her virginity would rouse her from her stupor, no doubt, but since she was still quivering from the bliss of her first orgasm, he'd soon be able to reduce her to mindless compliance again. She had not the experience to resist the power of what he could unleash in her body.

Oh, yes, he would make sure she enjoyed it.

Physically, at least.

Afterwards—well, when she was capable of thinking straight and her moral senses returned—he would reassure her that of course he would marry her.

She wouldn't refuse him, not once he'd taken her virginity. The act would make her his. Irrevocably his.

She was so honest, so straight about things like this, that once he'd had her, she could never marry another man. She'd feel obliged to confess to anyone who might propose to her that she wasn't a virgin, and even if the man was prepared to overlook it, she wouldn't.

Besides, by the time he'd finished with her, he would have convinced her that she'd only capitulated because she'd fallen in love with him. She'd seize on that excuse to salve her sensitive conscience, and then...yes, then she would be his.

He slid his hand from between her legs and went to unfasten his breeches.

But the action roused her a little. She stirred and turned her head to look at him, and smiled at him, shyly.

Trustingly.

His fingers stalled on the second button.

Nobody had ever trusted him before, because he was such a complete bastard. Not in the way his siblings could be described as bastards, because of what his mother had done, but because of his utter selfishness. He was a bastard by nature. He'd always done whatever he wanted, without considering anyone else's feelings. He'd habitually taken women for sexual gratification, then despised them for letting him use them.

But this was worse than all of that. Worse than anything he'd ever done before.

He was about to abuse Henrietta's trust by robbing her of the most precious thing she had—and he didn't mean her virginity. It was her very freedom he wanted to steal from her.

How could he forget the way she'd burst out of her hiding place, determined at all costs to stop Miss Waverley from forcing his hand? She'd stood up for him that night, although he was a stranger, because she hated injustice. She hadn't been able to stand idly by and watch a wrong being perpetrated.

And this was how he was repaying her—by planning to rob her of her own freedom to choose whom she would marry.

Seducing her would be the worst kind of betrayal. She would feel as though he'd turned on her. It would shatter her trust in him, thereby destroying whatever small amount of goodwill she'd come to feel for him to date.

It would doom their marriage to misery. It would never be enough for him to just possess her: he needed her to love him.

He needed her to love him? He shook his head. No—it couldn't be. He'd accustomed himself to the thought of her being in love with her husband, that was all. He'd inured himself to the prospect of humouring her when she displayed affection for him openly. He did not need love. God, he'd lived long enough without it. What difference could it possibly make now?

All the difference in the world.

And she could never love a man who could stoop to such tactics to get what he wanted.

Had he really thought he could despoil her and then expect her to forgive him?

Or that he would ever have been able to forgive himself?

Even if he ever managed to convince her that he'd acted out of desperation, that he'd felt physically sick when she'd announced her intention to end their relationship, that he'd panicked and thought he would do anything, whatever it took, to keep her, this was a line no decent man ever had any excuse for crossing.

He couldn't hurt her like this.

For the first time in his life, Lord Deben had

discovered there was something more important to him than getting his own way.

It was Henrietta's happiness.

He could not be the man who betrayed her. Hurt her. Abused her trust.

Dammit, but she was far too trusting. Why wasn't that aunt of hers taking better care of her? She ought to be protecting her from bastards like him, not letting her wander off on to moonlit terraces and into darkened rooms where God knew what could happen to her.

With a tortured groan, he scooped her up and settled her on his lap. He pulled her head into his chest so that he wouldn't have to bear that trusting look for one more second.

And she, being what she was, promptly heaped coals of fire on his head by snuggling against him, trusting as a child, and looping her arms round his waist.

'Was that…was that…what *was* that?'

'That, my dear,' he said 'was your first orgasm.'

'I…I was only expecting a kiss. I suppose… you did so much more because you wanted to punish me…'

'Did it feel like a punishment?' He was the one who should be punished. He could not believe he had almost stooped to such measures, simply to get his own way.

'At times,' she admitted.

'You enjoyed it, though.' Whatever else he might be, he reflected savagely, he was a consummate lover.

'Yes. Though I suppose...' she began tentatively. Unfortunately, as she went to lift her head, the movement brought the soft curve of her hip up against the full aching urgency of his erection.

'Don't do that,' he said sharply, setting his hands to her waist and lifting her off his lap. He was only restraining himself from doing what would make her hate him by the thinnest of threads.

'And don't enquire into my motives. I am not proud of myself,' he said grimly. It was pathetic to attempt to excuse what he'd almost done by claiming he was desperate. He should not have allowed himself to become desperate. Not long since, he'd sworn no woman would bring him to his knees, but his desire to possess Henrietta was so strong that it had almost driven him to an unconscionable act. He'd never wanted anything, or anyone, as badly as he wanted her.

Except, it appeared, her respect. He could easier live without her in his life, than do anything that would make her despise him.

'I had better tidy you up, so that you may return to your duenna without looking as though you've been half-ravished,' he said. He hoped she wouldn't notice that his hands were shaking as he did up her fastenings. Fortunately, she wasn't looking at his hands, but at his face.

'I am not at all sure,' she said in a small voice, 'that I am capable of returning to the ballroom...'

'You will be in a moment or two,' he said bracingly, trying not to be moved by what looked suspiciously like moisture forming in her eyes. 'Here,' he said, plucking a handkerchief from his pocket and thrusting it at her. 'Use this if you mean to become emotional.' He knew he sounded harsh, but at least it had a bracing effect on her. She took the handkerchief mechanically, crumpling it into a ball rather than using it. And hanging her head.

'I don't think,' she said, her cheeks suffusing with colour, 'that I shall ever be able to walk again. My legs feel like cotton.'

'Wine,' he said abruptly, getting to his feet and walking to the study desk. Apart from anything else, it gave him the chance to do up his breeches again before she could notice he'd undone the first button.

'I brought some in, hoping to set a mood.' He winced. How could he have been so blind? Treating her with the same casual cruelty with which he'd treated so many other women? And expecting her to smile at him gratefully afterwards, perhaps thank him for the skill with which he debauched her, then embark on a marriage based on trickery and power play? She deserved far better. When he'd decided he wanted to marry her, it was to get away from all that. Start a new life, a healthy life, where loyalty to one another played a pivotal role.

He poured wine into two glasses. Maybe he could never break free from his heritage. Maybe he was such an inveterate rogue that he'd never be able to live in the full clear light of Henrietta's moral standards.

She ought to marry a man who was worthy of her. He rammed the stopper back into the decanter. Someone who would value her, someone she could respect in turn. Someone whose life hadn't been so irrevocably tarnished by vice.

'But now it can serve a better purpose,' he said, tipping his drink down his throat before returning to the sofa.

Henrietta took the glass he extended to her with fingers that trembled and drank with gratitude.

'I think I owe you an apology for this interlude,' he said. What he'd actually done was bad enough, but his apology was for what he'd planned.

'No. You do not,' she said, lifting her chin to stare back at him with her open, trusting eyes.

'Yes, I damn well do! Though at least it ought to act as a warning to you not to go apart with a man whose character is as stained as mine. With any man. You cannot trust any of us. We are none of us much better than brute beasts.'

Her eyes widened in shock.

'However,' he said, returning to the decanter, and pouring himself a second glass, 'let me reassure you upon one point. On this occasion you escaped paying the full penalty for your dreadful naïveté. You are still a virgin. You need not fear your husband, whoever he may be, will know that you have had a sexual encounter.'

Because his back was to her, he did not see the stricken look in her eyes. And by the time he turned round, she'd managed to cover her hurt. It wasn't just the implication that she'd deserved to be treated with contempt for breaking the rules that decreed no proper young lady should ever be entirely alone with a man. The wound which she thought might never stop bleeding had been inflicted by the casual way he'd spoken of a future husband. *Whoever he may be.* Which meant that he had no intention of it being him.

Stupid to feel devastated. She'd always known he had no thoughts of making her his wife. He was so far above her, socially, that she might as well dream of getting a proposal from the emperor of the Russias.

'Can you stand yet?'

His impatience to get rid of her gave her a solid motive for attempting to get to her feet. And once she was on them, her own pride stopped her from tottering across the carpet, flinging herself on to his chest and begging him not to send her away like this.

She knew he'd wanted to do much more. He'd begun to unfasten his breeches before thinking better of it. And even she, inexperienced as she was, could not fail to see that he was still massively aroused.

It couldn't have been easy for him to call a halt. Especially since he was not used to exercising any self-restraint. If she were one of his usual women, it would all have reached a natural conclusion by now and they would be sipping wine together, laughing and chatting comfortably.

No wonder he was so angry with her. Perhaps if she explained that she wouldn't demand, or even hope for, a marriage proposal from him, he would push her back down on to the sofa and carry on where they'd left off.

Though all that would accomplish, in the long term, would be her degradation. Her family would be dreadfully disappointed in her, should they ever find out, and as for him—he would despise her.

And she didn't think she could bear that, on

top of everything else. Better not to make the offer. At least then she could walk away clinging to the few tattered shreds of what remained of her dignity.

With an expression of exasperation, he started to twitch her disordered clothing into place with deft fingers. Removed pins from her hair, tweaked curls and fixed them back in place with a dexterity that spoke of years of practice, while she just stood there, incapable of either moving or framing words.

He hadn't had any trouble framing words. He'd given her quite a trimming, although she'd detected concern at the back of it. He'd rebuked her in the same way her brothers would have done, had they caught her doing something stupid and dangerous.

So he did care for her. Just a little bit.

If he didn't, he might have just used her to slake his needs, before walking away and leaving her to deal with the consequences alone.

But he hadn't. He was still, to judge from the state of his breeches, quite uncomfortable, yet he was tidying her up, ensuring she could return to her world without a stain on her character.

For him, that amounted to quite a sacrifice.

It made her love him all the more.

When he eventually stepped back and surveyed her appearance with a critical eye, she wasn't trembling any more.

It was amazing how swiftly the body could recover, when inside she felt as though she was dying.

'Go on, get out of here,' he said harshly. 'Even your aunt might start to notice you missing if you loiter much longer.' And he didn't know how much longer he would be able to resist her if she kept on standing there looking so woebegone. He would be sweeping her into his arms and on to that sofa, and condemning them both to hell for the rest of their lives.

'F-farewell, then,' she stuttered, then turned on her heel and ran to the terrace door. Fumbled her way through the heavy velvet curtains, and rattled the key in the lock.

Don't go...

The plea died on his lips as she finally managed to get the door open and fled through it, out into the night.

Leaving him alone. Utterly alone.

He sank on to the sofa and buried his face in his hands.

Chapter Twelve

Henrietta did not go to Lady Carelyon's dress ball. Lord Deben ensured she had no need to, by disappearing.

At first, most people said he must have gone to one of his estates to lick his wounds in private, though some maintained that was nonsense, he wouldn't care about a skinny little nonentity that much. He'd probably just gone to the races.

When he did not return to town along with the other racegoers, the rumourmongers became more inventive. Perhaps he'd taken off with Mrs Yardley, an attractive widow in straitened circumstances who'd been resolutely refusing offers of protection from various well-heeled members of the aristocracy for the past two years. It would certainly account for the fact that she'd disappeared at about the same time.

For three days Henrietta tortured herself by imagining him slaking his desires in some out-of-the way love nest with this glamorous, beautiful widow, until Mrs Yardley appeared in Green Park, walking with the maiden aunt who acted as her companion and chaperon. They were both, according to the buck who'd accosted them, stunned to discover they'd been thought missing and indignant to hear of what Mrs Yardley was suspected. They had both merely been suffering from a minor indisposition which had made them stay within doors for a few days. To judge from the redness of both their noses, came the report, and the bleariness of their eyes, they'd most likely had a summer cold.

Henrietta soon perceived she'd been incredibly naïve when she'd imagined Lord Deben would be the one who'd have to face the aftermath of their public quarrel. Because he was a man, he didn't need to face up to anything. He had the power to order his carriage and slink off to one of his estates. Or go to the races. Or snap his fingers to some eager, experienced woman, who would be only too glad to satisfy his needs in a way *she* could not. A woman who would, when he was done with her, leave him absolutely free. If not Mrs Yardley, then another.

* * *

It became increasingly difficult to pretend she didn't care about the spiteful asides being whispered behind gloved hands wherever she went—loudly enough to ensure she overheard every one. Even her aunt conceded that there was no need to accept every invitation that came from what Mildred had taken to referring to as 'the top-lofty set'. And so Henrietta began, discreetly, to remove herself from the sphere in which Lord Deben would naturally move, when eventually he did return.

Apart from anything else, she did not know how she would cope with seeing him, knowing he'd spent the intervening time with some other woman, touching *her* the way he'd touched Henrietta. Kissing *her*. Driving *her* wild with desire. And then taking his own pleasure in *her* body. To the full.

For what else could he be doing?

Every night, in her lonely bed, she lay there, wondering. She could think of nothing else, when she had nothing else to distract her. Every time she almost drifted off to sleep, the weight of the blankets on top of her became the echo of his body, pressing her into that sofa. Her skin reminded her of the paths his hands had traced. She grew heated and restless, and didn't know what to do with herself. In vain did she throw off the covers. He haunted her. And she had nobody to blame but herself. He'd warned her that if he kissed her she would never be the same again. That he would make her a woman, aware of her body.

He'd also said she would look at men and wonder if their lips could rouse her to the heights he'd boasted he could show her.

It was no consolation to discover he'd been wrong about that. That the only man whose lips she would ever want on her were his.

Sometimes, when she had a few moments to herself during the day, she would take out the three monogrammed handkerchiefs she'd never quite been able to bring herself to return to him, close her eyes and press them to her lips. It wasn't the same. They were cool and dead, and, having spent weeks tucked at the bottom of her underwear drawer, they no longer bore even the remotest trace of his uniquely masculine scent.

But, because she did not want anyone to suspect how badly Lord Deben had hurt her, she took far more care over her appearance than she ever had before. She applied rice powder to the shadows under her eyes, made sure her gowns were taken in so that her loss of weight did not become apparent and even went so far as applying a little rouge to disguise her pallor.

It had been bad enough to have had her aunt

accusing her of moping, after the Richard fiasco. At least then she'd been able to believe everything would have been better if she could return to Much Wakering. Now she knew it would be useless to go anywhere else. Wherever she went, it would be without him, so she would still feel as though she was slowly dying. Besides, he'd rather taken the gloss off the life she'd lived in Much Wakering. She'd always thought of herself as indispensable to her family's happiness. She'd assumed her brothers loved her as much as she loved them. It had taken the cynical Lord Deben to point out that they'd all been taking her for granted for years.

No, if she was going to be miserable, she might as well be in London, with at least the benefit of theatre trips and art exhibitions to act as a distraction. Besides, her aunt and uncle were planning a lavish wedding for Mildred and Mr Crimmer. She did not want to spoil their happiness by waving her own misery in their faces like a banner.

Then one day, about a week after Mrs Yardley put paid to the rumours she was Lord Deben's latest mistress, Julia Twining and Lady Susan Pettiffer came to call on her.

She received them gladly, since they had been about the only people who had never treated her any differently, while she'd been entangled with Lord Deben, or afterwards.

'I have come,' Julia began, once they'd taken a cup of tea, and after Lady Susan had nudged her in the ribs, 'to speak to you about my literary evening. You have to buy a ticket, you know. It is in aid of the foundling home.'

'What Julia means,' put in Lady Susan with a quick frown of reproof, 'is that we very much hope you will attend. We have both noticed you are not going about as much as usual and, in certain ways, I can understand why not. But this,' she said leaning forwards to make her point, 'is important.'

'I think we are supposed to be going to dinner with some business connections of my uncle's that evening.'

Lady Susan looked annoyed. 'There is no reason why you have to go, too, is there? Don't you think you might be excused? You could still reach Julia's house in time if I sent a carriage and a brace of footmen to fetch you.'

'Surely my attendance won't make any difference…'

'Oh, yes, it will,' Lady Susan snapped. 'We need you there because of Cynthia Lutterworth. Cynthia means to read us some of her poems. You do remember Cynthia, do you not?'

She put the term 'poetess' alongside the name

of Lutterworth and came up with the image of
a wild-haired creature, just as Lady Susan went
on, 'And I'm quite sure, having been the target
of malicious gossip yourself, that you understand
how cruel some people can be. How unfair. Just
because she is a woman, and her parents' money
comes from trade, *some* people will take delight
in mocking her.'

'It isn't fair,' put in Julia. 'When she is just
doing her part to raise money for charity.'

'But surely, if her poetry is any good, people
will have no call to mock...' Henrietta trailed
away as the two visitors exchanged a signifi-
cant look.

'It isn't that her verses are *dreadful*,' said Julia.

'No, they're certainly no worse than many
others I could name,' finished Lady Susan. 'And
if she were only pretty, or had a title, they would
garner a great deal of rapturous applause,' she
added with a sneer.

Henrietta promptly changed her mind about
Lady Susan. Though she had not been able to
warm to her to begin with, it seemed that once
Lady Susan had made a friend, she was loyal.
And that counted for much, in the circles she inhabited. She could so easily have bowed to the
prevailing opinions and joined in the mockery
of one who had no means of defending herself.
But for some reason, Lady Susan had decided

she liked Cynthia, or her poems, and was not afraid to say so.

And had Lady Carelyon not predicted she would be in need of friends, once she and Lord Deben were finished? Having friends would help. Not that she would dream of confiding in them, but at least it would be comforting to think there were *some* people who actually wanted to be with her for no other reason than that they appeared to like her.

'Very well, I shall come and applaud with great enthusiasm, no matter how dreadful I find her verse.'

Julia beamed at her.

'Thank you,' said Lady Susan. 'That will be a great help. I have already persuaded Lady Twining to have Mr Wythenshawe go on first.'

Henrietta wondered briefly why Lady Twining had allowed Lady Susan to have any say in the running order of the evening at an event to be held in her house. But then she decided there were probably not very many people who could put a halt to Lady Susan once she'd got the bit between her teeth.

'His poetry is so awful,' explained Lady Susan, 'that Cynthia's offerings will come as a positive relief to the audience. There is nothing we can do about Lord Smedly-Fotherington, unfortunately,' she said with a frown. 'He is of noble birth, has long curly hair and has lately taken to dressing like a Turkish prince.'

'But is his poetry any good?'

Lady Susan's lip curled. 'What does that matter? He out-Byron's Byron.'

'He is actually very accomplished,' put in Julia.

'And very vain.'

'I promise,' said Henrietta, feeling for the first time in days that she was no longer completely without value, or completely without friends, 'that I shall not be in the slightest bit impressed by him.'

'You haven't seen him push his curls off his forehead with his long white fingers,' Julia warned her.

'That will have no effect upon me.'

'No,' put in Lady Susan with approval. 'If you have managed to stand firm against a man of Lord Deben's breathtaking masculinity, you will be quite immune to a young fop like Smedly-Fotherington. Didn't I tell you so, Julia? Miss Gibson has a mind of her own.'

It didn't occur to Henrietta, until she was actually entering the house two nights later, that the guest list would be much the same as it had been on the night of Julia Twining's ball. Not until the moment, in fact, when she saw Richard—with Miss Waverley on his arm, smiling up at him coquettishly.

The sight left her almost entirely unmoved, apart from a brief spurt of something like annoyance that she had to see either of them at all.

As far as she was concerned, Miss Waverley was welcome to Richard. And he to her.

Unfortunately, good manners dictated that she not ignore them, for Richard hailed from her own home town. And whatever he'd done to her, he not only had no idea that he'd done it, but he was, still, her brother's friend.

When, therefore, she was on the point of passing them, she stopped and dipped a brief curtsy.

'You here, Hen? Well, it's good to see you,' said Richard. 'Though I must say you're looking a trifle hagged. London too rackety for you, eh? Told you it would be. Don't say I didn't.'

Miss Waverley arched a brow at him. 'You know Miss Gibson?'

'Lord, yes! Practically grew up together. Like brother and sister.'

Henrietta gave him a level stare. Brothers did not grab sisters and kiss them under the mistletoe with such enthusiasm, thereby leading them to expect that feelings ran deeper, or rather, sprang from a source that was very far removed from filial affection.

'There you are!' Lady Susan was bearing

down on the trio with a determined look on her face. 'Miss Gibson,' she said, 'I am saving a seat for you next to me, on the front row. Once Miss Lutterworth puts on her spectacles to do her reading I don't suppose she will be able to see us, but at least on the way to the dais, she might notice some friendly faces among the crowd. You will excuse us,' she said to Miss Waverley and Richard dismissively.

'Of course, Lady Susan,' said Miss Waverley.

'Had no idea you was friends with Lady Susan,' said Richard at the same time, looking a bit put out.

Lady Susan smiled at them both, that cat-like smile which Henrietta was coming to recognise as preceding one of her acid barbs.

'I value Miss Gibson so greatly that I sent my own carriage and footmen to make sure she would be here tonight. It is so rare that one finds a person who does not delight in tittle-tattle, in spiteful speculation, or stabbing her acquaintances in the back,' she said to Richard, whilst darting a meaningful look in Miss Waverley's direction.

Henrietta felt a little winded by Lady Susan's spirited defence. 'I had no idea you were aware that Miss Waverley dislikes me so much,' she said as they moved further into the room.

'She makes no secret of it. I do not know what

you can have done to put that vain creature's perfect little nose out of joint, but I am inclined to think whatever it was, she deserved it.'

They were the only two people moving with any purpose. Everyone else was milling about, greeting acquaintances, taking drinks from circulating waiters, or, in the case of most of the men, edging towards the exit that led to the card room. She noticed, though, a knot of people gathered around a rather beautiful young man with flowing silken curls, dressed in flowing silken robes.

'Smedly-Fotherington's admirers,' muttered Lady Susan, noticing the direction of her gaze. 'They are the ones who will be most inclined to snigger when Cynthia steps on to the stage.'

At the front of the room, to which they were steadily making their way, was a small raised platform, containing a lectern, upon which the various speakers would be able to rest their pages of verse. Four rows of chairs were arranged before it, in a semi-circle, with a break every few chairs to allow ease of access.

As she took a chair upon the very front row, Henrietta glanced over her shoulder. Richard, she was certain, would be longing to join the group of men sidling out of the doors. He had no interest in poetry whatsoever, and, by the sound of it, he was about to be treated to several samples of the very worst sort. But from the looks of things, Miss Waverley had no intention of letting him off the leash.

Henrietta unfurled her fan and raised it to her face to conceal her smile, which was bordering on a most unladylike grin. Richard was about to undergo a most fitting punishment. If he'd gone to the bother of offering to escort *her* anywhere, she would at least have chosen something he might enjoy too. Miss Waverley was too selfish to care whether he liked poetry or not. His purpose was merely to play the part of devoted swain. Which, she reflected with a mental sneer, he did to perfection.

'Is this seat taken?'

She jolted out of her reverie to see Lord Deben standing before her, indicating the empty chair to her right.

'No,' she said, her cheeks burning. It had been almost three weeks since they'd last been together, and yet, because she'd relived that encounter so many times, it felt as though it had happened only yesterday. It was impossible to look him in the face, considering how wantonly she'd behaved. Yet she wanted to look. She'd been so parched of his company she wanted to drink him in. Yet all she dared do, since they were in such a public place, was sip by darting a series of thirsty little glances at him as he took his seat beside her. And when he had done so, his thigh was so close to her own that she could feel the heat from it. For a second, she relived, incredibly vividly, the sensations she'd experienced when that very leg had pinned hers beneath him as he unfastened her bodice. Oh, lord, she hoped nobody could tell that her heart was pounding. And were her cheeks as flushed as they felt? She plied her fan rapidly, hoping against hope to dispel at least some of the heat that was making her face burn.

'My presence unsettles you,' he observed.

'Considering that nearly all the other chairs are as yet unoccupied, everyone must be wondering why you have chosen to sit on the one next to mine.'

'Obviously,' he said, draping his arm along the back of her chair, and leaning in to murmur in her ear, 'I cannot bear to be apart from you one moment longer. Though I have nursed my broken heart in private, I cannot endure not to see you. Though you spurn me, I had to return to your side.'

'Stop it,' she hissed out of the corner of her mouth. His voice had shimmied all the way down her spine, making it almost impossible for her not to arch her neck in a silent invitation to him to nip it.

'I cannot play such games any more,' she said with a catch in her voice. 'I told you…'

'And yet you did not tell me I could not sit beside you. If you will give me such encouragement, you will never shake me off.'

'As if it would do any good to tell you I didn't want you to sit next to me. You would have just ignored my objections and sat down anyway.'

'True. But you could have got up and walked away, quivering with indignation at my temerity. Instead of which, you are darting me hungry little looks out of the corner of your eye.'

Oh lord, she'd forgotten how good he was at interpreting her without her having to say a word. Could he tell that it was taking all her concentration to keep her unruly body in subjection? That she wanted to clamber on to his lap and shower his beloved face with kisses, whilst simultaneously wanting to slap that mocking expression from his face, and scream at him to stop tormenting her?

'I have good reasons for staying exactly where I am,' she retorted. 'And they have nothing to do with you.'

'You have painted your face,' he said. 'In an attempt to replicate the natural bloom I so admired, and which you appear to have lost. Does that mean you have spent some sleepless nights since we last met? Dare I hope it is because you have missed me?'

'I think you would dare anything.'

'*I* have missed *you*,' he said silkily. 'I only returned to town yesterday and have spent most of today discovering where I could find you tonight.'

'Have you?' Henrietta's heart leapt. He'd done this before. Sought her out, when she had truly thought she would never see him again. But she dared not assume that he'd done it because she really meant something to him. She needed to find out why he'd so particularly wished to speak to her tonight before she said something stupidly revealing.

Knowing her attractiveness to the males of the species, it was more than likely that he wished to make quite sure that she really had relinquished all claims on him. That thought was so depressing that it had the effect of dousing nearly all the physical reactions that had been thrumming through her. But that was probably it. He'd been so keen to get her out of the room that he had not told her how he expected her to handle future meetings, should there be any. And he was so used to females pursuing him that he would probably need reassuring that she would not make capital of the intimacy they'd shared at their last meeting by...by... Well, actually, she couldn't see how she *could* make capital of it, except by confessing to someone that she'd met him in private and let him…

Her physical reactions surged back. Every one of them.

She plied her fan with a hand that trembled.

'Admit you have missed me, too,' he said. 'And ask me where I have been and what I have been doing.'

Her stomach tied itself into a knot. She'd ached to know where he was, every minute of the last eighteen days, and had tortured herself by imagining what he was doing, and with whom, every single one of those nights. She could not bear it if he confirmed all her worst fears. So she said, primly, 'Your movements can be of no possible concern to me, my lord.'

'Ah,' he said, sitting back and frowning down at the programme, 'I see.'

He removed his hand from the back of her chair and used it to crush the printed sheet into a tiny ball, while he gazed straight ahead, a muscle in his jaw working. There were a few moments of silence so tense she didn't quite know what to do with herself. Yet she dared not break it with some inane piece of chatter. Not while Lord Deben had that particularly devilish look on his face. So she just sat and watched out of the corner of her eye, and fanned herself, while he smoothed the programme over his knee. And then began to methodically tear it into tiny strips.

After what felt like an eternity, but was probably no more than a minute or two, Lady Twining climbed up on to the dais and clapped her hands to try to attract everyone's attention.

'Honoured guests!' Conversation became muted. 'Honoured guests, friends, would you all be so good as to take your seats now, please?'

Those who were about to do readings strode forwards at once, trailing their satellites, taking their places on the front row, or on the edges of aisles. Others began to shuffle forwards more slowly.

Except for one person, who strode to the front of the room and came to a halt before Henrietta.

'Get up, Hen,' said Richard, for it was he. 'And come with me. I am taking you home this minute.'

'What? Why?'

'Because Miss Waverley has just informed me that it's all over town that you're making a fool of yourself over this blackguard,' he said, pausing to glower at Lord Deben. 'And I promised Hubert I'd look out for you. I thought those people you are staying with would have done so, but it's obvious they've been dazzled by his title. Or they just don't know about his reputation. But I do, Hen. And I won't stand for it.'

Most of the other guests had taken their seats by now. Lady Twining was shooting the back of Richard's head a disapproving frown, though since he could not see it, it was having no effect upon him whatsoever.

'*You* won't stand for it?' Henrietta snapped her fan shut.

'That's right,' he said, grasping her wrist and tugging her to her feet. 'We are leaving. Now.'

'Mr Wythenshawe,' said Lady Twining, loudly. 'Would you please take your place at the lectern?'

To a smattering of applause, a portly young man climbed on to the dais.

'Surely,' Lord Deben said to Richard in that deceptively lazy drawl of his, 'that is for Miss Gibson to decide?'

'Precisely,' said Henrietta.

'Mr Wythenshawe is to commence our evening's entertainment,' said Lady Twining, including Henrietta in the dark look she was shooting Richard's way, 'by reading his latest work, "Sylvia by Moonlight".'

To the background of polite applause, Henrietta tried in vain to extricate her wrist from Richard's determined grasp.

'Do let go of me, Richard, you are hurting me.'

'Now that,' said Lord Deben, slowly uncoiling himself from his chair, 'is something that *I* cannot permit.'

The portly poet laid his sheaf of paper on the lectern and cleared his throat noisily.

Richard let go of Henrietta's wrist, but only to round on Lord Deben.

'Who are you to say you cannot permit it? You have no authority over me, my lord.'

'I claim the right of any gentleman to intercede when he sees a lady being mistreated.'

'Hark!' said the poet on the podium, shooting a dagger-like look in their direction.

'Mistreated? Fustian,' said Richard. 'I'm doing the very opposite. I'm here to rescue her, same as any of her brothers would do if they knew the company she'd fallen into. We've known each other so long that a little tussle like that between us don't signify.'

Lord Deben raised one eyebrow disdainfully. 'You may have known her since she was in the cradle, but that does not mean you can take liberties with her person.'

'And you would know all about taking liberties, wouldn't you?'

'Richard, will you keep your voice down,' Henrietta hissed. 'Everyone is staring.'

For they were. Nobody was paying the portly poet on the dais the slightest bit of attention.

They were far more interested by the drama playing out on the front row.

'And you shouldn't pay any attention to gossip.'

'Especially not if it originates from the scheming jade I saw pouring her poison into your ears earlier,' said Lord Deben.

Richard opened and closed his mouth a few times, clearly trying to make up his mind whether to pursue the argument he'd started, or veer off to defend Miss Waverley.

Encouraged by the brief cessation in hostilities, Mr Wythenshaw started up again.

'Hark!' he said. *'The vixen's tortured cry...'*

But Richard had decided where his priorities lay. 'I don't believe the bits about you, of course, Hen. I know you wouldn't demean yourself by chasing after a man,' he said, making Henrietta blush for shame, since she'd done exactly that in his case.

'What I do believe is that he—' he jerked his head in Lord Deben's direction '—might have turned your head with a lot of insincere flattery. Stock in trade of a rake. Shouldn't have to tell you that sort of thing, but there, you ain't up to snuff. Not your fault. Led a very sheltered life.'

Henrietta couldn't help bridling at his assumption that any flattery Lord Deben had poured into her ears must naturally have been insincere.

But what was worse was the way he would keep talking to her as though she was about five and needed a nanny.

'So you think it is your job to rescue me from him, do you?'

'Well, obviously it is.'

Out of the corner of her eye she noticed Lord Deben's lips twitch. Well, she was glad he was finding this funny. It was clearly her mission in life to provide him with entertainment.

Her eyes smarting, she let her frustration out on Richard.

'So, where have you been then,' she demanded, 'all these weeks since I have been in town, if you think I am too hen-witted to defend myself from the wiles of all the rakes and rascals who stalk London's ballrooms?'

'A man has…a man…' His eyes flickered guiltily to where Miss Waverley was sitting. 'That is not your concern,' he said pompously. 'The point is that I happen to know that it is downright dangerous to permit a man like *that* to flirt with you. I can see how you might have been taken in. But it has to stop now.'

She lifted her chin and noticed Lord Deben's mouth slide into an appreciative grin. In spite of feeling that at that moment she had never come so close to hating anyone, she kept her eyes fixed on Richard.

'Well, it won't,' she said. 'I shall flirt with whomsoever I wish,' she said, making Lord Deben's grin widen to something that looked, had she not known better, triumphant. 'You do.'

Richard blinked and for a moment his mouth hung open.

Wythenshawe took the opportunity to deliver his next line. *'Doth echo o'er the moonlit grass...'*

Then a knowing look came over Richard, and he said, 'You've been trying to make me jealous.' He laughed. 'And I never even knew about it until tonight. Don't that beat all!'

That remark wiped the smile from Lord Deben's face. It looked as though he'd realised that *this* was the man over whom she'd been weeping, the first night they'd met. And now, because of Richard's arrogant assumption, he would think she had been using him all along.

No wonder he looked murderous.

'I have not been trying to make you jealous,' she denied hotly, for Lord Deben's benefit as much as to puncture Richard's over-inflated opinion of himself. 'I have not spared you a thought for weeks and weeks.' How could she, when she was completely obsessed with Lord Deben?

'Of course not.' Richard grinned. 'You've probably been enjoying yourself immensely, too, while you *haven't been trying to make me jealous.* Look, we'll say no more about it, if you just come along nicely now. I only joined Miss Waverley's court because it's the thing to do. See? And as for the other—I'm not angry with you. Not a bit. Can even see how he might have turned your head. After all, a girl like you ain't used to masculine attention.'

'A girl like me? What, pray,' said Henrietta in a dangerously polite voice, 'do you mean by that, Richard?'

'You, ah…well, you…' Richard floundered for a few seconds, which was all the encouragement Wythenshawe needed to shout the next couplet.

While blanket-tossed I sleepless lie,
Pondering Sylvia's peerless…

'You ain't a flighty piece,' Richard burst out, apparently struck by inspiration. 'That's what I meant. And your brothers took good care you weren't exposed to the wrong kind of men. *His* kind,' he said, shooting a dark look at Lord Deben. 'The kind that will steal an innocent girl's heart for sport, then toss it aside when he's sure of his conquest.'

He looked into her eyes with the kind of concern she had once dreamed of seeing.

And then shattered her by saying, 'Face facts,

Hen. It cannot go anywhere. Fellows like him don't marry country girls with…well, let's be honest, plain faces.'

This was not news to her. She'd *always* known Lord Deben would not stoop to marrying her. Yet to have somebody say it to her, in a crowded drawing room so that everyone could hear, was just about the nastiest thing anyone had ever done to her.

From the back of the room she heard someone snigger. She suspected it was Miss Waverley.

For a moment, she was so shattered, she was incapable of making any decisions as to how to handle this.

What did a girl do, when she'd just been completely humiliated in public? Walk out with her chin up? Faint?

But then Lord Deben spared her the necessity of having to do either of those things, by producing yet another handkerchief from his tailcoat pocket with a dramatic flourish, spreading it on the floor and kneeling down on it. On just the one knee.

'Miss Gibson,' he said, placing one hand over his heart, 'if only I could steal your heart, I would consider myself the most fortunate man in London. For mine beats only for you.'

A collective gasp went up from the audience.

With a strangled cry, Wythenshawe seized his pages of poetry and stormed from the dais.

Henrietta wanted to weep. Was Lord Deben mocking her? She hadn't thought he could be so cruel.

But when she looked into his face, there was no trace of mirth. She had never seen him looking so deadly earnest.

A lump came to her throat. This must be his idea of coming to her rescue. He could see Richard had hurt her, publicly humiliated her, and he was trying to mitigate the damage by publicly denying he found her unattractive. And it was very sweet, but what good could it do?

'Now that's doing it much too brown,' said Richard. 'Don't listen to him, Hen, he don't mean it. Doing it for a wager, I'll be bound.'

'What a horrid thing to say,' she said, rounding on him. And, though she'd never aspired to such dizzy heights, she was absolutely sick of Richard putting her down.

'Why shouldn't he wish to marry me?'

'Well, ah, that is, nothing exactly wrong with you, Hen. But—'

'Since the sight of me on my knees, telling you that my heart belongs to you, is not clear enough,' Lord Deben interrupted, 'let me clear up any misapprehension and put it in such plain words that even this chawbacon—' he shot Richard a look of contempt '—could not misinterpret them. Miss Gibson, will you do me the very great honour of marrying me?'

For a moment, everything seemed a bit unreal. But at the back of the room, Henrietta noted the men who'd been sidling off into the card room come pouring back.

And then, as though from a very great distance, she heard Richard saying, 'She can't marry you. She's going to marry me.'

The outrageous statement shocked her so much she recovered the power of speech.

'How dare you tell such a lie, Richard? We are not betrothed!'

'As good as. That is, everyone knows you're going to marry me.'

'Everyone except me, apparently,' she snapped. 'For I don't recall you getting down on one knee and saying I would make you the happiest man in London if I gave you my heart.'

'Well, that's because I'm not such a sapskull,' he retorted. 'Anyway, what would be the point? I've known for ever that you have no greater ambition than to marry me. And…look, old girl, I admit I'm not ready to settle down quite yet—'

'Not. Quite. Ready.' It was no consolation to hear, now, that he'd been thinking of marrying her when he *was* ready.

He took her so much for granted that while

she'd been in London, right before her eyes, and with her full knowledge, he'd joined the set that hung round Miss Waverley, jockeying with them for position as favourite.

Thank heaven she'd had her eyes opened to his true nature. If she really had ended up married to him, he would have treated her with as much consideration as though she were a piece of furniture.

'But I know that when I *am* ready I couldn't do any better than you,' he added hastily. 'Oh, come on,' he blustered, going red in the face. 'It's been understood for ever. M'father...your brothers...and then when we kissed, I thought...'

So that kiss had been in the nature of an experiment. To see whether he could stomach the notion of marrying to please his father.

'You went off to London, thinking your future secure,' she spat. 'Thinking you'd conquered me with one paltry kiss. Well, you are correct in saying you could do no better than marry me,' she said coldly. 'But I can most certainly do better than you. Lord Deben...'

As she began to turn away from him, Richard seized her by the shoulders and gave her a little shake.

'Stop right there, Hen. Do not commit yourself to anything in a fit of pique. I admit, I may not have given you as much attention since you've been in town as you would have liked, but I thought we'd have our whole lives ahead of us.'

'You didn't even have the common courtesy to call on me, as a family friend, never mind accord me the kind of respect the woman you planned to spend the rest of your life with deserves.'

'At least I didn't make myself a subject for gossip with indiscreet behaviour, like you did. What do you think your father will say when you get home and he finds out you've been making a fool of yourself?'

'If anyone has been making a fool of themselves this Season, it has not been me. Watching you trotting round at Miss Waverley's heels like a spaniel has to be the most revolting display of idiocy in which you have ever engaged. And that includes the time you harnessed those poor cows to your father's gig and they pulled the entire rig to bits in the middle of the high street and tipped you into the midden.'

'That was for a wager,' he said. 'And leave Miss Waverley out of it. She...'

'She what? Is worth a dozen of me, is that what you were going to say?'

'No. But perhaps it is the truth. My God, it would serve Lord Deben right if you did accept him.'

'Serve...him...right?'

While the two of them had been bickering,

Lord Deben had remained very quiet. In fact, everyone in the room had gone very quiet, as though they were taking the greatest care not to remind those involved in the brangle of their presence. At one point Lady Twining had clambered on to the dais, opened and closed her mouth, reached out her hand imploringly, then pulled it back to her chest. And instead of saying anything, she was just standing there, wringing her hands. For there was nothing, in any of the books of etiquette, that covered interrupting a lovers' quarrel that had turned into a marriage proposal from an earl in the middle of what was supposed to have been a poetry reading.

Henrietta wrenched herself out of Richard's grip, turning to look at Lord Deben, to gauge his reaction. Did he look like a man who was waiting for the axe to fall? Did he look as though he dreaded what she might say next?

No. He looked completely calm.

For a second.

Just until he smiled at her. A lazy, devilish sort of smile that seemed to be daring her to do her worst.

Chapter Thirteen

Henrietta's heart began to beat very fast. He'd said nothing on earth would have induced him to marry Miss Waverley. And she was sure nothing would pressure him into marrying anyone, if he didn't want to. So the fact that he was kneeling at her feet, with that devilishly teasing grin on his face, must mean that he…that he…oh, dare she hope that he actually *wanted* to marry her?

He'd told her he would have to marry one day. That it was part of his duty. But from the way he'd confided in her, she'd assumed he'd already ruled her out.

But then just now he'd said that while he'd been away from town he'd missed her.

And he'd promised her, once, that he would never lie to her.

Did that mean he'd come to the conclusion

that since he had to marry somebody, and he got on with her as much as he was ever likely to get on with any woman, he thought they could make a go of it?

Or had this proposal been a spur-of-the-moment thing? Was he just acting out of some fit of gallantry because Richard had been so insulting?

Gallantry? She almost laughed out loud. There was nobody less likely to indulge in a fit of gallantry than Lord Deben. And he never did anything on the spur of the moment. He laid careful plans. After giving everything a lot of thought.

If he really meant this proposal…

But then, supposing he didn't? Supposing he felt secure in the knowledge she would turn him down?

His kneeling at her feet like this, expecting a rebuff, would therefore be a very dramatic act of…well, what, exactly?

Perhaps he still felt he was in her debt. He had gone to absurd lengths to repay her for coming to his rescue on the terrace in the first place. Or perhaps this was his way of repaying her for… well, for having so very nearly ruined her, that night on the sofa at the Swaffhams' ball. Could he be suffering from a guilty conscience? He had looked rather tortured at one point that night. And again, earlier, when she said his movements were of no interest to her. Perhaps this was his way of offering her the chance to have her revenge upon him.

She could do so very easily by turning him down. It would be the talk of the town. How he had gone down on one knee at Lady Twining's literary evening, for all to see, and claimed his heart beat only for her. He was laying his pride, his future, and his reputation as a consummate lover on the line here. If Lady Carelyon were here, she was sure she would be urging Henrietta to grind his pride into the dust.

If she had wanted to take revenge for the liberties he'd taken, and the harsh way he'd repudiated her afterwards, now was the time to do it.

But then, he was giving her the chance to make this anything she wanted it to be. If she refused him, she would have revenge on him. If she accepted him, she would have revenge on Richard for his neglect, and then the litany of insults he'd just heaped on her head. If she were to repudiate them both, and stalk out of the room with her nose in the air, she would not only have paid them both back, but would become a minor celebrity. Everyone would be talking about the girl over whom two men had practically come to blows at what was supposed to have been an elegant, intellectual evening held in aid of a worthy cause.

And to top it all, Miss Waverley would be beside herself with envy, for both of the men on whom she'd set her sights were fighting over Henrietta.

But had he really thought about what would happen if she accepted his proposal? Because he'd made it in public, he wouldn't be able to back out, as Richard had warned him.

Though he really didn't look as if he cared.

Perhaps he didn't.

And that was where her deliberations came full circle. He had to marry someone and so it might as well be her.

Well, she didn't want revenge. Not on anyone. She wasn't a vengeful person.

But she would like to marry Lord Deben.

If only…no, she thrust aside the little voice that clamoured *if only he loved me*. A girl who waited for Lord Deben to fall in love before accepting a proposal would wait for ever. If she was going to marry him, she had to take him exactly as he was and hope that, over time, her love for him would melt away one or two layers of cynicism.

But she was not going to let him walk all over her in the meantime.

'My lord,' she began tremulously, 'I am well aware that you do me great honour by proposing to me. And I thank you for it.'

'Henrietta,' said Richard. 'I'm warning you…'

'And, upon certain conditions,' she said, blocking him out by keeping her eyes fixed on Lord Deben's wicked smile, 'I rather think I might accept.'

'Name them,' said Lord Deben swiftly.

'Hold hard, Hen,' said Richard, at the exact same moment.

'Speak your mind, my angel,' said Lord Deben. 'Tell me what conditions I must meet to win your approval and your hand.'

Taking her courage in both hands, she said, 'If I agree to become your wife, I shall expect you to be completely faithful to me. If I ever discover you have broken your marriage vows, I shall…I shall…' The thought was so appalling that she found her eyes sting with tears.

'Break my nose?' he supplied helpfully.

'Oh, for heaven's sake! A man like him will never be faithful to you! Look at him. He appears to think this is funny. When it's my whole future at stake.'

'Not yours, Richard,' she said firmly. 'Mine. For I must tell you that whether I choose to accept this proposal from Lord Deben or not, nothing on earth would ever induce me to make the monumental mistake of becoming your wife. Should you ever,' she said pointedly, 'get round to asking me.'

'What?'

'You heard her, Bishop,' drawled Lord Deben with a smug smile. 'She has far too much intelligence to throw herself away on a country bumpkin like you.'

Hearing someone fling the words Richard had used to belittle her right back at him made her want to cover his face with kisses.

'She was born,' said Lord Deben with a touch of hauteur, 'to preside over the houses of a man of influence in this country. To act as his hostess whether he invites politicians or peers, foreign ambassadors or tenants to his table.'

A sudden qualm struck her. 'Oh, no, I couldn't. I'd be rude to them. You know how outspoken I can be...'

'When you are a countess,' he countered smoothly, 'you can be as rude as you like to people and they will just say you are charmingly eccentric.'

'No, but I wouldn't want to let you down.'

'You could never do that. And I will endeavour never to betray your trust in me by giving you cause for jealousy.'

'Really?' Hope timidly tried to push aside her doubts.

It didn't quite succeed. He was not exactly saying he would be faithful. Only that if he strayed, he would be discreet about it.

She supposed that was quite a concession, from a man like him.

His face softened. 'Unlike your country swain,' he told her, 'I will not regard marrying you as *settling* for anything. There is nobody else I could consider trusting with my future. My children. My heart.'

She looked at him. There was a pulse beating at his temple. It was beating very fast. His eyes were so intent upon her that she felt as though he was willing her, with every fibre of his being, to accept.

But then, if she didn't, he was going to look perfectly ridiculous.

She closed her eyes and bowed her head. What she wished she could do, more than anything, was to bend down, cup his face in her hands and tell him to go away and think about it. Then, if he really meant it, to ask her again in a couple of days. In private.

During which time she could seriously consider whether she could cope with a lifetime of wondering where he was, and what he was doing, every time they were apart.

For several agonisingly long seconds it felt as though the entire room was holding its breath.

'He will never be faithful to you, Hen,' said Richard. 'He will make you miserable.'

Yes. She'd accepted that one way or another, Lord Deben was going to break her heart.

Because if she didn't marry him, he would certainly go out and find someone else. She'd already had a taste of how painful it could be, imagining him in the arms of another woman.

And at least if she was his wife, she would know that he would always come back to her once he'd tired of his temporary diversions.

'On the contrary,' said Lord Deben vehemently. 'I shall be faithful unto death, now that I have found a woman to whom it will be worth being faithful.'

There was a collective gasp from the bystanders.

Henrietta opened her eyes and looked at him again. 'Do…do you really mean that?'

'Of course he doesn't mean it!'

'Richard, will you please keep out of this. Just because you don't think I'm worth making any effort for, does not mean that I'm not worth it. And whether he means it or not, I'm jolly well going to marry him.'

She couldn't let this chance slip through her fingers. She would never forgive herself. He might be asking her for all the wrong reasons, he might never make her happy, but at least there was a *chance* that he might. A chance she would never have if she refused him now.

'Thank goodness,' said Lord Deben, getting to his feet. 'You have no idea how uncomfortable it is kneeling in such a fashion, in evening breeches. At one point I began to fear you had forgotten me altogether while you were squabbling with your childhood playmate.'

What a ridiculous thing to say. As if anyone or anything could make her forget him.

Though at the same time, it was good to hear him reduce everything that had passed between her and Richard to its proper perspective, for her own sake, as much as the assembled company. They had never loved each other. They had just grown up together, and almost, disastrously, drifted into a marriage that would have pleased both their families. Richard would be able to see that in time, too, though at the moment he looked absolutely furious.

There was just the tiny matter of her own conscience still to come to terms with. For whatever had prompted Lord Deben to propose to her, she was well aware she had just taken full and shameless advantage of the situation to get exactly what she wanted.

Him. For better or worse. For the rest of her life.

She hung her head.

'Oh, no, you don't,' Lord Deben growled softly.

And then she felt his hand under her chin, lifting her mouth to his so that he could kiss her.

And being Lord Deben, he did not deliver a chaste kiss, the kind anyone might expect a newly betrothed man to bestow upon his bride-to-be.

No, he crushed her into his chest and kissed her fully and thoroughly.

Almost as though he was staking his claim upon her.

She could dimly hear gasps of outrage, then murmurs, and finally giggles as the kiss went on and on, and she was reduced to clinging to his lapels to stay upright, since her knees had turned to jelly. At one point she dimly registered the sound of footsteps stomping away. Richard, she supposed, furious at being balked of control of what he would consider her substantial dowry.

And then an increasingly strident female voice, repeatedly saying, 'My lord! I must protest!'

Lady Twining was desperately attempting to restore decorum.

'Please, my lord…' She was still wringing her hands, Henrietta noted as Lord Deben turned to frown at her over his shoulder. He looked fierce enough to make her quail, yet she managed to squeak, 'Please try to remember that this is a respectable drawing room. You cannot carry on like this here.'

From within the charmed circle of Lord Deben's arms, Henrietta was incapable of feeling guilty for embarrassing her hostess. Once she'd recovered from the initial shock, Lady Twining would thoroughly enjoy recounting every detail of the dramatic events that had disrupted her evening. Everyone would want to know all about it and Henrietta could just picture her quavering voice, her recourse to the smelling salts as she teased out the details of the sordid squabble, the shocking proposal, and the subsequent depraved behaviour of the newly engaged couple. For weeks to come, she would have the cachet of being the woman in whose house the notorious rake, Lord Deben, had finally surrendered his bachelor status.

Lord Deben caught her eye at that point and it was clear to her, from the spark of amusement that flared between them, that he was thinking more or less the same thing.

'I am sure my fiancée agrees with you,' he said to Lady Twining, though he did not take his eyes from Henrietta for a second. 'A respectable drawing room is the last place we wish to carry on.'

She knew he was about to do something even

more scandalous before he'd swept her into his arms and off her feet.

'We need privacy, do we not, my heart? Besides,' he said to the room in general, 'you all came here to listen to poetry, did you not? And Miss Lutterworth, I believe, has some ready to read to you.'

'Yes, yes,' said Lady Twining, making frantic beckoning motions in Cynthia's direction.

Nobody watched the hapless poetess as she mounted the podium. They were all enthralled by the spectacle of Lord Deben carrying his fiancée out of the room.

'Poor Cynthia,' said Henrietta as they reached the hall. 'Nobody will pay her the slightest bit of attention now. They will all be far too busy discussing…us.'

'At least they won't be laughing at her behind their fans,' said Lord Deben curtly. 'Which is what you dreaded, was it not?'

All traces of amusement had left his face.

Now that they were alone in the hall, with no audience to perform for, it was as though he no longer saw any need to pretend to be deliriously happy. Or totally besotted. Or whatever impression he'd been trying to give in there.

He just looked weary.

'What…' she swallowed nervously '…what happens now?'

'Now,' he said, striding out of the front door and down the steps, 'we go home.' He nodded to the footman who'd come trotting out after them. 'Fetch us a cab, would you?'

'A cab? Don't you have a coach waiting somewhere? And I have left my coat and outdoor shoes behind in the ladies' retiring room.'

'The reports of our betrothal, and the manner of it, and our hasty departure will soon reach my coachman. He can make his own way home. After all, he has the transport.'

'Yes, but...'

'And you don't need outdoor shoes,' he said, carrying her across the pavement to the cab, which had drawn up. He deposited her inside, stripped off his own tailcoat and wrapped it round her shoulders. 'Nor do you need a coat for the short journey to Deben House.'

'Deben House? Why are we going there?'

'Because we need to talk. Somewhere where we won't be interrupted. My servants will not dare to question my movements, in my own home. If I take you anywhere else, there's bound to be someone who'll try to make us pander to the conventions. We may be betrothed, but we still ought not to be alone with each other. So people will say. And I—hell!' He raked his fingers through his thick dark curls as though almost at the end of his tether. 'I cannot go on like this. It's unbearable.'

She shrank into his coat and into the corner at the same time. It was unbearable?

'Being betrothed to me, do you mean?'

'No! How could you think that?' He winced. 'No, I know exactly how you could think that. I have not behaved…but—no. What I regret is the manner of my proposal. Kneeling there in silence, practically willing that oaf to goad you into it. He said he grew up with you. How could he not know that giving you a direct order would result in you doing the exact opposite? You all but said, *so there*, and stamped your foot when you told him you would jolly well marry me. How do you think it makes me feel, knowing you only accepted my proposal to spite him?'

'I…I don't know,' she said in amazement. But it sounded almost as though it mattered to him. Which implied that he cared. More than just a little.

'I thought it would be enough that I'd got you to say yes. But it seems where you are concerned, my conscience is particularly acute.' He shut his eyes and threw his head back against the squabs. 'God, before I met you I was not even aware I possessed a conscience.'

'B-but you have done nothing you need feel guilty about.'

He gave a bitter laugh. 'Oh, haven't I? Do you not understand what I have done to you yet? I have robbed you of all choice. You have to marry me now, or for ever be condemned as a jilt. And do you know what is worse? Nobody will reproach me. Nobody. I can behave as badly as I wish and still be accepted everywhere. But if you make a bid for freedom you will be ostracised. You will have to spend the rest of your life hiding out in the depths of the countryside and even there you will not completely escape the repercussions of this night's work.'

She laid a hand on his arm when he would have run his fingers through his hair again.

'None of that will happen, if that is what is worrying you, because I am going to marry you. I will not back down.'

'No. You are not the sort to back down from a challenge. That is just the trouble.'

The cab juddered to a halt and Lord Deben flung the door open.

'I gambled on you doing just that. It was unforgivable,' he growled, stalking away from her without a backwards glance.

She clambered out, unaided, and followed him up the front steps of the imposing mansion into which he'd just disappeared.

'Oi,' cried the jarvey as he saw both his passengers vanish without a backwards glance. 'Wot about my fare?'

From inside, she heard Lord Deben order someone, in far-from-polite terms, to see to it.

As she stepped into a massive hall, a footman scurried past her and out into the night. Another stood gaping at her. She supposed she was quite a sight, draped in a man's coat over her evening dress, but worst of all, unchaperoned and clearly the cause of his lordship's ill humour.

She clutched the coat to her throat, wondering what to do next.

A door to her right flew open and Lord Deben emerged from it. 'This is Miss Gibson,' he told the perplexed footman. 'Soon to be Lady Deben, unless she can come up with some way to overturn the damn-fool proposal I made her tonight.' With that, he retreated into the room from which he'd briefly emerged, slamming the door behind him.

The footman blinked just once upon reception of that astonishing news, but then recovered his professional demeanour and asked if he could relieve her of her coat.

She shook her head, steeled herself to face up to whatever lay behind that door and went in pursuit of Lord Deben.

He had gone into a room that looked as though it was kept in readiness for when he returned in the evening. A fire was blazing in the grate. And Lord Deben was standing on the hearthrug with his back to it, already in possession of a drink.

Glaring at her.

'If you wanted me to have some means of escaping our betrothal,' she pointed out tartly, 'then you should not have physically carried me out of the Twinings' house, into the cab and brought me to your home.'

'I know,' he said grimly. Then he laughed harshly. 'Even when I decide to reform, the best I can do is make my mouth say the right words. I am incapable, it seems, of preventing myself from behaving in a completely and utterly self-ish manner.'

'Are you telling me,' she said, reaching behind her to close the door, 'that you feel as though you ought to release me from this betrothal, but find yourself incapable of doing anything so... chivalrous?'

'Yes, dammit.' He tossed back the entire contents of the glass he'd been holding, then dashed the empty vessel into the fireplace. 'I have taken ruthless advantage of the opportunity that idiot handed me to bind you to me irrevocably. Letting him run to his length, silently urging him to goad you into accepting my proposal has to be the lowest, meanest thing I've ever done. Just when I'd been congratulating myself these past few weeks for drawing the line at forcing you into marriage by taking your virginity, I went and did something just as underhanded. Just as manipulative.'

'Wh…?' She shook her head, thoroughly confused. 'Underhanded? Manipulative? You sound as though you truly want to marry me, my lord.'

'Of course I do, you little idiot! I've been besotted with you practically since the moment you erupted out from behind those plant pots with your hair all over dead leaves and your nose running, to rescue me from making the biggest mistake of my life…'

She sank down on to the nearest piece of furniture, since her legs suddenly decided to give way.

'Mistake?' She shook her head again. 'You said nothing would have induced you to marry Miss Waverley…'

'That was not the mistake I was about to make. It was far worse. I had just decided that all women were so untrustworthy that it didn't matter who I married. I had just decided to walk into the ballroom, ask the first relatively attractive one who batted her eyelashes at me to dance, and, if she didn't bore me too greatly, to propose to her and get the whole wretched business over and done with.

'But then you showed me that there *are*

women who have a sense of honour and decency. And that if I married just any woman, I would doom myself, and probably my children, to a lifetime of regret. I decided that I wanted to marry a woman like you, Miss Gibson. A woman who would be loyal, and decent, and honest. Even painfully honest, if she didn't agree with the way I tend to act as I wish. And before much longer, I didn't want to just marry a woman *like* you,' he bellowed. 'I wanted *only* you.'

'You have always wanted me? Even when I—?'

'Wore the most ridiculous outfit and made a spectacle of yourself, just to teach me a lesson,' he agreed gloomily.

'So then, why are you trying to find ways to get out of it? I have said I will marry you. And I won't go back on my word.'

'It isn't enough. I thought it would be, but it isn't.' He turned round and gripped the mantelpiece with both hands, his head bowed as though he carried the weight of the world on his shoulders.

'Dammit, you must be the only woman in London so innocent that you haven't noticed how hard I've been trying to seduce you. The depths to which I've stooped to get you to this point. I wove a sensual web round you, lured you into that room, then reduced you to a state of mindless passion, deliberately, so I could take your virginity that night. Haven't you realised it yet?'

'No, I...' She sat back, stunned. It hadn't been farewell then, that night. He'd been trying to stop her from ending their relationship in the only way he knew how.

And yet when it came to it, he hadn't been able to go through with it.

'Why did you stop, then?'

'You smiled at me,' he groaned. 'You looked so trusting... How could I abuse that trust by robbing you of your right to choose? After you'd shown me how important it was? That was the moment I realised that I didn't just want to possess you and make you do what I want. I wanted you to...' He paused. His knuckles went white. 'I want the impossible. I want you to love me.'

'Oh, that's...' a little sob escaped her throat '...that's wonderful!'

'What?' He spun round so quickly that for a moment he lost his balance and had to clutch at the mantelpiece to regain it. 'What is wonderful?'

'That you want me so much you were prepared to go to those lengths. That you cared enough about me to put my wishes before your own for once. I know how much that must have cost you.'

'Yes. You know me for the selfish bastard I am,' he said bitterly.

'But if all this is true,' she said, suddenly puzzled by one glaring inconsistency in his argument, 'why on earth didn't you just propose to me in the conventional manner? Why did you have to make it all so *complicated*?'

'You wouldn't have accepted,' he said with conviction. 'Why would you? You hadn't been in town five minutes before you learned of my reputation. How could a girl with such high moral standards stoop to consider an alliance with a serial adulterer?'

She looked thoughtful. 'It has often occurred to me to wonder why you consider yourself so very bad. You don't frequent brothels, or keep a string of mistresses, tossing them and their offspring aside once you've grown bored, like so many other men of rank. And I have never seen you the worse for drink.'

He grimaced with distaste. 'I do not like having my wits addled. Drink dulls the senses and makes fools of men I could otherwise respect. Do you think I wish to figure in society as a fool?' He made a slashing motion with his hand. 'But like all men of my class I did commence my sexual career in a brothel. It was just that I soon found out I'm too fastidious to frequent such establishments. I graduated to keeping a string of

mistresses, though that...' he snorted in derision
'...palled swiftly, too. There is something so very
mercenary about the arrangement.'

'Oh, I see! At least a married woman genuinely wants you for yourself, not for what you
can buy her.'

'You are elevating those encounters to something they never were,' he grated. 'They didn't
want *me*. They just wanted *someone* in their bed
to alleviate the boredom they experienced with
their own husbands. Don't make excuses for me.
I treated them all abominably. I demonstrated
how much I despised them for breaking their
marriage vows even while I stripped them naked.
They liked it,' he said with a curl to his lip. 'The
more brutal I was with them, the more my reputation for being an exciting lover spread,' he said
with disgust.

She shook her head. 'I don't understand how
you can have driven yourself into such a miserable state. Why did you not—?'

'What?' He laughed bitterly. 'What alterna-
tive did I have? I have a healthy sexual appetite,
but I dislike women intensely. As people,' he
added swiftly when he saw her eyes widen in
surprise. 'I enjoy women's bodies. I hunger for
the satisfaction that I can find only in bed. But
as for forming any kind of connection outside
the bedroom...' He shook his head. 'I cannot

believe I am talking to you about such a sordid topic. I could excuse myself by saying that right from the first, you have had the power to make me blurt out thoughts I have never had any trouble concealing from everyone else. But it is not sufficient. Instead, it is just one more sin,' he drawled darkly, 'to chalk up to my name.'

'We are going to be married,' she said softly. 'We should be able to talk about anything. And from what you have just told me, it sounds as though you have been at war with yourself for quite long enough. There is nothing wrong with wanting a woman to love you, and only you. Nor in disliking visiting brothels. Nor keeping a mistress, if you have not been able to find a deep and fulfilling relationship with a woman. Lord Deben,' she said with a twinkle in her eye, 'I rather think you have more moral values than you like to let the world suspect you of harbouring.'

'Nonsense!' He drew himself up, affronted that she should suspect him of harbouring moral values. 'This is just one more example of why it would be quite wrong to make you marry me. You won't face the truth. You keep looking for the good in me, and there isn't any!'

'This, from the man who drew back from taking my innocence when he was so aroused his breeches must have been positively painful? A man with no good in him would have taken what he wanted and probably tossed his victim aside afterwards.'

'What would you know about such things?'

'I have four brothers,' she said with a wry smile. 'And the two older ones have not always been as discreet as they might be when embarking on their own adventures of that nature. They talk to each other and forget that, in the dead of night, when they roll back from the tavern, my window might be open and I might not be asleep.'

'Nevertheless,' he said, pushing himself away from the fireplace and walking across to the sideboard, 'I should not have exposed you to my lust.' He picked up the decanter. 'It was wrong.' He slammed it back down again. 'I am not good enough for you. That was, in the end, the only thing upon which your father and I could completely agree,' he finished morosely.

'My father? How do you know my father?'

'Where the hell do you think I've been these past two weeks? Or do you still maintain it is of no concern to you?' he said bitterly, swinging round to scowl at her.

'No,' she said, completely entranced by the sight of the self-contained, suave, sophisticated Lord Deben in the throes of an emotional crisis.

Over her.

'I should like to know, very much, where you have been and what you have been doing, now that I begin to suspect,' she said shyly, 'that you might not have spent the whole time in some secluded love-nest with a woman who was able to give you what you didn't seem to want to take from me.'

He looked at her sharply, his brows lowering even further.

'You thought I didn't want you that night? You thought I was with another woman?'

'Never mind that,' she said, making a dismissive motion with her hand. 'You said you were going to tell me how you met my father.'

'So I did.' He regarded her thoughtfully. 'After allowing you to escape me, at the Swaffhams', I indulged in a fit of despair that lasted almost two full days.'

'Really?' She curled her feet up on the sofa and made herself comfortable. 'Go on.'

His eyes flew to where his coat, still slung over her shoulders, gaped to reveal a hint of her figure, then rested for a few seconds on the rapt expression on her face.

'I took myself off to Farleigh Hall. And strode about the estate, hacking at the undergrowth with my cane, cursing the fates that had me falling for the only woman I'd ever met who was completely immune to me. And then I began imagining one of those bucks who've been hanging about you finally breaking through your indifference and persuading you to marry him instead of me. Then I realised that it was not as far from Farleigh Hall to Much Wakering as it is from London to Much Wakering, and I could do no worse than start all over again with you, by going to visit your father and asking for his permission to pay my addresses to you on a formal basis. Once I had that, I thought, you would have to see that I was in earnest. That you would have to at least think about me as a potential husband, and not…well…' He ran his fingers through his hair. 'I do not know how to describe the relationship we've had so far. But I knew that it would be the devil's own job to change it from what it had been to the kind of conventional courtship you deserved.'

She swallowed. It took only two days to reach London from Much Wakering. That left a lot of time unaccounted for.

'Should I enquire where you were for the rest of the time?'

'I have just told you,' he replied with a touch of impatience. 'I have spent the entire time in Much Wakering, trying to persuade your father that I would make you a suitable husband.'

'He argued about it?'

'I made the error,' he said, 'of assuming he would be flattered to think an earl...'

'Two earls,' she corrected him.

'Oh, God, you can just picture it, can't you? I went up there all full of myself, announcing my intention to make you my wife, boasting of my titles, my lands, my income...'

She couldn't help it. She giggled. 'He n-never set much store b-by such things.'

'I am glad you find this amusing,' he snapped. Then sighed. 'But there. A more intelligent man would have known it was the wrong approach to take with your father from the snippets you had told me about your childhood. All those scientists and inventors thronging his house, then the way he appeared to think the Ledbetters were suitable people to introduce you to London society...'

'Oh, my goodness. What did he do?'

'He looked at me over the top of his spectacles and said it was all very well, but he would never give his consent to let you marry an idiot. Told me you were a highly intelligent girl, used to using her mind, and that a stupid man would never make you happy. Then he wrote something on a sheet of paper and told me he would consider my suit if I returned with the correct answer.'

'Oh, how wonderful.'

'It bloody well wasn't. It was in Greek!'

She had meant, how wonderful that her father had not just granted the first man to ask for her hand permission to marry her, but had set him a test. She'd begun to think he did not love her overmuch. But he did, in his way. He wanted her to marry a man who would make her happy.

How fortunate she was in him. Many parents, from what she'd gathered during her time in town, had ambitions for their daughters which did not take their happiness into account at all.

Lord Deben began to pace up and down. 'I did not attend university. I was educated at home. I have a passing acquaintance with Latin, but my father saw no need for me to learn Greek. He wanted me to learn how to manage my estates and behave like a gentleman, that was all. I was in flat despair. I considered going to Farleigh Hall and employing my secretary to translate it for me. But then I thought your father would consider that cheating. So I asked if I might borrow a lexicon and set about attempting to decipher the symbols, at least.'

'Gosh. That is very impressive.'

'There you go again. Imputing me with virtues I do not have. I could make neither head nor tail of it!'

'I didn't mean…' that she assumed he'd managed to translate it. She was just impressed that he'd spent the better part of two weeks wrestling with some Greek epigram in order to win her father's permission to court her.

'And then,' he said as he got to the end of the room and was turning to pace back, 'at the end of the first week, he informed me that he'd been lenient setting me a riddle to solve written in Greek, since he might well have done so in Aramaic. Eventually, well, you know me better than anyone has ever done. You must already have guessed that I gave up. And gave up in the most dramatic style,' he said in self-disgust. 'I tore the cursed thing to pieces and stormed out into the orchard.'

'And then?'

'He followed me outside, sat me down and told me that although I would not be his choice of husband for you, that at least I appeared to be very much in earnest about you. And that if you wanted to marry me, he would not forbid the match, because there was no accounting for women's tastes, after all.'

She could just imagine the dry way he'd said it. He always did think women a very great puzzle.

'That was when I confided that I wasn't at all sure you did want to marry me, which was why I'd gone down to see him. I had hoped if I could

win him over, that would count in my favour,
seeing how very highly you regard his opinion.'

'Oh. Did...did that win him round?'

'Not really. He just said he was glad to hear
you had not entirely lost your head, just because
you'd gone to London. Nor did he wish me luck
with you when I left. He just said I must not be
as big an idiot as I looked, since I had fallen for
a girl with as much sense as you, and that at least
if you married me I was bound to improve.'

'Oh...dear.' Henrietta put her hand over her
mouth. What a very unpleasant time Lord Deben
had been having.

'But I won't,' he said grimly. 'Tonight's performance has proved beyond all shadow of doubt
that I am beyond redemption. I came to town determined to court you in form, and what did I do
instead? The very first chance I got, I made it
impossible for you to do anything but marry me.'

She shucked his jacket aside, uncurled her legs
and crossed the room.

When she reached him, he caught her hands.
'I have done only one thing tonight of which
I'm not ashamed. And that was to show that oaf
that you have brought a peer of the realm to his
knees. At least if you had chosen him, that might
have made him treat you with just a little more
respect. He was the one, wasn't he? The one over
whom you were weeping, the night we met?'

'Yes. But I got over him remarkably swiftly. Because,' she admitted shyly, 'I met someone who cast him completely in the shade.'

She squeezed his hands, encouraging him to understand she meant him. He gripped them hard.

'I taught you to want me, physically,' he said. 'I know that, but...'

'It has always been more than that. But I dared not let anyone know how I felt about you. There was already so much gossip flying about. I did not want to appear in it all as a lovesick fool.'

He searched her face. 'I always thought I could tell exactly what you were thinking.'

She shook her head.

'You were so often cross with me,' he persisted.

'I have never been so angry with anyone in my life as I have been with you. You made me want things I thought were impossible. I...' She flung up her head and looked him straight in the eye. 'I didn't want to love you, because I thought you could never love me back. But I couldn't stop loving you, no matter how hard I tried. Can't you see what a deleterious effect that might have had on my temper?'

The breath left his lungs in a great whoosh.

'You never needed to attempt to seduce me,' she said, 'or back me into a corner where marrying you seemed like the only way out. All you ever had to do was ask.'

'I didn't dare,' he said. 'I didn't think you would believe I was in earnest.'

'I might not have done,' she conceded. 'Not at first. You might have had to ask me several times before I believed you meant it, because you always seemed to find me amusing. I might have thought you were teasing me. Besides, how could I really believe that a man as experienced as you, a veritable *connoisseur of female beauty,*' she said, making him wince, 'would really want to marry a woman whose only claim to attractiveness was curly hair?'

'Oh, the things I said…'

She smiled at him fondly. 'You called me Hen.'

'So did that oaf.'

'He'd called me that since I was a little girl, because he maintained a hen was just what I looked like, with my beak of a nose.'

'I adore your nose,' he said. 'It is a nose of distinction. I hope all our children will have it. I will be delighted if it gets passed down through our line for generations to come.'

'Really?'

'Really,' he said, dropping a kiss on it.

She shivered with delight. 'And I adore everything about you. Before you start saying I cannot possibly,' she said when he frowned and drew breath to do just that, 'because you are such a rogue, then let me tell you, my lord, that I do love you. With all my heart.' She placed her palm on his cheek in a gentle caress.

'You have been very lonely, I think, for a very long time. From what I have learned, nobody has ever really loved you as they should have done and it has made you feel unworthy of love. But I do love you,' she said firmly. 'And we are going to love each other in a healthy fashion. We will communicate outside the bedroom as well as in it. And I don't care if you do despise all other women, so long as you never despise me.'

'You mean it,' he said, studying her face intently.

She nodded.

'What have I done to deserve this?' He snatched the hand she'd lain against his cheek and pressed a fervent kiss into the palm of it.

'You have loved me,' she said, running the fingers of her other hand through his already disordered curls, 'in a way no other man ever has. You are what I need.'

'And God, how I need you,' he growled, pulling her into his arms and kissing her. It was a passionate kiss, which spoke both of his need, and his relief. It was so powerful that it drove them both to the sofa, on to which they tumbled, eager hands tearing at buttons and pulling aside fabric.

'I warned you that I'm utterly selfish,' he growled in self-condemnatory tones, as he freed her breasts from her bodice. 'But no power on earth could make me deny myself the pleasure of your body,' he said, fondling them, 'while we wait for your aunt, or my godmother, to organise the society wedding you deserve.'

She subsided back into the cushions, watching, with intense feminine satisfaction, the rapt expression on his face as he cupped and stroked her breasts.

'I have been on fire for you for what feels like for ever,' he groaned. 'It will do you no good to say going without will be good for my immortal soul, or some such nonsense,' he warned her.

'I wouldn't dream of talking such fustian,' she replied. 'Because then,' she added with a wicked smile, 'I would have to go without as well.'

He made a low growl of approval and lowered his head to her breasts. She flung back her head and luxuriated in the sensations he aroused, crooning over and over again, 'I love you, I love you.'

It was so liberating to be able to say it, at last. Especially while he was showing her how very much he loved her, too, with each kiss and urgent caress.

'I can't resist you any longer,' he gasped, pulling himself up to look at her.

'I don't want you to try,' she said. 'In fact…' She struggled to sit up and pushed him away.

'What are you doing? I thought you said…'

His look of dismay faded as she began to peel off her gloves.

'I don't think,' he said in a thickened voice, 'I have ever seen a more erotic sight.' For he understood the implication of her needing to bare her hands. There were to be no barriers between them.

He raised his own hands to untie his neck-cloth.

'No!'

'No?' He paused, uncertain now that he'd made the correct assumption about the gloves.

She shook her head. 'I want to do it,' she said, pushing him back down amongst the cushions at the other end of the sofa.

She was more efficient at dealing with his clothing than he'd expected her to be. In no time at all she'd stripped off his waistcoat and shirt. But then her touch could not be described as efficient at all. It was reverent, almost, the way she stroked and explored his torso.

And when she hitched up her skirts so that she could straddle him and kissed her way down his neck, then flicked her tongue over his nipples, it was more arousing than the most expert ministrations of those women who'd never put their heart into it. That was the difference, he decided as he ran his hands up the outside of her thighs. Her shy yet eager touches were prompted by love, not lust. His hands reached their destination and squeezed her soft flesh, whilst delving both his thumbs inward. She squirmed on his lap.

And, hell, but the sofa was not the place where he ought to take her, not the first time.

He sat up, and took hold of both her hands.

'No. Stop. We should…a bed, at least,' he panted raggedly.

'You really expect me to walk through your house, to find a bedroom, with all your servants to see, in this state?' Her hair had half come down. Her bodice was gaping and her dress was rucked up round her waist.

'Though I suppose they might not be all that shocked,' she finished doubtfully.

'I have never brought a woman here,' he assured her, having caught her meaning at once. 'I have always conducted my *affaires* elsewhere. I have never wanted to encourage a woman to think she might have some hold on me, by inviting her into my home,' he declared with vehemence.

'And yet you brought me straight here,' she marvelled.

'Yes. Because I *want* you in my house, in my life, in my arms, for ever.'

She leaned forwards and kissed him again, flinging her arms round his neck.

'You have started to make love to me twice already on a sofa. I think it is exactly the place you ought to take it to its natural conclusion.'

'If you're sure.'

'More sure,' she gasped, flinging back her head as he ran his hands under her skirt for the second time, 'than I have ever been about anything.'

'In that case,' he growled, flipping her on to her back and coming down hard on top of her, 'who am I to argue?'

'Ooh…' She sighed as he sucked one breast into his mouth, whilst employing his fingers to devastating purpose. 'Oh, that is positively scandalous.'

'Not yet,' he murmured into her ear. 'But we have all night to create a real scandal.'

'All night?' Her eyes widened in surprise.

'Easily,' he vowed, with a wicked grin. 'In fact, I doubt very much if I will be able to let you out of my sight for some considerable time to come.'

She said nothing, but from the curve of her lips and the way she ran her fingers through his hair, Lord Deben knew she had no complaints.

And nor had he. For once, he had found perfection.

And her name was Henrietta.

* * * * *

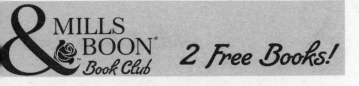

MILLS & BOON Book Club

2 Free Books!

Get your free books now at
www.millsandboon.co.uk/freebookoffer

Or fill in the form below and post it back to us

THE MILLS & BOON® BOOK CLUB™—HERE'S HOW IT WORKS: Accepting your free books places you under no obligation to buy anything. You may keep the books and return the despatch note marked 'Cancel'. If we do not hear from you, about a month later we'll send you 4 brand-new stories from the Historical series priced at £4.49* each. There is no extra charge for post and packaging. You may cancel at any time, otherwise we will send you 4 stories a month which you may purchase or return to us—the choice is yours. *Terms and prices subject to change without notice. Offer valid in UK only. Applicants must be 18 or over. Offer expires 31st July 2013. **For full terms and conditions, please go to www.millsandboon.co.uk/freebookoffer**

Mrs/Miss/Ms/Mr (please circle)
_____

First Name
_____

Surname
_____

Address
_____

_____

                                    Postcode
_____

E-mail
_____

Send this completed page to: Mills & Boon Book Club, Free Book Offer, FREEPOST NAT 10298, Richmond, Surrey, TW9 1BR

Find out more at
www.millsandboon.co.uk/freebookoffer

Visit us Online

0113/H3XEb